PUMPKIN PIE

A HAP-PIE-LY EVER AFTER STORY

Katelyn Brawn

D1367009

The Omnibus Publishing
Baltimore, MD

The Omnibus Publishing
5422 Ebenezer Rd.
POB 152
Baltimore, MD 21162

www.theomnibuspublishing.com

Publisher's Note: This is a work of fiction. Names, characters, places, and incidents are a product of the author's imagination. Locales and public names are sometimes used for atmospheric purposes. Any resemblance to actual people, living or dead, or to businesses, companies, events, institutions, or locales is completely coincidental.

Book Layout ©2018 BookDesignTemplates.com - Cover Design by dissectdesigns.com

Ordering Information:
Quantity sales. Special discounts are available on quantity purchases by corporations, associations, and others. For details, contact the "Special Sales Department" at the address above.

Pumpkin Pie/ Katelyn Brawn. -- 1st ed.

ISBN 978-0-9986811-3-9   Library of Congress Control Number - 2018942261

This novel is dedicated to two people who always had faith in me and my dreams. Making me believe in my happily ever after even when I couldn't see if for myself.

Andy and Jackie Brawn, my incredible parents, none of this would be real without you.

This one's for you.

"You yourself, as much as anybody in the entire universe, deserve your love and affection"

—BUDDHA

Chapter One

There are a finite number of crystals inside a shaker of salt and yet I know I will never be able to count them. There's something unsettling about not having that kind of control, even over a thing so inconsequential. I play with the tab of the industrial sized container of table salt as my eyes flick between the salt shakers lined up like soldiers in front of me. My chin's resting on the edge of the checkered table of the booth I'm sitting in, and I try like crazy to ignore the tacky substance that's sticking to me there. It's taken me almost ten minutes to remove the lids from the shakers at my banana slug pace. Truth be told, I have the easiest of all closing jobs, refilling the salt and pepper shakers. I always get through the pepper pretty fast, but my brain majorly slows down whenever it comes to the crystals in the salt.

"Hey dumb-dumb, pour the sodium chloride," a voice exclaims from across the room as a rag hits me in the head. It soaks my face with the three day old water we use to clean the tables. I look up to see my friend Rosie smirking at me from behind the counter. She wipes her hands on the white lace apron she wears around her waist. Her red painted lips curl up into a smile as she piles a few empty pie tins on top of one another to take back to her kitchen.

"How about you worry about yourself?" I mumble as I bang one of the shakers against the counter to break up the clumps. I hate clumps. Not that she's wrong. I only have one thing I need to do while everyone else does the hard cleaning. I flip open the tab of the wholesale salt and pour about a tablespoon of the crystals into my palm and rub my hands together. I focus on the feeling of coarseness cutting into my hands.

"Darling, I will always worry about you before me," she says with a smile as she makes her way back through the swinging doors into the kitchen with her pile of empty pie dishes. The clinking and clanking of the metal and ceramic pans against one another, mixed with the harshness of the salt in my hands pushes the rest of the room, including my responsibilities, away.

Bella pops up from behind the counter as Rosie finally exits. "How is my ray of sunshine?" she asks me as she begins her nightly fight to count out the money from the register. Bella's black framed glasses slip down her nose as she turns to the ancient money machine that Beattie, our boss, insists on keeping. It's older than all of us combined and barely ever works, but it's Beattie's prized possession and it's not going anywhere. She lugs an oversized toolbox from under the counter and fishes around inside for the pieces she needs to conquer the beast. Victoriously she emerges with a flathead screwdriver to wedge the cash drawer open. It screeches and screams in protest as metal rubs against metal, but Bella doesn't seem to hear it.

I remember moving that massive eyesore in here months ago, my back still hurts at the thought. It's crazy for me to think that this place hasn't always been here. It's hard sometimes for me to remember how I survived without it for the first sixteen years of my life.

Allow me to welcome you to Hap-PIE-ly Ever After Pie Shop and Restaurant! Where all we serve is, you guessed it, pie, pie and MORE PIE! We make everything from my favorite pumpkin pie to your traditional apple and cherry to crazy things like Midnight Madness (a chocolate cookie crust with a dark chocolate and caramel cream, yum). Breakfast quiches and pasta pies (you haven't lived until you've had lasagna in a flaky crust). It's one of the most popular places to eat in our small town. Especially considering it's us or the questionable diner. For years mystery meatloaf and week old cannolis were the only option in our little corner of the East Coast, but that's all changed now.

Beatrix Cod, whom we call Beattie, moved to our town a year before and bought the old place that used to be a hardware store. She'd covered the windows in newspaper and I swear no one ever came or went. The only inkling to there being people inside were the sounds of saws and hammers. Walking by, we were overwhelmed by the smell of wet paint and sawdust, but we never heard voices. Being the nosy people that we all were in Harpersgrove, Maryland we couldn't NOT know what was going on in there, so we did our best snooping at all times. When you think of the gossipers in a small town you probably think of little old women sitting under dryers in the local hair salon. Not so in Harpersgrove. In our town it's everybody, from the principal of the elementary school to the captain of the high school football team and even us, the girls who would come to work here. We're all guilty of spreading gossip about what was going inside the shop of mystery. The rumors stretched in every direction the imagination could go. My neighbor thought it was an S&M shop, my English teacher thought it was day care, and my sisters thought it was a vegan cupcakery.

So, the day came for the opening and Beattie, being her normal secretive self, hung the sign outside, under the cover of darkness. Then she actually covered it, like with a sheet. In front of the door stood Beattie, a woman about twice my age even though you couldn't tell by looking at her. Her dark red hair piled up on top of her head in a messy ponytail with pieces flying loose across her eye. Her flawless, freckled skin showed no trace of makeup. She wore paint splattered and ripped jeans and a tee shirt that actually read, "Frankie Says Relax." Beattie was not a woman for the pomp and circumstance of appearance and I loved that about her. The people in town, I was sure, expected her to be in a dress or suit. I know they assumed she'd be in something quasi-professional, anything but what she was wearing. And yet she was the most strikingly beautiful person I'd ever seen. I can't tell you what it was about her, but she looked like a goddess or something. Maybe it was the eyes. She has amazing blue eyes, like a cloudless sky in the middle of summer.

The mayor had insisted on doing a grand opening. He wanted an event when the library bought a new set of shelves. The opening of a new business was a must for pomp and circumstance. Everyone in town showed up for this. I mean, we barely filled Main Street, but everyone was there. I was standing with my mother and younger, twin sisters. Two truly annoying thorns in my side who spent the entire time complaining that they had to be there at all. The mayor gave a little speech about something that to which I wasn't paying attention. When Mayor Byron got talking you tuned him out after about a minute. It was a necessity for your sanity. The man could talk about nothing forever in his monotone and boring voice that sounded like a fog horn assaulting your ears. I was still looking at Beattie. She seemed as annoyed by this as I was. Her head thrown back in a way that if I hadn't known better I would have sworn she was sleeping. I did my best not to laugh, but it wasn't working and I let out a giggle. My mother reached over and pinched my arm, actually pinched me, and hissed, "Stop that, pay attention!"

To what? I wanted to ask her, but I kept my mouth shut and looked back to the stage. My mother stiffened beside me. My very existence annoying her as the Bobbsey twins, squawking beside me, bickering over who would get to have the sparkly pink phone case. I was in hell.

"Now I would like to welcome the woman of the hour, Miss Beatrix Cod," and finally Old Byron loosened his death grip on the microphone and handed it to Beattie as the sound of feedback hissed through the speakers on either side of the shop. Everyone in attendance cringed.

"Thank you," she said pushing the loose curls of red hair away from her face. "I appreciate your welcoming me into the community. I'm incredibly happy to be here."

She seemed sincere enough, the town was pretty idyllic. Since we're so small we're virtually untouched by chain stores. An ideal spot for a small business. She reached up and grabbed the end of the sheet over the sign and continued, "I'm sure you're all curious as to what I've been doing. You've done pretty much everything besides break the door down."

It sounded like a swarm of angry bees as a hum of mumbles and grumbles settled amongst the crowd. It was of course, completely true, but that wasn't something people in my town wanted to hear.

"Anyway, this is what I've been doing." She pulled the sheet down and we all stared at the sign she revealed. It had a huge, round pie in the left corner and read, "Ha-PIE-ly Ever After" in a pretty black script. She threw the sheet off to the side and shoved her hands in her pockets.

"I like pie, I make pie. That's all. I don't serve anything else, but this is the fourth place I've opened and I'm good at it." I knew to everyone else she sounded cocky, but to me she just seemed honest.

"So, I'll be opening in seven days and my door will be open all week for interviews. Thanks."

There was some applause, but it was forced and sporadic, like something you'd hear at a fourth grade piano recital. Beattie disappeared back into the shop and the crowd slowly dispersed, disappointed in the lack of any type of show. My family was among the few left.

"Who on earth would work for that vile woman?" my mother mumbled as she tried to operate her expensive cell phone that she had no idea how to work. The clicking of her acrylic fingernails against the screen matched perfectly in time with the tapping of her stilettos against the asphalt in a way that was almost hypnotic. I shrugged as I walked behind her. My sisters were fighting over a tube of lip gloss that was actually mine as they filed in line behind mom.

"I wouldn't mind working for her," I said, more to myself; but who respects those boundaries anyway? Not my mother, Eleanor Conner, that's for sure.

She stopped dead on her designer pink pumps, my sisters nearly falling over her as they slammed to a stopped and grabbed each other for balance.

"What did you say Michelle? You'd actually want to work for that woman?"

The look of horror that flashed across her perfectly winged eyes was worthy of a Hitchcock leading lady.

I really hadn't wanted her to hear me, mainly so I could avoid this conversation. My mother was quite a difficult human being to handle most of the time, and that was when she was making effort to be pleasant. Otherwise I couldn't even be in her presence. She made it her constant mission to change me into something she could be proud of, it wasn't something I was any good at accomplishing on my own. At the age of nine she'd enrolled me in charm school to make me a lady and I'd begged my father to leave after two lessons. I found no joy in learning how to set a proper table and walk with a book on my head. I don't think she ever forgave me for that.

I shoved my hands in the pockets of my jacket and rocked back on my heels.

"I don't know mother. I think she seems kind of cool. Plus you're always saying I should get a job." My being an irresponsible and freeloading teenager was one of her favorite subjects of discussion.

Her left eyebrow, nothing but pencil now as she'd waxed the real one to smithereens, arched, meaning that I had made a valid point but she wasn't going to openly acknowledge it.

"Well, that is true, it's about time you start taking on some responsibility."

As though I didn't already do the mountain of housework she and my sisters refused to do.

"But I don't think I want you working in a place like that." She had such a superior attitude, it was disgusting. I knew it was because of the way that Beattie looked and she made me so mad. But I knew how to deal with her.

I shrugged and said, "Well, I mean I could always work for you."

My sisters, Megan and Tyler, glanced up from their phones to see how she'd react. The idea of me going to work for my mother at the posh boutique she owned in neighboring New Shiloh was probably the worst thing she could imagine. She flat out told us all, on many occasions, that the only reason she went back to work in the first place was to get away from us. Well away from me anyway, she worshiped the twins. My entering her dome of solitude would put a major damper on that. After thinking about it for a good long moment she rolled her eyes and said, "Just do whatever you want." In other words, "Don't even think about stepping a foot into my place of business!"

She started to walk a little faster towards her car, her heels clapping like a galloping show horse as she called over her shoulder, "And do something with your hair! We're in public and you're embarrassing me."

I smiled and pulled up my long brown hair into a smooth ponytail, if that wasn't good enough she'd have to do it herself.

"I swear to God," Bella exclaims as she hoists her foot onto the register, still trying to force the drawer open. Rosie, who stands beside her, giggles and offers no real form of support, moral or otherwise. Classic Rose.

"If anyone ever tries to rob us they'll be sorely disappointed when I can't get into this thing for an hour!"

Thank God we've entered the technological age where most people pay with a credit card and we don't have to rely on the dinosaur as much. I mean, our credit card system still uses a dial up connection, but it's at least a little faster than the register.

"You're hanging around for testing tonight right?" Rosie calls as she swishes her way back toward the kitchen. I'm not into girls, but if I was it would totally be over a girl like Rosie. She's petite, definitely under five foot five, but curves in every direction, windier than a country road. She channels this aura of Slutty Sandy from the ending of "Grease." Total rockabilly. She sprays and curls and teases her naturally platinum blonde hair high on her head. Usually in barrel rolls or a bun. She covers her olive skin in thick, white pancake makeup that she doesn't need. Most girls would kill to be that naturally tan. Her eyes are always painted the same black as her nails and she keeps her lips a bright red. I've always been jealous of her fearlessness. Rosie Peters will never be anyone but herself.

I turn around and shrug. "Depends. Are you going to try and kill us all again?" I look up to see her glaring at me through narrowed eyes. Her blonde hair is plastered away with hairspray from her face and the pies she's making.

"Never going to let me forget that are you?" she growls. Rosie can be a little scary sometimes if you look at her the wrong way. I wouldn't want to come up against her in a dark alley. She'd kick your butt and serenade you with show tunes while she did it.

"You undercooked chicken and we all ended up in the hospital with salmonella poisoning. What do you think?" My stomach flips at the memory. I had never been so green, dehydrated, and sick in all my life.

Rosie gnaws on her bottom lip, trying to come up with a quippy and Rosie-worthy comeback. When she finds herself unable to summon anything, she shrugs and says, "No, I guess not."

We both laugh as the door behind us swings open and in walks the self-proclaimed princess of this place. I already knew that Blanche was here after hearing her rickety orange VW bug make its way down the street. The poor thing is always hanging on by a thread.

"Hey ladies!" Blanche exclaims with a smile, not caring who hears her, very Blanche-esque. My best friend has a larger than life personality. Her mom had been Chinese and her father is Irish and the result of Blanche is beautiful. She has thick, smooth black hair that she keeps cropped close to her chin. She has thin black eyes like her mother with a flutter of freckles across her pale nose that she definitely gets from her dad. She's tall like her father and thin like her mom. She's a beauty and a presence that can't be ignored.

I roll my eyes and give up on pouring the salt.

"Hey Blanche, what are you doing here? You're not working tonight."

Blanche looks at me like I'm nuts then she peers down at herself.

"Do I look dressed to work silly girl?" she poses with a laugh. She's in her regular running outfit. Blanche is the star sprinter for her school's track team that's just outside of our town. My guess is she's just come from practice.

She smiles and says, "No buddy, I came for the tasting. I mean as long as Rosie isn't making pot pies again."

A loud bang sounds behind as Rosie holds up a carving knife, a murderous look in her green eyes. "I have apologized over and over. I officially hate you all."

"You love us and you know it," another voice says from the door. Nixie Waters walks in, her dark red hair dripping wet from the swim practice she probably just left. The gang is officially here.

"Did you all come for pie?" Goldie asks as she brings the plates from her last table back behind the counter. Goldie Rust is quite possibly the most beautiful person I've ever met. She has about a seven inch waist, straight blonde hair down to her knees and a few other lovely "assets," if you know what I mean. It's like being friends with Barbie. If, of course, Barbie had been the only child of a teen mom and a bit of a trollop instead of living with Ken in the dream house.

"Yeah, did you all come for pie?" Rosie scratches through her crunchy hair with an edge of panic to her voice. I guess there might not be enough to go around. Elbows will be thrown and switchblades drawn if everyone doesn't get their due amount of pie.

"As long as it's not chicken pot pie," Nixie says with a menacing giggle.

Rosie starts to come from behind the counter and we all do well to get out of her way. She does, after all, have a very sharp carving knife in her hand and with the flour on her face and clothes she looks a bit like a reject from a slasher movie.

"Okay, no pie for any of you! I didn't come here to be insulted-"

"Where do you usually go?" Bella chimes in with a smile in her eyes over the rim of her glasses as she continues her fight with the cash register. She has a fork under the lip of the drawer, trying to force it open.

Blanche reaches forward, across the counter to tousle Rosie's hair. With the amount of hairspray in it, it will not be budged. It's like a blonde football helmet.

"Beattie said that if we wanted to come to the tasting we'd have to come and help you guys close."

"Coach was not pleased." Nixie adds. "But no way was I missing pie night."

Pie night, is a monthly tradition for the staff of Hap-PIE-ly Ever After. We try all of Rosie's newest concoctions and experiments. Every month we turn out a new pie or two, or seven, so our customers never get stuck with the mundane and boring.

"Seriously though, did you make anything with chicken?"

Rosie sticks her tongue out, "No, I did not make anything with chicken. And just for that you get to do dishes with me."

Nixie smiles, dropping her gym bag by the register next to Bella, and follows Rosie behind the counter.

"Lead the way master," she continues with a smile.

When all the work is finally done and my salt shakers finally filled, it's pie time! We line up along the neon stools in front of the checkered counter and Rosie resembles Julia Child as she dishes out the first pie onto the mismatched plates.

"What do we got?" Goldie asks as she twists her miles of her hair onto the top of her head in a messy bun that makes her look like a supermodel, but would have made me look homeless.

Rosie sighs proudly and as she admires the dish in her hands. Girl loves her pies.

"First up, we have a new creation of mine that I really like. It's an apple and sour cream pie."

She fiddles with the hem of her simple black tee shirt that's such the Rosie staple, and shows off her perfect boobs. It's so unfair that all my friends are super models and I'm a shapeless string bean.

Blanche whines, throwing her head down on the table in an extremely dramatic fashion that we barely notice. Blanche can be the queen of drama. She narrows her eyes Rosie and demands, "Aw, come on now, apple's my favorite pie! Why would you bastardize that?"

Rosie rolls her eyes and purses her perfectly painted red lips.

"Will you just try it?"

I won't lie, I'm a little wary of doing so. I take a deep breath and bite into it. Rosie never fails to impress. It's brilliant. The taste is rich and creamy, like heaven in your mouth.

"Well," Rosie poses to Blanche with a smug smile, balancing her hip against the counter and waiting. Her purple rose tattoo peeks out ever so slightly at her collarbone on her left shoulder.

My friend avoids eye contact, focusing her dark eyes on her plate, and tries to be nonchalant, "It's not bad, I guess." Everyone sitting around the counter shoots her a look.

"Okay, fine it's pretty good, but I still like the traditional better."

As the words leave her lips her purse begins buzzing feverishly. She pulls out her phone and sighs at the screen before answering it.

"Hello," she begins and then listens intently for a minute as she rubs the space between her eyes with the thumb and forefinger of her free hand.

"Is it a rash or is it chicken pox? Well where's dad? Fine, fine, fine. I'm leaving now. Keep him in the tub and no one touch him."

With an aggravated sigh she clicks off the call and throws the cell back into her purse with more force than necessary.

"Well my pie night just got cut short. Shiloh may have the chicken pox and my father is out on a date."

"Which one is Shiloh? Is he the scrawny one with the chicken arms?" Goldie asks.

Bella shakes her head and mumbles through a mouthful of pie, well into her second piece, "No, you're thinking of Wilson, Shiloh has glasses."

"Nope," Nixie corrects, tying her long red hair that has dried into its frizzy, bright normalness. "Thomas has glasses, Shiloh has freckles."

"No-" I begin, but Blanche cuts me off.

"Shiloh is the baby everybody, can't you get them straight?" she snarls as she pulls on her coat. She's already wearing a hoodie over her tee shirt, but only shorts on the bottom. The girl only gets cold up top.

Rosie extends a paper bag with a few pieces of pie inside to Blanche.

"For later," she explains. "And besides, you have about a thousand brothers. It's a little hard to keep them straight."

Blanche snatches the bag, but there's still gratitude to it.

"I have seven, thank you very much. And thank you for the pie." She runs a hand over her short black hair and crinkles her freckled pale nose, a classic sign that she's upset.

I touch her arm as she turns away.

"Do you want me to come with you?" I ask, really hoping she'll say no. Not just because it was pie night, but also because I didn't want to go. There's far too much testosterone in that house. My role as best friend can only stretch so far.

She smiles and kisses the top of my head.

"No my darling, I'm fine. It's not my first rodeo. See you all tomorrow."

"Bye," we respond in unison.

Rosie has truly outdone herself on this run. We try fifteen different pies and I'd be lying if I said my stomach isn't killing me by the end, but we've successfully picked three new pies for the menu. The apple and sour cream, a quiche with the flakiest crust ever, and a black-bottom cheesecake that Nixie instantly chooses as her favorite.

We all do the dishes, a little less to be put on Rosie's plate, and turn over the stools. The girls say their good byes and I wait around a minute for Rosie.

Rosie pulls down a heavy sack of flour from the highest shelf in the kitchen. She's already busy making another pie. Never slows down for even a moment.

"You should go home. Your mother already thinks I corrupt you too much as it is. That will only be worse if I have you out past curfew." Everyone in town knows my mother pretty well, which means they also know her attitude.

"Oh my mother thinks I'm corrupt all on my own. It has nothing to do with you. Besides, my dad's coming home tomorrow so I think I'm the last thing on her mind." My father travels all over the world for business. What he does? I have no idea. For all I know he's a hitman for the mob. It would be a perfect profession for my bald, short, fat, middle-aged father of three. No one would ever suspect him.

"Where is he this time?" Rosie asks as she adds flour to concoction in the mixture, causing a cloud to puff up and out of the bowl. It's no wonder Rosie's always covered in the stuff.

I shrug.

"Paris? Singapore? Cleveland? I don't know, which I think is kind of the point. That way we can't find him. My mother's freaking out about her solitude being broken, so the further out of the way I am the better. Megan and Tyler are the only ones she really cares about anyway." Rosie nods. It's pretty bad when your friends don't try to say, "Oh that's not true, your mother loves you just as much as your sisters." They know the reality and we all accept it.

I glance down at my watch and sigh, "But perhaps you're right. Even Eleanor might notice I've been gone this long." Soft dark circles cloud the undersides of Rosie's eyes. I'm always so worried about her.

"Are you getting any sleep? It's starting to show."

Rosie turns on the mixer, the sound of the motor breaking our silence.

"Oh my dear Elle, there's plenty of time for beauty sleep when I'm dead."

It's completely dark by the time I walk home. Not a huge feat in the state of Maryland in October, but still it makes me tired. All the lights in my house are on and burning brightly. My mother's in full freak out mode about my father coming home.

I walk through the front door and Megan's leaning over the sink in the kitchen turning the water on and off, her version of doing the dishes. I don't know what surprises me more, that my mother gave Megan a task, or Megan actually doing it.

"Somebody's in trouble," she singsongs in a very musical way. The girl can easily play a Broadway villian. Creepy.

"What're you talking about?" I ask, nearly getting it all out before my mother booms down the stairs.

"Young lady, where have you been?" she shrieks as she clears the bottom step. I know that she's been working all day and yet there's not a hair out of place or a wrinkle in her perfect pantsuit. I'm a hot mess with a cheese-doodle powder stain across my black tee shirt and hair frizzing at the sides of my face.

"Working," I say sheepishly, a little afraid of my mother at that moment.

"Michelle Antoinette Conner, I told you I needed you home early tonight to help with the house. The dishes need to be done, the floors need to be mopped, the chimney needs to be cleaned, and the trash taken out. Who exactly did you think was going to do all that?" she demands.

I almost don't speak, but finally I open my mouth and say, "Megan and Tyler?"

The sink shuts off and you could hear a pin drop in the silence.

"Don't be stupid," I hear Megan say from behind. "These are your jobs."

"And what exactly are your jobs then? Or Tyler's for that matter?" I ask, ignoring my mother for a minute. Megan bites her bottom lip and thinks for a long pause. It probably takes that long for the hamster running the wheel in her brain to get moving.

"Well, there's, and, well, we keep our room clean."

"You do not," I argue back quickly and she knows it's true.

"Well, there's also, we do the laundry." I just smile. "I do your laundry." She just crosses her arms. "You suck."

"Good comeback Meg," I mumble with a grin. This is worth what I'm bound to get from my mother later. But Eleanor's too preoccupied with her own crap to even notice that I'm making fun of one of the golden children.

"Will you just get started please? There's a load of laundry to do and the floors all have to be done."

It's not worth the fight. I could stamp my feet and whine and cry like the twins would. I could tell her that it's unfair and I shouldn't have to do so much when my sisters don't have to do anything. I know that won't get me anywhere and I'll just be later getting started.

"Fine, I'll get it done. Is there any dinner left?"

My mother's already onto the next thing as she absentmindedly answers, "Oh I took the girls out to eat."

"Thanks for letting me know," I mutter, grabbing the new bottles of Rain Water detergent and fabric softener that I recently bought, off the breakfast bar and stuff them into my overloaded purse.

"Excuse me, young lady. Did you say something?" she hisses, narrowing her long lashed eyes at me.

I sigh heavily and make my way to the pantry to grab a Pop-Tart, the dinner of champions. "Nothing mother, I'll go start on the laundry." How I ever get anything done, like homework or a life, I'll never know.

Our basement's a rather cold and unwelcoming place. The only lighting is a swinging bulb from the ceiling and there's a general smell of mildew that never quite goes away. The laundry sits in whopping piles all over the floor. No rhyme or reason, nothing's even separated, but why would they do that when they have me to do it for them? I start wading through the sea of pajama pants, tee shirts and dresses on my way to the far side of the laundry room in search of dryer sheets and laundry baskets. I find what I'm looking for, but am momentarily distracted by a box sitting beside the bottles on the shelf.

Everyone, I feel, is entitled to a hobby that's special and strange. Something uniquely theirs. For me that's salt and pepper shakers. I know it sounds stupid, but you'd be amazed what pairs they put together to make these things. Nothing better to me than spending a Saturday morning at a yard sale digging up what I can for my collection. This particular box is full of the ones I love too much to get rid of, but don't love enough to display in the glass case I keep in my room. I remove a Garfield Salt and Odie Pepper and smile at the chipped paint around their faded eyes and smiles. They clip together in the middle like they're hugging and it makes me incredibly sad.

I started going to the flea markets with my dad when I was little. He would wake me up at the crack of dawn most Saturdays between April and October and we'd go off on an adventure together to find the cleverest things we could. Dad looked for old records and I looked for salt and pepper shakers. After a long morning of hunting we would always stop at the town's diner for waffles before heading home. I got to know my dad on those Saturdays. I wish I still knew him as well. He had started to grow apart from us when I was twelve. I didn't know what happened exactly. I mean I can't pinpoint it down to any specific moment, but something changed. I can't say if it was my mother, my sisters, or even me, but one day he was always there, spending as much time with us as he could and the next he was going on trips that took him away for weeks and weeks. I'd be lying if I said I didn't miss him sometimes and seeing the remnants of our old adventures only makes that harder. I wrap Garfield and Odie back into their protective newspaper with its familiar newspaper smell and tuck them back to safety before closing the box. I grab the detergent and softener from my purse and turn my back on the memories. There's no time for them now.

As I load the laundry machine for the fourth time, my sisters wear more clothes in a week than the population of a small country in a month, my cell starts buzzing in my pocket. It's Blanche.

"Hey," I start as I measure out the blue goo detergent.

"Blah! This has been the longest night of my life! I'm covered in freakin' cornstarch!" she shouts into the receiver. This is a big reason why our friendship works. Blanche is good at talking and I'm good at listening.

"Cornstarch? I thought Shiloh had chicken pox?" I question as turn the washer on and move to sit on the steps. I have a feeling this one might take a while.

"Oh yes, that's what I thought too, but you only have to see the kid to know that it's not chicken pox. He looks like he has some kind of flesh eating virus or something. I called the doctor and he said it probably wasn't anything bad, but to try and keep him away from the other boys until tomorrow when he can see us. Elle, have you ever tried to keep seven boys away from one another in a small house? I had to make three of them sleep in the living room," she huffs into the phone and I keep up with my job of listening, "hmm"ing and agreeing when necessary.

"And, of course, if it does turn out to be chicken pox, Wilson and Martin have never had them so I have to be doubly sure to keep them away."

I have this feeling that what I'm about to say is a bad idea, but for some reason I say it anyway.

"Is your dad home yet?"

She's silent only a moment before continuing on with her rant.

"Oh, that's a whole other can of worms! Where is he is the better question. He's not answering his phone. He didn't leave a note as to where he'd be. I mean these are his kids, he should be here with them. But is he? That's a big no red rider! He's out dating... Dating!"

Blanche's mother had died five years before, giving birth to the youngest boy, Shiloh. Blanche hasn't coped or grieved at all and Mr. Summers' recent decision to start dating again isn't helping matters any.

"Blanche, Blanche," I chant, trying to get back into the conversation, but she's mumbling on about Martin's math homework that he refuses to do and Leo getting a note sent home from his teacher. "Blanche!" I finally have to scream to get her silent for a second.

"What?" she yelps, shocked that I'd interrupt her.

"Blanche," I start again calmly with a sigh. "Just listen. I know you're not going to like what I have to say, but listen with an open mind." I take her silence as confirmation. "I know you feel like your father is somehow abandoning your mom by dating again, but it's been five years. Your dad is still relatively young, he might just be lonely."

"Lonely? Lonely!" she shrieks, obviously the open mind approach didn't work. "Elle, he has eight children! Who could be lonely with eight kids?"

She's getting hysterical, and I try my best to sooth her.

"Just talk to him if you don't like this. He might not even know that it upsets you, and he'll never know if you don't tell him." I coo softly in the most comforting voice I can muster. This is not usually my job. Normally Blanche calms herself down.

"It's like I know that you're right, but I'm tired and I'm frustrated and there's a little man in my head telling me that you're wrong." Her voice catches on the end and I know that she's fighting tears. Blanche doesn't cry.

"Sweetie, I think they call that schizophrenia," I say and she laughs. The buzzer on the dryer goes off, it's time to switch clothes around. Balancing the phone between my shoulder and ear, I open the dryer door and shovel a mountain of socks and underwear into a blue laundry basket. The smell of the fabric softener is heavenly and I want to bury myself in the warmth.

"No, no, not those kinds of voices. Like a reverse conscience or something. I don't even know anymore," she says simply and I hear her plop, probably down onto her bed. I smile as I sit back on the step to fold the clothes I've just retrieved.

"Look, try to put the boys to bed. Get the older ones to help you and then go to bed yourself. In the morning, talk to your dad. You'll feel better once you do."

She breathes out heavily and it sounds like static in my ear.

"Yea, I guess you're right."

"Michelle!" I hear a scream from upstairs. My mother has such a subtle way about her.

"The evil queen of the household beckons," I lament with as much sarcasm as I can muster.

"Ew, I think I'll stick to the seven screaming boys," Blanche replies back, and I can tell she's feeling better.

"Michelle!" she screams again. "You need to do these floors, now!" I push away the pile of laundry, I guess that's going to have to wait

I roll my eyes and call up to Mom, "I'll be right there mother." To Blanche I say, "I've got to go before her head pops off and I have to clean that too."

"Night!" Blanche responds and clicks off.

I shove my phone in the back pocket of my jeans and as I climb the stairs I mutter to myself, "Wash the clothes Michelle. Mop the floors Michelle. Do the dishes Michelle. Michelle, Michelle, Michelle."

I'd like to see the woman just once pick up a mop herself or make her two other spoiled brats do a damn thing. Yeah, that would be the day.

Chapter Two

My body hurts something fierce the next morning after my full night of scrubbing. My sisters had been sent to bed hours before because they were in need of beauty sleep, like my mother. While I, like my father, have a body built for work, so I can obviously handle all of it on my own. Oh, how I long for May to come so I can graduate and get out of here! Unfortunately, it's only the fall. Far too long left to go. I'll have to make due for the time being. The true question and biggest dilemma seems to be where to go. Blanche and I have been through all the pamphlets and nearly live at the college fairs in the bordering town, usually in Blanche's high school cafeteria.

Blanche and I have this dream of going to the same school and being roommates and maybe even studying the same thing and living happily ever after in a city far, far away from Harpersgrove and never coming back. There's only one seemingly large flaw in our perfect plan. We don't agree on any of it. Blanche wants to go to a school up north, probably NYU, while I want to get as far away from my mother and sisters as possible. I'm even considering schools in Hawaii I'm so desperate. More realistically I think somewhere in Cali, or maybe Washington State. And as far as our being roommates? Forget about it! I'm a neat freak and Blanche has grown up with seven younger brothers (need I say more?). She's a bit of a night owl and I'm in bed by nine thirty, yep just like a ninety year old woman. So, the chances of our ending up in the same place doing the same thing are slim, but we don't like to talk about such things.

I take a quick shower and it seems to ease my aching muscles a bit. I wish I could stay in there forever. But, of course, school can't wait. I dress in a black sweater and a pair of jeans. I'd have work after school so I figure it's best to dress in something simple. I'll get some crap from my mother about it, but I don't really care. I mean I'll get an earful if I try too, so it's easier to wear what I want.

Sure enough, as soon as I clear the last step into the kitchen my mother starts in on me.

"Good Lord, Michelle! Are you even going to make an effort? I buy you all those nice clothes-" Yeah, the last time my mother bought me an outfit I was still in Granimals. "-and you never, ever wear them."

Tyler rolls her eyes, barely even looking up from the screen of her phone.

"Yeah you look like a freak Elle, but that's nothing new." The other half of her brain (also known as my sister Megan) snorts and it rolls into the world's most annoying laugh that reminds of a woodpecker going to town on a tree.

My mother's jaw clamps down. She HATES that laugh. Any imperfection in the wonder twins is a thorn in Mom's side.

"Michelle, you really must try harder. Remember you are a reflection on me."

Well that makes way more sense. She doesn't want me to look good for me; she wants me to look good for her.

I decide to change the subject and throw her off course.

"What time do you have to get dad from the airport?" I ask as I pour myself a glass of orange juice, the only breakfast I have the stomach for today.

It works. She sighs and runs her finger around the rim of her coffee cup, ignoring the lipstick ring forming on her hand.

"He decided to take a car service."

Wow. It's something of a drive from the airport in Baltimore to our house in southern Maryland. He must really not want to spend a lot of time in the car with my mother, not that I can blame him or anything.

"He'll be here when you get home from school."

I pack up a lunch with a pleasing spread of a PB&J sandwich, a banana, and a few salt and vinegar chips as I mention, "I won't be home until late, Mother. Remember I have work on Fridays."

I look up just as she slams her palm down on the table. Even Tyler and Megan stop what they're doing to watch what's happening.

"Michelle, your father is barely ever able to come home and the one time he does you choose this ridiculous job over seeing him. I will not stand for it."

I hop down from the breakfast bar stool and shove my lunch into my book bag.

"Well, Mother, he doesn't choose to spend his time with us. I don't plan to rearrange my life to spend time with him."

My mother looks like I've just slapped her.

"You don't speak to me that way young lady." I expect her to yell, and yet her voice comes out so soft and calm that I'm nearly thrown off my feet.

I have a brilliant comeback that's equal parts mean and smart, but luckily Goldie (my ride to school) blares her horn outside. Saved by the bell. I groan and swing my bag over my shoulder, wincing as it hits me in the back. My generation will be a group of old ladies with hunchbacks due to the weight of our books.

"I'll be home when I'm home Mom. I'll see Dad then."

She so desperately wants to say more, but I zip out the door before she has the chance. Out in my driveway putters Goldie's beautiful golden metallic Pinto with a thick and continuous fog pouring from the exhaust pipe. Ah, what good we're doing for the environment. Inside sits Goldie in the driver's seat and Rosie in the passenger. Rosie lifts her seat forward so I can I slink into the back. The seats are made of some kind sparkly plastic blend that sticks to your skin even in the cold of winter. The car looks like a moving ray of sunshine, much like Goldie.

"What's shaking?" Captain Sunshine asks as she pulls out of the driveway.

"All four cheeks and a couple of chins," I answer jokingly as I buckle my seat belt. I sigh and run my hand over my face. Yet another moment I'm so thankful I don't wear makeup. How girls can go without scrubbing at their faces all day I'll never understand.

"My father comes back into town today and my mother is acting like a crazy person."

"More than usual?" Rosie asks as she unbuckles herself and turns in her seat. Ever the rebel.

I scrunch a little lower in my seat, my chin digging into my breast bone, really giving me four chins.

"Yeah, hard to imagine, right? How was work last night, Rosie?" I ask, trying to avoid the discussion of my father. I always kind of hate it.

She smiles all the way up to her eyes and crinkles in her forehead.

"Fantabulous! I made a few of the quiches and cheesecakes for today. Far ahead of schedule, mind you."

"Did you get any sleep?" Goldie questions as she makes a dangerously sharp left turn.

The town is small and the distance is short to school and yet Goldie always treats it like the Indy 500 or an eighties movie police chase. You learn quickly how to hold on and embrace the ride when she's driving.

Rosie shrugs, her low-cut black top falls off her shoulder revealing the entirety of her tattoo.

"Who needs sleep?" We're both quiet for a moment and she finally huffs, "I got like three or four hours. Happy?"

"No!" I bellow as I pinch her shoulder near the tattoo. "We'd be happy if you actually got a good night's sleep."

Rosie bites the inside of her cheek as her eyes scan quickly around the car, "Damn Goldie, does your hair get caught in the pedals?" Rosie and I are both good as switching the subject when we're uncomfortable.

Goldie's long blonde hair hangs down past her waist and twists around into her lap as she drives. She narrows her eyes at Rosie and mocks, "Oh. Ha, ha, no! It only comes to my knees."

"Ever thought about cutting it?" I ask as she makes the final death-defying turn into Harpersgrove High School.

She shrugs as she finds the nearest parking spot, the brakes screeching to a screaming halt, alerting all our classmates in the lot to our arrival. Goldie loves an entrance.

"I've thought about it, but I've just never been able to bring myself to that place. And I'm pretty sure my mother would kill me if I did. She's kind of obsessed with it."

"Parents are lovely aren't they?" I mention as they get out of the car, me behind them.

Rosie puts her arm around my shoulders and says, "Yeah, I wouldn't really know."

Rosie's mom has pretty much been out of the picture entirely and she'd never known her dad.

"But now it doesn't matter because we're here at this beautiful and wonderful school." She pauses and we both look at her like she's was crazy. The only thing Rosie hates more than sleep is school. "Where we have a whole other slew of problems," she continues making Goldie and I both laugh, and together we walk into the glory that is Harpersgrove Senior High School.

Every school has one. You know who I mean, the princess, the quintessential beauty, the top of the social food chain, and the biggest witch that the school has to offer. At Harpersgrove that royal pain is Lucy Wilcox. Shockingly enough, Lucy and I had actually been something of friends when we were little, but then the inevitable happened. Lucy got boobs and suddenly became greater than God and no time for me anymore.

That morning, as I remove books from my locker the dark princess graces me with her presence. I really do have to admit it, much to my disdain, the girl is pretty damn perfect. She has long, unaturally shiny black hair that hangs in loose curls down her back. She has a super slim waist, much like me, but then also hips, a butt and boobs, much unlike me. She can pull of a sweater and a miniskirt better than any girl I've ever seen. Cosmically unfair.

When Lucy walks down a hallway it's like a bad 80's teen movie. Everyone parts like the Red Sea so she and her minions won't have to brush up against anyone. If I didn't know better I'd swear that she moved in slow motion as her hair created its own wind and power ballad whispers in the background. She has a pack of perfect clones that follow her blindly. Mainly it's the fellow cheerleaders that all strive to be just like their fearless leader. Makes me want to vomit. The one bright spot on the entire situation is actually my sisters. So rarely do they ever bring me any joy, but when it comes to Lucy they are most entertaining. Tyler and Megan so badly want to be two more of Lucy's mindless drones. Lucy doesn't even know they're alive. The twins do everything short kiss Lucy's feet and she still has no idea that they're around. It's delicious.

Lucy however does not pay me the same kindness. She's acutely aware of me. As she passes my locker with her hoard of bubbly idiots she decides to hit the large pile of books and papers in my hands so they scatter like a mushroom cloud of homework all around. I sigh and stare at the pile, planting my hands on my hips before beginning my rescue mission. This is, unfortunately, not a one time occurrence.

"Whoops," Lucy sneers with her perfectly straight, pearly white smile. "Your books fell. They must have seen your face." That isn't even funny. She's losing her touch.

"Thanks for that, Lucy." I say flatly as I sink down to my knees.

She snaps the wad of gum in her mouth like a couture cow chewing cud.

"You're such a freak." At that her zombies all let out a cackle and turn to laugh at me. Suddenly my sisters appear as if from nowhere and snicker behind Lucy.

"Yeah, you're such a freak!" they shout together.

Lucy gawks blankly at them and turns away, her girls close in toe. Tyler and Megan stay right on their heels. As the last few pass me with their snide glances I continue to smile and pile up books.

"Ladies, always a pleasure."

"Freak," a few of them mutter. You might think in all those years they'd come up with a better insult, but alas they have not. It's rather disappointing really.

I turn my attention down to the sea of papers at my feet and try to make sense of the chaos as two pairs of shoes enter my line of vision. One set of flip flops owned by a pair of freckly pale feet and the other olive skinned with great calves in some Mary Janes. I peer up to see Nixie and Rosie.

"She's just the most pleasant little thing, isn't she?" Nixie asks as she bends down to help me. Her red hair's slicked back and dripping on my geometry book.

"Did you have swim practice this morning?" I ponder as I snatch them from her. I appreciate the help, but not if she's going to get everything wet!

Nixie rocks back on her heels and stands up. "Heck yeah! Every morning at five a.m. Beat my best time in this morning."

Rosie sighs dramatically and scoops up the rest of my loose papers. "Trust me, don't ask any more questions. I've had to hear all about it all morning."

Nixie narrows her eyes and flicks some of the water in her direction, hitting me in the process. Luckily, I like the smell of chlorine.

"Oh yeah, you've been with me a whole fifteen minutes."

Rosie thinks for a moment and shakes her head in horror.

"Was that all? It felt a heck of a lot longer than that."

"Ha ha." Nixie mutters flatly.

"Anyway," I continue, turning my attention to Rosie. "I don't really let Lucy bother me anymore."

"Why? She bothers me, and I don't even know her," Rosie snips as we start down the hall. The three of us look like a group ready to trek on an African safari by the size of our packs. There's definitely a chiropractor and a back brace in my future.

Nixie looks at Rosie like she's the most stupid person in the world, "Of course you know her. You've gone to school with her forever," Nixie is a year behind us, only a junior. "And she's always lived in this town with us."

"That doesn't mean I know her. Paul Flats, the town drunk, has lived here my whole life too, but I don't pretend to know him." Rosie exclaims sharply. Unlike me, Rosie has never been close with Lucy. In fact they've pretty much always hated each other. Rosie and I have only become friends in the past few years. Before that she honestly had always scared me.

Nixie and I say goodbye to Rosie and head to our English class. This is one of the many times I wish Blanche went to school with us. We're both taking the same AP course load and it would be nice to be able to study with her, but of course we learn things at different times. Luckily, Nixie's advanced for a junior and I have her in my corner, for this class at least.

Lucy looks straight at me as I come through the door. Yeah, Lucy is also smart on top of being beautiful and popular. Bitch. Nixie and I claim our seats in the back row just as Mr. Peters schleps into the room with his suitcase and cup of coffee. He's one of those middle aged men that always looks permanently exhausted with bags under his eyes and constant labored breathing. Technically Nixie and I came in late, which he doesn't like. So, we're getting a bit of the evil eye as he starts with the class.

"To be early is to be on time ladies," he reminds us as he writes the date on the green board with white chalk. The old timer had pitched a major fit when they'd tried to trade his classic chalkboards for dry erase boards.

We've been reading *Romeo and Juliet* in class, said to be the greatest romance of all time. I don't get it! Okay, so I am just about the most unromantic person in world. I rank right down there with Ebenezer Scrooge and Hitler, but normally I can see where people are coming from in the lovey dovey stories. This one I never get. Romeo's an emo little pain in the butt who whines and complains through the whole play. I'm happy when he offs himself. Is that wrong of me?

Of course, Lucy has a whole other opinion.

"I think it's so romantic and so lovely. I wish I could have a story like that," she muses with a whimsical sigh. I make the awful decision of chuckling at her. She does not approve. She whips around in her seat and demands, "Something funny Conner?"

Crap, now I have to talk. I swallow hard and look over to Nixie to help me, but she shrinks down in her seat. Traitor. Mr. Peters decides to help me along. Yeah that's what I need. "Ms. Conner, please," he encourages with a smile. He's all about lively debate, no matter what it may do for your social life.

I shift my weight and decide just to go for it. I'll be gone to college in a few months, how much damage can the evil princess really do in that amount of time. I look Lucy square in the eye and say, "We all wish you'd have a story that was just like this. And I do mean just like Romeo and Juliet's story."

"Wh-What did you just say to me?" she stutters, I've never heard her do that. Her porcelain white cheeks pink up as her fists ball in rage straight down at her sides.

My stupidity decides to kick in, because I just can't let it go. The word vomit is too strong for me to stop. To make matters even more dramatic and worse, I stand up.

"I'm sorry Lucy, did I stutter?" The entire room falls silent and I suddenly feel a rush of heat flush up the back of my neck and a flare of total humiliation and embarrassment rise up my throat. You don't talk to Lucy Wilcox like that. It's just not done. I look to Nixie for comfort, but she turns her head away, pretending not to know me. If she could subtly get under her desk to get away from me I'm sure she would. I settle back into my seat and mumble, "I apologize, Mr. Peters." He just grumbles something under his breath and goes on with his class. I'm sure that's not the kind of debate he'd been hoping for from his two brightest students.

I do everything in my power to keep my eyes locked on my book. Mainly, so I won't make the mistake of looking up at Lucy. Of course, I'm so far from perfect that I have to slip up sooner or later. Just as we're packing up our stuff to leave, which I do faster than I ever have, I see the hem of Lucy's too short skirt enter my line of vision. I can't help but to look up at her. Her face is cold as stone. "You're dead Conner, I hope you know that." And then she walks away. The lump in my throat can't be swallowed. Maybe she's capable of more damage than I thought.

Nixie reaches across the aisle between our seats and punches me in the arm. "Ow!" I exclaim. "What was that for?"

"What were you thinking?" she demands, her hair frizzing around her face, like a ginger halo, as it dries. "What happened to staying under the radar and out of the way of Lucy Wilcox?"

I blow out a deep breath that flutters through my lips, sending the vibration through my entire body. "I don't know. I'm mad at my mother and sisters. I'm frustrated and I just snapped. I wanted to stop, but I couldn't."

Nixie shoves her seashell covered binder into her bag. "Well, I hope you have a will all ready to go."

I stand up and swing my bag over my shoulder. "Comforting, thanks Nix."

She shrugs. "Hey, you insulted Lucy Wilcox, not me."

"You know, you can just refer to her as just Lucy. I'll know who you mean." I inform her as we make our way into the hall.

Nixie considers this a minute and says, "I don't know, there's some so much more dynamic about Lucy Wilcox, compared to just Lucy."

"Yeah, that's just what Lucy needs, more dynamics," I grumble as I turn the combination on my locker. It pops open and something falls out at my feet. I lean down and pick it up, flipping it over as I do. It's a note, written on simple loose-leaf paper and on the front it reads, *To the most beautiful girl I've ever seen.*

Is that supposed to be me?

Chapter Three

❝ To the most beautiful girl I've ever seen," I read to the girls at the pie shop later that afternoon.

"Is he talking about you?" Blanche interrupts. She pulls the elastic headband out of her hair and starts running it through her thin fingers.

Rosie leans across the counter and smacks Blanche in the back of the head. "Will you shut up and let the girl read?" she demands. Rosie's traded her high topped Mary Jane's for sensible flats which turns her into a curvy, fashion forward hobbit.

I grin and continue, "When I saw you last Saturday at Lucy Wilcox's party-"

"Oh, he's definitely not thinking of you then," Goldie and Bella call out at the same time. Oh, the sweet comfort of my friends. I'm beginning to forget why I wanted them to hear this in the first place.

Rosie's in my corner though. "Shut up and let her read it, or I swear to God I will poison you all on purpose next time." The room falls eerily silent to the point that you can hear the hum of the ice maker two rooms away.

"When I saw you last Saturday at Lucy Wilcox's party I knew that I'd needed to talk to you. Normally I'm not shy around girls. I know that sounds kind of cocky, but I just want to tell you the truth. Girls are the one easy thing to me, but something about seeing you that night made me clam up and I just couldn't come up to you. I think I'm only telling you all this so you won't find this note to be a coward's way out, but I needed to talk to you in some way."

"So, I don't want you to feel any pressure to respond, I just wanted to contact you. But I do hope to hear from you... but no pressure. Your Secret Admirer."

I finish and fold the note back up. All of my friends have a different expression. A few look intrigued, the rest look confused. All the while the only sound between us is the buzz of the ice maker and the tapping of Goldie's long red nails on the cash register.

My best friend's extreme levels of sensitivity fly out first as Blanche exclaims, "What a freakin' pansy!" Rosie reaches forward to slap her again, but Blanche flips around and grabs her wrist with ninja like speed. "Hit me again and see what happens," she hisses, the breathlessness of her s's coming across like an overheated tea kettle.

Rosie twists her hand away and rolls her eyes. "You are so dramatic Blanche. The letter was nice Elle," she says in my defense.

"Sorry to be Johnny Raincloud here, but the letter's not for her. We can agree on that can't we?" Blanche says as she hops to her feet. She steps away from Rosie before she can be swatted again.

"Blanche, I'm aware that the note wasn't for me," I bark as I fiddle with the rough edge of one of black tiles that's been eroding on the counter. It makes a loud clicking sound as it snaps from my finger back to the table. I wouldn't have even noticed it if Bella hadn't slammed her hand over mine to stop me.

Blanche looks confused and her brows furrows in annoyance. "Then what are we discussing?" she demands

"What should she do? Right?" Goldie asks looking back at me with a question in her eyes.

"Exactly," I say motioning to Goldie, at least she understands. "I mean, I know it was kind of corny and everything, but he did sort of lay out all his feelings and stuff. I kind of feel bad for the guy, he lays his heart out and it wasn't even to the right person."

"Why are you assuming it's a guy?" Blanche asks as she bites at a hangnail on her thumb, taking a bit of chipped New Shiloh blue nail polish with it.

Everyone grows silent for a moment as they consider this. "It's a guy." I snip after a minute. "It has to be a guy."

Blanche shrugs as she throws her arm over my shoulder. The girl perpetually smells of clean sweat and sunscreen. It's a smell you want to snuggle into. "What do you care? It's not even for you."

"It's a guy Blanche." I hiss through my teeth and she laughs.

Suddenly Beattie emerges through the kitchen door.

"I'm sorry ladies, maybe you could clarify something for me. Am I running a pie shop or a sorority house here?" she snaps, pushing up the sleeves on her flour covered navy blue sweater. Normally, Beattie's fine with our messing around, but not when it's all of us, at the same time, and it's busy, busy.

Nixie snorts. "We'd be Pi-Pi-Pi." Beattie is not amused. Nixie hops down from the neon pink stool where she sits.

"You're right Beattie! This isn't a sorority house and I love pie. I have a table, in fact I think I have two." And with that she bolts to the other side of the restaurant, kicking up a gust of wind like an old school cartoon character as she passes.

Beattie sighs and shakes her head. "That girl has a screw loose somewhere."

I smile. "Yeah, but we love her."

"I think that might be the only reason I haven't killed her yet," she says as she turns back to me. "So what's going on?"

"What do you mean?" I ask, tucking the note into my pocket. I'm a little embarrassed about the whole thing, especially in front of Beattie.

She's smarter and faster than me though, as she snatches the letter from my pocket. I make no move to stop her. Once Beatrix Cod wants something it's futile to resist her. She scans the letter holding it a distance away because she isn't wearing her glasses.

"What is this?" she asks when she's done, looking up at me from under her pale lashes, a smirk lurking at the corner of her mouth.

"It was in my locker this afternoon," I admit as I chew on my lower lip, ignoring the metallic taste when I bite down a little too hard.

"Well, it's not for you? Is it?" she asks as she hands the letter back.

I shake my head and tuck the paper safely into my pocket, patting it there for security. "No, obviously not. But I'm not sure what I should do about it."

"What could you do?" Beattie asks as she wipes the counter down with a rag.

I let out a breath that hums between my lips as it's released. "I don't know. I feel bad that this guy wrote this letter and it's not even going to get to the girl it's meant for."

Beattie leans against the counter, throwing the rag back into the sketchy looking bucket where it leaves. "Well, I wouldn't worry your head too much about it. Do you have any idea who it might have been for?"

I sigh. "No, not a clue. But man do I wish a boy would write a letter like this for me."

Beattie puts her hand under my chin and says, "It'll happen sweetie, just give it time. Kids in your generation are in such a hurry to grow up and find your soulmates. I still haven't found mine and I'm more than twice your age."

I put my hand over hers and say, "Thanks Beattie." And I try not to be panicked at her admission that I may still be alone at forty.

Suddenly she stands up straight and chuckles, "I think we have company Ms. Conner."

I swivel around on my favorite green stool to look where Beattie is motioning. In the doorway stands a short, middle aged man. He has a bald head with peaks of salt and pepper hair around his ears, a nice dark gray suit with a red tie with a pair of wire framed glasses at the end of his nose. "Hello Elle," he says his voice comfortable and familiar to a point that I want to cry.

I hop off my stool and walk in his direction.

"Hi, Dad."

We glare at each other for a long while and I swear a tumbleweed from the wild west blows between us in our standoff.

"How can I help you?" I ask him coolly. My father and I are by no means close anymore. A lot of time has passed since our flea market adventures.

"Michelle-" he begins crossly, put off by my demeanor, I'm sure.

"Anthony," I interrupt mockingly. "How can I help you?" I ask again.

He crosses his arms over his chest.

"Young lady, your mother said that you refused to come home and see me." He shifts his weight between his expensive Italian dress shoes and pushes his glasses up his thin nose. I hate sometimes how much I look like him, thin features and all.

"No father, I told her that I had to go to work. Don't you always tell me that nothing comes above work? Or is that just your job?" I argue. Suddenly it's very important that I make sure all the menus are perfectly straight. It's difficult for me to maintain extended eye contact with him.

"You know that's not true. Everything I do is for my family." he says as he moves to sit in one of the booths by the front counter. Unfortunately, he picks one right in my section. The sign says "Please Wait to Be Seated" for a reason, I could have easily passed him off on one of my lovely friends instead.

"Are you going to order something? Because I kind of live on my tips you know," I demand as I stare down at the blank notepad in my hand. I can feel my palm getting sweaty underneath, but I focus all my effort into holding onto it. Conners don't show their weaknesses.

Shockingly, my father decides to play along.

"What's good?" he asks, slipping his glasses off and placing them on the table in front of him.

Now I'm just annoyed. This is my place, I don't want him here.

"Why don't you go home? Mom's been running around like a chicken with her head cut off getting ready for you to get here."

He sighs, adjusting uncomfortably in his seat and pinching the space between his eyes. I understand the feeling. I too now have a headache.

"Yes, I'm sure she has."

It's not an accident that my father chose a job where he travels nonstop. Being around my mother is not his favorite pastime.

"So what's good to eat?" he asks again, pushing his glasses even further away.

I don't have time for this.

"I like the pumpkin," I answer curtly, waiting for this weird experiment of his to end.

He smiles, actually smiles. It's terrifying.

"I'll take a pumpkin then."

"Fine, a piece of pumpkin pie." I mumble as I scribble it down on the pad in front of me. I obviously can remember it, but it's a good excuse to advert my eyes.

"No, I think I'll take a whole pie." he says with a smirk. Even the way he smiles, with just the corner of his mouth turning up, looks so much like me I want to smack him. Can't any part of my identity be my own?

I huff and sit across from him in the booth.

"Why? So you can sit here and watch me during my whole shift?"

"I promise to give you a big tip," he says with that same big smile. Mocking me I was sure for my earlier outrage over his wasting my time.

I push my thumb down on the plunger of my pen, channeling some of my angst on the inanimate object before sliding it into the hair of my messy bun.

"Fine, whatever." I sulk as I walk away, doing my best to not stomp my feet like a child. This is so like him to make me miserable.

I skulk back to the window where Rosie's waiting for me. "I need a whole pumpkin pie," I gripe as I hand her the ticket with my father's order.

"Your dad's going to eat a whole pie?" she asks, her eyes wide with surprise. I don't know why she seems that way. My father's a rather pudgy guy. At least that's one way we're different. He's short and lumpy and I'm tall and thin as a rail.

"Yes, isn't it lovely?" I gripe as I cut myself a very large slice of my signature pie. I'm upset. It's allowed.

She scratches her head as if she has no idea what to say to me. Rosie doesn't do well with emotions. They aren't her style and she especially doesn't do well with parents. She's never really had them. She points her thumb in the direction of the stove, my attention caught by the perfect black nail polish she wears. She never seems to reapply it, but it's always there and flawless. Some kind of Voodoo black magic.

"I'll just go put the pie in for you," she murmurs as the front door jingles behind us.

To my overwhelming, oh so overwhelming, displeasure, another member of my family stands in the doorway of the pie shop. Eleanor makes every effort to never, ever come to this place. So what's she doing here now? That's really a stupid question. The answer is taking up one of my booths awaiting his pumpkin pie.

"Michelle," my mother notions as she slides off her slim brown leather jacket. It's too warm for it, but I know that comfort isn't why she wears it. The jacket costs more than I even care to think, and she knows that people will notice. That's all.

"He's over there." I say with a sigh, pointing to my father's seat. My eyelids are impossibly heavy. Five minutes with both my parents and I'm exhausted.

"What makes you think I'm here to see him?" she asks as she straightens out her perfectly smooth black hair, looking around as if it's not for anyone in particular. Who's she really trying to fool?

I could definitely crawl under the counter and take a nap I'm so exhausted. Eternal slumber seems like a valid way to avoid my problems.

"Please mother, you never come here to see me. Just go over there to him." I'm aware, of course, of what's bothering her. The fact that after all his time away and all her efforts to make it a pleasant homecoming for him, he only wants to see me.

"Why is he here with you, when I'm home waiting for him?" she mutters through a clenched jaw. Her eyes are now locked on the spot where I know she wants to focus. My father's doing his best not to look at us. No one cares that much about the pie menu to be studying it as intensely as he is.

I grumble and turn back to the counter. Mrs. Reed approaches with her check and outstretches her credit card to me while wrangling her twin five year olds. The boys slap and poke at each other under heads of cowlicked hair and whine in unison about wanting to go home. Mrs. Reed has a finger looped through the back of each boy's shirt and seems oblivious to their protests as she waits for me to run her card through our ancient system. I can't imagine my mother ever tolerating that kind of behavior from any of us, out in public or otherwise.

"I don't have time for this mom. Go over and talk to him if you want, or just leave. Or maybe I'll get you a booth and you can sit and eat a whole pie on your own too. I don't care. I just don't want to be a part of it."

"You do not speak to me like that young lady," she hisses, grabbing my wrist hard. I hate when she does the young lady thing with me. And any kind of physical aggression on her part has always seemed like lazy parenting to me.

Today I'm in no mood for her. I pull my wrist away, and I know that it's not the best idea, but I can't stop myself.

"You don't touch me."

I brace myself, unsure of what her response will be. Neither of us has the chance to say anything however. Like always, Beattie comes to my rescue. She steps in front of me, facing me, her face strong and serious.

"Go in the back."

Her hands are warm and urging on my shoulders and I know it's not a question, but my feet refuse to move.

"I'm fine," I mutter, ungrateful for her saving me. My jaw is throbbing from the grinding of my teeth and angry tears burn the backs of my eyes.

Beattie takes a step toward me even though she's already too close. She smells like cake batter and fabric softener. It's the way I imagine mothers are supposed to smell. My mother reeks of floral perfume and judgment. Bella emerges from nowhere to finish up with Mrs. Reed. The boys have started pulling at each other's hair and she's ready to get out of here.

"That wasn't a request Elle. Go."

I turn on my heel and storm back into the kitchen. I know Beattie will handle it and I should appreciate having someone so ready in my corner. It's just that sometimes I'd like to fight my own battles.

I burst through the kitchen door and slam into Rosie and the uncooked pie in her hands. Cherries and their juices ooze down the front of her and squish into her cleavage. She slides the sad, empty pie dish onto her stainless work table. She purses her lips and plants her fists on her curvy hips.

"Why?" she whines softly as she stares at her ruined black shirt.

I pace back and forth across the kitchen, ignoring Rosie and her cat eyes of as they follow me.

"Why are they even here? They ruin everything. This is mine, not theirs."

"You yell about this constantly," Rosie begins, dabbing and wiping at the scarlet stain on her skin with a green towel she uses to do her dishes. She's sitting cross legged on her counter, trying not to make eye contact with her dearly departed pie.

"I don't know what to tell you anymore. What is it you want to hear?"

She's right. If it's not about the pie shop, it's something else involving my family. I don't want them to be a part of me and yet they seem to be everything I talk about.

"I guess I don't have much else to talk about," I admit with a frown.

The timer on the oven beeps and Rosie smiles as she points to it.

"Your dad's pie's done."

I turn out of the kitchen with my father's pie and run into Beattie. She smiles, and asks, "You okay Elle?" The maternal concern in her voice as she places her hand on my shoulder makes me want to cry. The tears are already on the brim, it won't take much to make them fall.

"I don't know what to do Beattie," I weep, slamming the pie a little too hard onto the counter. Rosie will not be pleased if I break her dish.

She sighs and rubs my shoulder with her hand.

"Well, your mother and I had a little discussion and I don't think she's going to be a problem."

"Why?" I wonder in surprise. The mere fact that anyone would yell at my mother is shocking enough, but the fact that my mother would take it kind of pushes me over the edge.

"Because I told her that if she came in here again and acted like that I would have to call the police and make sure that they take her to the station… in handcuffs. Sheriff Elroy has a bit of a crush on me so I know he'd do it if I asked."

THIS WOMAN IS MY HERO! I only wish I could have seen Eleanor's face when she heard it.

"Wow. I've never heard of anyone doing anything like that to her."
Then a thought settles over me and I'm not quite so jubilant anymore.
"What about my dad?"

She twists my shoulders toward the direction of the tables. My father's still waiting in the booth and waves to me. I grimace and turn back to Beattie. She grins, sadist.

"He said that he wants to talk to you for a minute and then he'll leave."

"Want to be me for a minute?" I groan, kicking my foot into the solid counter in hopes of breaking a toe and winning a trip to the hospital to avoid all of this.

She laughs and pushes me gently away and toward my dad.

"I have my own parents, thank you very much. You go deal with yours."

I whine for a moment and kick my foot one more time before heading to the booth. I slide the warm pie in front of him and he beams at me. I don't like this stranger masquerading as my father.

"Want a piece?"

"I'm good." I answer waving my hand at the pie. I'm even madder than before. My father has made me refuse pie, PUMPKIN PIE!

He shrugs, completely ignoring my angst.

"Okie dokie, more for me then." He picks up his fork and dives in like cheetah after a wildebeest. It's disturbing.

I take a deep breath. I want this over with and to go back to pretending that he doesn't exist. Well, what I actually want is for him to go home, do his laundry and get back on the road where he belongs. It's too strange and dysfunctional to have him home.

"What did you want to talk to me about dad? I have to get back to work."

He looks up at me sadly and there's hurt it his eyes. I don't know how to take it.

"I was really looking forward to seeing you Elle. I miss seeing you."

"Since when?" I demand. It comes off a little shriller than I want it to and I'm attracting attention. When I'm mad I'm not exactly rational.

He seems generally upset, which is generally creepy.

"Now come on Michelle, that's not fair. I always miss you. You're my daughter."

Who is this guy? I know that it cannot be my father. Through my entire childhood my dad had always seemed more pleased with ignoring my existence than spending any time with me. Our weekly flea market trips were the exception of course, but even that hadn't lasted. What on earth is going on now? Only one thought pops into my mind and in common Elle Conner fashion, I let it spill right out. "Dad," I begin, grabbing his attention. "Are you dying?"

He nearly spits his pumpkin pie out he's caught so off guard. Blanche, who happens to be walking by, stops at the table. Since my best friend has no sense of boundaries she decides to sit down in the booth next to me.

"You're dying Mr. C?" I narrow my eyes at her, willing her to go away. Oblivious as always, Blanche picks up a fork and digs into the middle of dad's pie.

Dad wipes his mouth and questions, "I'm sorry, who are you?"

I bite down on my lip hard, and for once Blanche lets me take the conversation. Her mouth's too full of pie to interrupt me anyway.

"See, this is what I mean, Father. If you cared so much about my life you would know that this is Blanche Summers, my best friend. Damn, she's practically the sister I never had."

My father scratches the back of his bald head, quite confused.

"Elle, you have two sisters."

My expression remains unchanged. "Like I said," I turn to Blanche. "Can you let me talk to my dad for a minute?" She smiles and nods, placing her fork in my hand. She returns to her aggravated table that has apparently been waiting not so patiently for her.

I round back to my dad, who's cracking the knuckles on his left hand, a sound that rips at my ears. He's staring at me so hard, I worry he'll burn a hole through my forehead.

"What? Seriously?" I bark in a harsh tone, completely freaked out by this imposter.

He lets out an exasperated breath that whistles through the small gap in his front teeth.

"No Elle, I'm not dying. I'm not sick. I'm fit as a fiddle."

His gut disagrees with the last part. My rotund, roly-poly of a parent needs to jog a few laps around the block.

"I'm just interested in getting to know my oldest child."

"Why?" I know that I already asked, but I can't get away from it. "Why now? Why after all this time do you suddenly want to know me?" It hurts me enough that we've grown so far apart over the years. His sudden need to wiggle back in makes my stomach ache.

He looks down at his pie and pushes it towards me. He pulls his wallet out of his pocket and thumbs a fifty out of a wad of cash, placing it on the table in front of me.

"Keep the change, Pumpkin," I approve of neither the pun nor the cutesy name. "I'll see you at home." And with that he slowly wedges himself out of the booth and leaves. Cryptic.

No sooner is his second foot out the door before Blanche is back at the booth eating my father's pie, with my father's fork. I would have been disgusted, if it hadn't been Blanche. Growing up with seven brothers, I'm sure that sharing a fork was the least gross thing she did on a regular basis.

"So, what's the dealio?" she asks.

My eyes stay locked on the door, "I don't have a clue."

For the first time in my entire life I'm actually interested in going home. Something isn't right about dad and I know I won't feel right until I clear it up.

Chapter Four

When I get to my house after closing I know that something's really wrong. The twins pace the front lawn, in bare feet. Tyler and Megan don't leave the house without shoes, ever, and they certainly don't pace.

"What's wrong?" I ask Tyler as I approach the yard.

Her face twists into something resembling concern.

"I don't know, they're yelling." Another first, my sister doesn't throw a sarcastic comment my way. Just as unsettling as my father's kindness. My universe may be dysfunctional, but it's mine and I'm used to the way it spins.

Suddenly, the door behind us flies open and I have to grab Tyler around the waist and pull her out of the way as my father comes storming out. My mom's close on his heels. They seem to have no idea that their children are even here.

"Where are you going?" Eleanor cries, her black mascara streaming down her cheeks. Another serious indicator something's wrong, my mother would only step outside looking her pristine best.

"I'm leaving again in the morning. I'm staying at the hotel tonight," he howls as he rips his car keys from his pocket. His breathing is heavy and labored, probably the most exertion he's had in years. Our nosy neighbor, Mrs. Thompson, peeks out through her kitchen blinds and I'm sure hers won't be the last eyes to watch us if we stay out here.

I've had enough. I jump in between them, flailing my arms back and forth to shut them up for a second.

"Hey, someone want to fill the kids in?"

They both seem surprised. My mom actually seems vulnerable, nearly human, for a moment.

"You're father's leaving, he wants a divorce." My heart catches in my throat as a silence settles around the five of us. Crap.

The twins start wailing hysterically. My mother's crying just as hard. My dad begins to yell. I want to join them and cry and scream myself, but apparently there's only one member of the Conner family with the capability to act like an adult. It has to be me. I place two fingers in my mouth and whistle as loud as I can. They all fall silent, staring at me. They're not the only ones looking. Other neighbors have joined Mrs. Thompson and pop their heads out to see what the commotion is and now they're looking at me as well. Embarrassed, I march over to my dad and yank his fleshy arm.

"We're not doing this outside. We look like extras from Jerry Springer," I whisper harshly in his ear. To the rest of my family I announce, as silently as possible, "Everyone inside now."

My father tightens his jaw and proclaims, "The only thing I'm doing is leaving, Elle."

I strengthen my grip on his arm, in no mood for insubordination, especially from my dad.

"No, the only place you're going is in the house." He doesn't fight me now. I suppose he's shocked by my tone and the mere fact that I'm standing up to him at all. I'm usually the passive one of the Conner family.

I herd everyone into the front door, send the weeping twins into the living room and my parents into the kitchen. Mom and Dad immediately start arguing. I'm forced to whistle again.

"Shut up!" I yell. Normally my mother would have thrown a tizzy, screaming and throwing things, but I think she's too distraught to react. "Now both of you take a breath and let's talk about this calmly. At 17 years old, I refuse to be the only rational person in this room."

They both stand there silent for a long moment before my father says, "I don't see what we have to talk about." He pulls out a breakfast bar stool and hops his round little body up onto it.

"We're going to talk about why out of the blue, you two are discussing divorce." I demand, leaning back against the breakfast bar. My back goes slack and my eyes are heavy as the weight of handling a situation far beyond my maturity level overcomes me.

"Come on now Elle," my father begins with a huff that comes out like a wheeze after his physical activity. "You're a smart kid. You know that this hasn't been working for a long time."

"Well, then why the sudden need to change it? You've been living apart forever. What's different now?" I screech, stomping my foot like a little kid. My adult abilities for the evening run thin. The quiet in the room is so intense that I swear I can our hearts beating out loud. "Well, somebody say something."

"Would you like to tell her Anthony, or should I?" my mother jeers coldly as she leans against the sink, her arms crossed over her chest. It's the most relaxed I've ever seen her, which only lets me know that it's the most uncomfortable she's ever been. If my mother doesn't have a giant stick up her butt then she's far, far off her game.

"Tell me what?" I insist. They're silent, which just makes me mad. "Tell me what?" My fists slam down into my legs, but I barely feel it. Fear settles in the pit of my stomach as my vision blurs around its edges.

My mother shifts her weight off the sink and takes a step toward me.

"Well, if your father's going to be a coward then I guess I'll tell you," she voices with what appears to be a smile.

"Eleanor, don't do this. This is about you and me, not them." my father urges with a hiss, hobbling off the stool to approach her.

"We're your family too, Dad." I shout, failing to keep my composure at this moment as my voice betrays me and breaks with a crack. "Don't we have the right to know what's going on?"

The silence is deafening again as I wait for them to tell me. Finally my mother sighs and takes pity on my fragile sanity. "He has someone else."

That's not what I'd been expecting.

Angry and surprised tears spring to my eyes and my hearing drops with my blood pressure down to my feet.

"What?" I breathe out, my voice nearly inaudible. "What!" I scream as my heart pounds viscously against my ribs.

"Elle, I'm sorry-" my father apologizes as he reaches out for my arm, but I pull it away as though he'd burned me.

"No, no, no, no, you don't get to be sorry," I growl. My teeth clench so tight I think they might shatter. "Is this why you came by the diner and tried to be sweet to me? Were you trying to soften the blow of all this?" That turns the anger I feel into betrayal which is so much worse. I had thought that maybe, just maybe, he was actually trying to make a change. That he actually missed me, but apparently I'd been wrong. He just doesn't want me to hate him. The heat starts rising up my shoulders and flushes my face. I'm so angry I can barely contain it.

"Jesus dad, couldn't you at least have made a little effort to win me over. I mean, I always wanted a puppy." I hear my mother snicker bitterly. My eyes snap over to her.

"What?" my voice clips. I'm mad at her too. I mean, my father is the one who's leaving, but my mother doesn't exactly do a wonderful job of making anyone want to stick around.

She bites the inside of her cheek and says sharply, "Look in the living room." She has to be kidding.

I duck my head around the corner and see my sisters playing with a golden retriever puppy in the middle of the living room floor. I whip my head back around.

"Seriously?!"

My father shoves his hands in the pockets of his suit pants and rocks back and forth on his heels. "I don't know, Becky thought that it would help you and your sisters with the change and-"

"Whoa, whoa, whoa!" I shout, cutting him off before he tells me anymore about... Becky. "First of all, we're not in kindergarten. You can't distract us with a puppy while you run out the back door-" I of course ignore the fact that my twin sisters seemed to completely forget about my father's abandonment once they saw the dog. "And second, don't you dare say her name to me. You don't have any right to say her name to me."

"Elle, sweetie, I think you'll really like her once you get to know her. I mean she's really not that much older than you are. I think you'd have a lot in common-"

That was all he was able to say, all he can say before I hit him. I slap him so hard my hand stings. A sharp intake of breath sounds around the five us as we process what's just happened.

"How dare you! How dare you say that to me! You want me to get to know the woman, well girl apparently, that you're leaving your family for? You know what Dad? Screw you!" I reach out and grip his arm and pull him toward the door, pushing him outside.

"Leave! Get out of here and don't ever come back!" Before he can say anything I slam the door behind him and melt down against it. I pull my long legs up to my chest and balance my forehead against my knees.

My mother kneels down beside me and places her hand on top of my head. The smell of her floral perfume makes me want to vomit.

"Thank you for defending me like that Michelle."

I look up at her with fire in my eyes and slap her hand away.

"I wasn't defending you! I was defending me. If it wasn't for the fact that you're so nuts he might have been home every once in awhile and this never would have happened. This is your fault as much as it is his."

I jump to my feet and hurry into the living room. I steal the little puppy off the floor, much to the dismay of my sisters.

"Hey! Give him back!" Tyler cries. But I don't hear her. It's taking everything in my power not to break down in a puddle right here.

I run up the stairs to my attic bedroom and pull the steps up behind me. I collapse on my bed and snuggle the innocent puppy up to my chest and let myself cry a little. As if my life doesn't have enough problems already. Now a divorce gets thrown into the mix and a toddler dating my father.

The puppy begins sniffing around me, like puppies often do, and he drags something out of my pocket. It takes me a second to get it away from him, but finally I win. His little tail wags with glee and I scratch his head. It's the letter from my locker that I wrestle away from him. I press it to my chest. Maybe it's best that I got this and not the person it's intended for. I probably saved this poor guy a ton of heartache over this girl. Matters of the heart never turn out the way we want. I've been stupid to ever think otherwise.

…..

"Whoa, whoa! Time out, your dad's leaving?" Rosie asks Monday at lunch, as I sulk over my turkey sandwich. Too much mayonnaise.

"Yup," I mumble into the bread.

"And he bribed you with a puppy?" Nixie adds, as she takes the cookies I didn't want from my brown paper lunch. I had been too distracted by the events of the previous night to really pay much mind into what went into my lunch. I accidentally packed a bunch of the twins' soy products, yuck! Thank God that with her training for the swim team, it's the only stuff Nixie eats. I do hate to waste food. "See, you always struck me as a person to be overtaken by a kitten, not a puppy."

Rosie kicks Nixie under the table. "That's not the problem with the puppy, dumb-dumb."

"Then what is the problem?" Nixie whimpers as she rubs her shin.

"The fact that he's leaving his family for a child and tried to make it all better with a pet," Rosie explains.

I give up on the turkey sandwich and nod. "Yeah, pretty much." I run my hands over my face, fighting the urge to start crying. I really, REALLY didn't want to do that in school. Lucy Wilcox could have been hiding around any corner waiting to mock me. "I can't believe that I'm getting so upset about this. I mean, I don't ever see my father, nor do I want to really. Why does it bother me that they're finally making it official? I mean, I've been betting this would happen since I was a little kid."

"There's a simple answer to that if you want to hear it." Nixie says as she bites her bottom lip.

I nod and lean back against the blue plastic chair supplied to us by the public school system. "Lay it on, my sister."

She sighs and wraps her red hair in a knot at the base of her neck. "Listen, it's one thing to imagine about what could happen, someday, maybe-"

"But it's a whole other ballgame when it actually happens." Rosie adds. "It's okay to be upset about this-"

"I think we'd be worried about you if this didn't bother you. This is normal." Nixie finishes. "So be sad, it's okay."

"Aw, is little Miss Conner sad?" Lucy sasses behind me. As if the day couldn't get worse.

"Go away, Lucy," I grunt to my apple juice, knowing there's nothing to be gained by making eye contact with the witch herself.

"Excuse me?" she crows, her hooker high wedges entering my field of vision beside our table. Not that I didn't already know she was there. There's a cloud that follows her of pure darkness and evil that you can practically taste before she even enters a room.

"She said, go away Satan spawn," Goldie calls from behind her, as she pushes her way around to the table. In her hands she's carrying a lunch tray with only an apple and a bottle of water. It's funny because I know she'll end up eating all the fries off Rosie's plate before lunch is over.

Goldie has absolutely no problem making Lucy mad, one of the few, if not the only one who can do it. I guess, beautiful people have the go ahead to call out other beautiful people. Lucy knows the code and yet she's so flabbergasted that she storms away from the table without another word.

Goldie rolls her eyes to the back of her head and takes the chair next to mine. I often envy how little she cares about what people think. This is no exception. "What's crack-a-lacking?" she muses as she grabs my potato chips. See, she never starves. When we meet her with silence she looks up from the chip bag. "Somebody die?" That's my girl, dumb as a post, but no problem with being blunt.

"Mr. Conner's moving out," Rosie clues her in as her fingers steeple under her chin.

Goldie's quiet a second, she's never quiet. It makes me sure that some profound wisdom is about to spill from her lips. "Damn," she mutters instead. Why is this such a shock to everyone? I mean I hadn't seen it coming (no matter how obvious it should have been to me), but my friends were blown away. Why? "I'm sorry, Elle."

My shoulders twitch, trying to brush it off. I know they'll be able to see right through me. And they do. "Don't even try giving me any of that 'it's not a big deal' bull, because I won't be buying it." Rosie snaps, jutting an ever black painted finger at me.

"Don't point that thing at me; it's got a nail in it," I murmur, pushing her hand away from my face.

Rosie opens her mouth to say something else, but a presence beside us stops her. The three of them look up, so I decide it's important enough for me to check out too. Standing next to me is this super pimply faced kid, only about five feet tall and 90 pounds soaking wet. His red hair sticks up in every direction and his Darth Vader breathing invades my ears. "Do you have locker 3788?" he asks simply, his nasally voice wheezing out like a whistle.

He's distracted me so much with his overall awkwardness that I almost don't hear him. "What?" I reply, pulling myself back to reality.

"Do you have locker 3788?" he asks a little slower, over enunciating every word, only making me feel a little stupid.

My head bobs up and down slowly, doing my best to keep my jaw from hanging open. My friends look as creeped out as me. Especially Nixie, our resident ginger who hates this stereotypical display of her kind. Her eyes narrow and her jaw locks in disdain as she crushes an innocent bag of teddy bear cookies in her hand. "Uh-huh." I mutter.

He narrows his eyes at me, clearly annoyed, "Well do you have a response?" he requests as he taps his dirty, untied sneaker against the cafeteria floor.

"A response? A response to what?" I ask, trading a glance with Rosie to see if I had missed something. Her jaw is slack and her brow furrowed, good to know she's as lost as I am.

"The letter I put in your locker" he explains further, so slow he's practically talking backwards. Of course. Of course this is the person. And yes, I'm still painfully aware that the letter was not intended for me. That doesn't mean that I wasn't holding onto the romantic notion (as anti-romantic as I am) that it had been written by some knight in shining armor. That has officially been shot to hell.

Disgust rises up on my face, crinkling at my nose and between my eyes. "Oh," I sing out, my voice several octaves too high, attempting to redeem myself. I mean for all I know he could be a nice guy, and he really put himself out there with that letter. I owe him the benefit of the doubt. "You wrote the letter?"

He rolls his eyes again. I start to feel a little less bad for the jerk.

"No, I just delivered it. I go to New Shiloh outside of town-" same school as Blanche. "A guy there asked me to put it in your locker." Thank God! And again I do know that letter wasn't for me. I'm not completely delusional. Not completely. "So," he holds out again, really impatient.

"So, what?" I question.

"Response? Do you have one?" he demands, sniffling in a congested breath that makes me gag.

I take a deep breath, resisting the instinct to reach out and strangle this guy, and ignore the nauseating stench of his acne cream and unnatural BO. "Um, can one of you give me a piece of paper?" I ask to my circle of friends.

Rosie furrows her brow and begins, "Elle, why would you-" I kick her, rather hard, under the table. "Ow!" she shrieks, pulling her injured shin up under her in the blue plastic chair.

"Just give me the paper Rosie," I hiss sharply. She reaches into her bag and hands me her black notebook and a pen, rather begrudgingly I might add. I know I'm getting an earful for this later.

I scribble down something quickly on the paper. I do it fast before my friends can read it and judge me. Or before I can change my mind and not do it at all. I fold the paper up and hand it to the pimply kid, turning my attention back to my apple juice. "Pleasure doing business with you." he says flatly before disappearing from the cafeteria. Gone as mysteriously as he'd arrived.

"Will you let it drop already?" I implore as the bell on the door of the pie shop jingles. Rosie and Goldie follow close behind me. Nixie had to go to swim practice, or else she'd be here nagging away at me too. They'd been on my case the entire day about writing the note back. I almost opted to walk to the shop rather than ride in Goldie's car and face more ridicule, but alas, it began to rain. Damn it.

"You kicked me. I demand an explanation," Rosie insists as she hangs her leather jacket on the coat hook inside the door. It drips water on the floor. I hate when it rains. I'll have to mop that up later.

"And you did use her paper and her pen," Goldie continues as she adds her yellow slicker on the rack as well. So much water! I'll have to get on it quickly before someone falls.

"Will you please, please, please let it drop? I beg of you." I don't want to talk about it. I really begin to think the response was a mistake and these people, who are supposed to be my friends, aren't making it any easier.

"What's going on?" Bella asks from behind the register with a smile as she adjusts her black framed glasses. Bella's always only half listening to you. Her nose is forever stuck in book. Today it seems to be an examination of abnormal psychology. The girl certainly knows how to party.

"She wrote a response to the note," Goldie answers, plopping down on the green stool and cutting herself a hearty slice of pie before starting her shift.

"The note that wasn't for her?" Bella confirms, her grin growing. I'm so pleased that I can be a walking punchline for all my friends.

"My darling girl, let's just say that today I'm very envious of the fact that you're home schooled," I say to Bella as I take the pink stool next to Goldie and rest my forehead on the counter. It's sticky with sugary syrup from some unknown pie. Perfect.

Bella pats the top of my head like I'm some kind of puppy. "I doubt that's true, but okay."

"It is true! I swear it!" I yelp into the table, slowly peeling my skin from the counter.

"So, what did you write?" Bella inquires as she wipes down the counter in front of me. Too little, too late for my poor forehead that itches something fierce from whatever had been on the tile a minute before.

They're nothing if not persistent and I know they're not going to let up. "Fine," I sigh as I throw back my head. Suddenly they swarm around me. Thank God, there are only three of them. "It's really not that exciting though, so don't be disappointed." They don't seem fazed. "All I said was that I was sorry, but he'd gotten the wrong girl. I found his letter really sweet and that the real girl was lucky. Whoever she was."

They seem disappointed. "Well that's lame," Rosie whines with a frown creasing between her perfectly plucked eyebrows.

"Yeah, I'm with her," Bella agrees, pointing a thumb at Rosie. Bella's as romantic as they come, I thought she'd be on my side.

Goldie's lower lip juts out in a pout and she adds, "I find myself disappointed and underwhelmed." She scoops the remainder of her pie into her mouth before pushing her plate to Bella, who narrows her eyes back at Goldie's inability to bus her own plate.

"What's wrong with it?" I ask, I think I did quite a good job. It was nice, kind and not meant to hurt him, exactly the letter I'd want to get.

Goldie shrugs. "I don't know. I guess I thought you were going to, you know, play along or something. It would have been more interesting." She wraps that impossible mass of hair into a twisted bun on top of her head. It resembles a cinnamon bun out of a diabetic's dream. She shoves two pens through it to keep in place before adjusting her skirt and sweater to show off some of her flawless midriff. Clearly she's assuming Beattie isn't here, because our boss would have a cow over that fashion choice at work.

"That would have been cruel. What if he had found out? I wouldn't do that." I exclaim as I pull my dark hair back. My shift's about to begin and Beattie doesn't like it when we start late.

Bella huffs, balancing her chin on her hand as she stares off in the distance at nothing, longing pools in her eyes. "I don't know. It would be kind of romantic to have this secret love affair through letters. Very old world." Now that's the Bella I know and love.

And of course Rosie is Rosie, she flicks Bella in the arm. "Snap out of it, crazy person."

I grin as the door jingles open again. Blanche, just the girl I've been waiting for, comes inside, soaking wet in her track clothes. She's covered in mud up to her knees and tracks it all over the nice, shiny floor. "Damn it, woman!" I shriek, pointing sharply to the floor.

She looks down at the floor. "Whoops." It's like she's trying to hurt my feelings.

"Oh, you and your whoops," I pout in a shrill tone.

Bella laughs and maneuvers around the counter. "I'll get you the mop."

"Thanks," I mutter as I scratch my head.

"What's up, buttercup?" Blanche asks as she pulls off her filthy shoes and throws them into her track bag.

"And you couldn't have done that outside why?" I demand as I take the mop from Bella. The pungent smell of the disinfectant makes my stomach turn.

Blanche looks up at me like I'm a crazy person. "My feet would have gotten wet." Oh, of course, how could I have been so stupid? "So what's with all the tension?" she asks as she waves a finger between all of us.

"She wrote a letter back to the mystery man," Rosie chimes in, her face popping up from the kitchen, already covered in flour. No idea how she always gets that way so quickly.

"Really? Why?" she wonders as she slicks back her wet hair. She ties her black apron around her lean waist and her white high tops squeak against the damp floor as she takes over mopping for me.

"Because it was the nice thing to do," I grumble. I don't get why this was so hard for everyone. "But I was wondering if I could ask you something?"

"Shoot, bumblebee," she says with a laugh as she wipes down her legs with a towel from her bag, balancing her weight against the mop.

"Well, you go to New Shiloh and I think maybe you can help me identify someone," I continue as I straighten the menus in their holder.

"Who are we talking about? I mean, it's a big school, but I might know who you mean," she asks as she resumes her mopping, intrigue in her voice.

Behind me Rosie snorts and I do my best to ignore her. "There's a guy, red hair, short, really skinny." She thinks it through, but it doesn't seem to set off any bells. "Pimply face and nasal voice." That ignites a light bulb in her brain as her eyes light up. She's practically giddy.

"What about him?" Blanche asks with sudden playful curiosity. I don't want to tell her anymore.

"Nothing, never mind." I hurry off to my table and away from this conversation. Mr. and Mrs. White wait patiently for me to take their order. They're always patient. I don't think it's because they like us so much, the pie's just so good. "I'll be right there." I bellow with a smile.

Mrs. White nods to me. "Take your time dear, we're in no hurry. We never are."

"No, no, no, no," Blanche cackles as she steps in front of me, blocking my path to the table. She's one of the few people I know who can really stand eye to eye with me. Why couldn't Blanche have gotten her mother's tiny frame instead of being an Amazon like her dad. "You ask me about Guy Feldman and nearly in the same breath tell me that you responded to the letter. You have to tell me more. Is Guy the mystery man?" She laughs and turns to all my friends who don't jump to my rescue and refute this. "Oh, this is too good!"

"It's not that guy!" I shout. Once again I remember that the letter was not meant for me, but did everyone have to insist upon bursting my delusional bubble? "He just put it in my locker and delivered back the response."

Blanche nods as if this makes some sense to her. "I guess, I get that. I mean, Guy is kind of known as the messenger at my school."

"What is that?" Goldie asks as she brings Mr. and Mrs. White two glasses of water. I smile to thank her. "You make it sound like you go to spy school." Goldie, in her childlike innocence, starts hopping up and down with excitement. "Holy crap, do you go to spy school!?" she shrieks at a level only dogs can hear.

Blanche narrows her thin eyes at her. "No, you idiot. All I mean is that Guy kind of goes unnoticed. You saw the guy, do I really have to explain?" Obviously not. "So for the right price he runs favors for other people." I won't lie, that sounds a bit like spy school to me.

"Well apparently he's running one for the mystery man." I say as pull out my note pad. The Whites have waited long enough.

Blanche shrugs and moves onto her table, a mother and four children (Blanche's least favorite situation in the world, lots of kids) and mentions, "Apparently."

I spend the night at Goldie's, call my mother and tell her we have a history project to work on, anything to keep from going home. My mother's distraction with her pending separation and inevitable divorce have occupied her so much that she wouldn't have known if I miraculously turned into a cat and started singing on Broadway.

The next morning Goldie's grandmother holds me hostage and force feeds me waffles. I try not to cry into the butter and syrup at the unfamiliar maternal gesture. She won't me leave until she holds me in an extra long bear hug. I practically melt into her tiny frame. It takes both Goldie and her mom to pry us apart. Lori, Goldie's mom, instead pats me on the arm and squeezes my shoulder to say goodbye to me. I don't know which gesture was harder for me to swallow, but they both hurt. Whenever my mother touches me she treats it like a chore that takes some extreme amount of energy.

I decide to walk to school and it takes me exceptionally longer to get there than it normally would have. I arrive with most of the other students. I get to my locker and drop my book bag to the floor. I reach in a pull out its contents, my binder, chemistry book and world history book. Suddenly, not that I need to guess who did it, the books are knocked out of my hands. "Always a pleasure Lucy." I mumble as stare down at my fallen books. The spine on the chemistry text is cracked; lovely.

"Freak." She giggles with some serious sinister undertones as she sashays passed me in her disgustingly well coordinated mini skirt and tight sweater. The devil really does wear Prada.

"Always a pleasure," I murmur again to myself as I open my locker. I turn the combination, six to the right, thirteen to the left and 23 to right. It clicks open and to my total surprise, something falls out. Another letter, in the same white envelope as before. I pick it up and flip it over so I can see the front. It reads, "To the owner of locker 3788." That's me all right. This one's meant for me.

Chapter Five

Clearly I've been missing something in the years I've spent mocking Goldie and Bella over their obsession with dime store romance novels, because the thrill of opening what has even the potential to be a retro love letter nearly makes me swoon. I feel the need to drop by Franny's Books on 2nd Street before heading to work to fall completely into the world of ripped bodices and heaving bosoms. The folks who write those books are onto something.

My finger slices through the seal on the white envelope as my shaky fingers remove the letter. "To the owner of locker 3788," I read to myself in homeroom. I don't alert any of my friends to this note. I figure it's better to wait and read the contents for myself first before I involve all of them. "I have to say I was rather relieved when I got your letter. As soon as I'd sent the first one I wished I could have taken it back. It seemed a little embarrassing, laying my heart out and everything. I don't know what I was thinking even sending it. I really appreciate your kindness. I feel like I should tell you who I am, I mean I did bare my soul to you (however unintentional). I don't know, I guess I like the mystery.

So to my mystery girl, the owner of locker 3788, I'll be the mystery guy. Until we speak next, and then who knows." And that's it. I fold the letter back up carefully and press it against my desk with my palm. Okay, so it's not exactly the virile masculinity and breathy feminine wiles that I had built up in my mind, but maybe it was something? Or it was a Dear Jane letter when I'd never actually been the Jane, I will opt for positive and hopeful side that doesn't make me feel like a loser.

"What's that?" I suddenly hear from beside me.

Crumbling the letter into my hand, my head snaps to the side so fast I'm sure I'd given myself whiplash. Rosie hovers over my desk, watching me suspiciously through long black lashes. "Nothing," I squeak out, my voice about seven octaves higher than normal.

"Nothing my eye," my overly perceptive friend exclaims as she snatches the paper from my hand. Between Blanche's speedy Asian movement and Rosie's cat like reflexes in eternal blackness, I'm living in a world of ninjas.

She scans the paper quickly and then lets it fall at her side.

"Is this for real? You've got to be kidding!"

Maybe it's possible that Rosie's even less romantic than me. In the beginning I'd thought Rosie was on my side, but that doesn't seem to be the case anymore. I'm not wrong, right? She was the one telling everyone to leave me alone when I'd been reading the first note, wasn't she?

"This is just sad."

I grab the letter back from her, folding it up and returning it to the safety of my pocket. "Shut up, it's nice. Sweet really."

She takes the seat next to me. "No, it's stupid." She leans far over the side, her forehead practically touching mine. Proximity will apparently emphasize her point.

I rest my chin against the desk. "You're stupid." Yes, this is one of my more mature comebacks.

"Yeah, yeah, if I had a nickel for every time I heard that," she says in her traditional nonchalant way. She leans forward, all the way across my desk. "Seriously though Elle, I get the creeps from this whole thing. What if he's some type of crazy creepy stalker?"

"Rosie, he didn't even know it was me until yesterday," I sigh with a roll of my eyes.

"Yeah, but maybe he's all obsessive and creepy now," she continues with a shrug, straightening back up. She pushes her blonde bangs out of her eyes and shifts her shirt back into place over her perfect boobs. It's annoying how pretty my friends are.

"How many times are you going to fit 'creepy' into this conversation?" I ask as I open my textbook and binder, hoping that Rosie would end this conversation and move on to her own class. She's not supposed to be here. My teacher really doesn't like it when she is.

She shrugs again. "As many times as necessary I suppose. Any-who, all I'm saying is that maybe you should just nip this thing in the bud right now and walk away."

Before I have time to respond my teacher walks through the door. Without even looking up he cajoles, "Ms. Peters, this is not your class, please go find yours. I'm not telling you again." It's a message set on autopilot. He's always reminding Rosie of her last warning.

Rosie smiles and stands to attention. "Aye, Aye, Captain!" she proclaims with a sarcastic salute. To me, she whispers, "Just think about it." She marches out of the classroom with military precision. Her red stilettos click all the way down the hall.

"What are you thinking about?" Lucy sneers in the most evil tone she can muster. I swear she sounds like a snake mixed with a black cat, with an extra dash of evil.

My hand flies to my pocket, making sure the note's still safely there. "None of your business," I mutter, turning my attention to the chalkboard and the important lessons Hamlet has to teach me.

My discomfort intrigues Lucy. I kind of knew it would. Damn it. "Oh, we'll see about that," she purrs in that same tone as she flips forward in her seat. Whatever's turning in that sadistic head of hers is surely destined to be something bad for me.

When lunchtime rolls around, I wait in the hallway that leads to the cafeteria. It smells like stale potatoes and teenage angst, and I don't want to be here. I assume, like the last time, my little redheaded buddy will show up to receive a response. Knowing my friends, specifically Rosie, will disapprove, I decide to wait for him out here. Just as I expect, twenty minutes into my lunch period that pimply little face shuffles toward me. "Do you have something for me?" he asks dryly. What a miserable existence he seems to be living.

I extend the letter I've been holding in my hand out to him. It's simple in content. I only ask him one question. The girl he'd been searching for, how does he know her locker number and not her name? And how then does he not know mine? It's simple, but I want to know. Since his letter hadn't delved into anything deep I didn't want to be the psycho crazy person that took things there. "Thanks," I say to the grubby guy, named Guy.

He rolls his eyes. "Whatever." He disappears into the crowd of Harpersgrove students, taking the smell of zit cream with him.

As he walks away, I hear footsteps come up close behind me. "What are you doing Elle?" Rosie asks. She leans against the door frame with a disapproving look on her face. She reminds me of an old photograph of Marilyn Monroe, which I know is what she's going for. She's a beauty outside her time.

"Oh my God, Rose, it's just a letter. Like having a pen pal. That's all," I state definitively as I move around her, back into the cafeteria.

"A very creepy pen pal," she utters, keeping close on my heels. I'm walking at full speed and yet somehow at half my height and in four inch heels, she's able to keep up right at my side.

"Again with the creepy," I voice as I stop dead in middle of an aisle. The group of freshman boys sitting at the table beside us gawk up at Rosie in wonder. They are right at boob level.

She nearly falls over me. "Look, I'm your friend. I want you to think about what you're doing. This isn't you, it's not logical," she says honestly as she braces herself against me. The girl's heels are as thin as toothpicks, I'm shocked she can walk in them at all.

"Not everything has to be logical, Rosaline," I snap sharply. Why am I fighting with her? This is stupid, but I can't swallow my tongue. "It's something for me, something that's all mine. Let me have it."

Rosie bites down on her lip. "Fine, but I'm only looking out for you, Michelle."

"I don't need anyone to look out for me, Rosaline," I huff as I storm away.

I walk into the shop with Goldie after school that afternoon and the place is frenzied. Every table is filled along with every stool at the counter. We toss our jackets to Bella who's behind the counter, her hair falling from her messy ponytail and her face flushed with frustration. "Where have you guys been?" she demands as she thrusts change to a woman with frizzy red hair that snaps her gum in my ear. She doesn't shut the drawer on the register. By the sheer number of people in sight I'm sure she's worried the line will spread out the door if she has to try and force it open again.

"We just got out of school, what going on?" I ask as I tie my apron and shove a pencil through my bun.

"Arbies," Nixie yelps as she barrels around the corner from the kitchen, her arms lined with plates.

Of course, I know what you're asking. What's an Arbie right? Allow me to explain. In my small town when summer ends and fall arrives, the leaves change colors. This brings the Arbies. We made up the word here in Harpersgrove for the people who come to see the leaves change and fall from the trees (hence Arbies, you know like arbor, tree). Most of them are scattered photographers, both professional and wannabe. Once in awhile we'll get the family from Idaho, the retirees from Florida or even a documentary filmmaker. For pretty much the entire month of October it's us, and our cozy little town, versus them. The dreaded Arbies.

"What the hell is this?" Beattie fumes from the kitchen. Beattie has never been here for the Arbies. She has no idea what she was in for. She looks at Goldie and me and seems a little more than annoyed. Her dark red hair is slicked with sweat against her skin and her clothes. "Where is Rosie? I need Rosie."

I laugh as I shove my order pad in my apron pocket. "Good to see you too, Beat."

She points a dough covered spoon in my direction and it's twitching with Beattie's every word. "Don't mess with me right now. Where is she? And Blanche too?"

"You gave them today off, Beattie," Goldie reminds as she leads a couple to the only open booth at the back of diner. Opening such a quaint little spot like this in such an idyllic little town is like catnip to Arbies. We'll be lucky if the place is left standing when they roll out in a few days.

"Well call them, I need them now," she yells as she disappears back into the darkness of the kitchen.

I pull my cell out of my pocket and turn to Bella. "Hey Bells, can you call Rosie," I'm not exactly in the mood for her. "And I'll call Blanche." The Arbies always bring craziness, but usually some excitement too and we can use a little more of that.

It takes Blanche 45 minutes to get to the pie shop. Beattie's not happy. In fact I'm pretty sure her head's going to explode. I pummel Blanche as she comes through the door, but something that follows her stops me in my tracks. It's about 30 people in New Shiloh High School track uniforms. "What the hell is this?" I bark, motioning to the mob behind her.

She rolls her eyes. "It's a long story, but the real question is, what is all this?" she asks as she surveys the chaos that has become Hap-PIE-ly Ever After.

"Arbies," I mutter as I glance at the stack, yes stack, of orders sitting idly in my hand. I fear submitting to Beattie and Rosie who feverishly bake in the kitchen. The last time I popped my head in there I swear steam was bursting from both their ears.

"Like the fast food place?" she questions, completely confused. I forget so often that Blanche isn't from Harpersgrove. She lives just far enough outside our little bubble to know nothing about this.

"No, they come to see the leaves change on the trees. And we don't have room for all your track people here today. Why today?" I hiss, feeling my face flush. Stress management is not one of my mastered skills. I pick up a tray of pies, all for customers somewhere out here. I'll find their homes eventually, worse comes to worse I'll start shouting out descriptions of what's on the plates. I swing around, hitting something on the other side, the tray flying from my hands. It's like a scene from a movie. Everything moves in slow motion before colliding with its final target. Blueberries and apples and peaches ooze all down the front of the most attractive boy I've ever seen.

"Oh my god." I shriek, collapsing to my knees in front of him. He's covered in fruit and syrup, pie crust and crumbles and yet he's still so beautiful I'm fighting the urge to drool. He has piercing blue eyes and a face that seems to be chiseled from marble, oh his chin is perfect. I have a thing for chins. All types of pie drip and gush through his full head of coal black hair. I'm such a klutz idiot. "I'm so sorry. Are you- are you okay?" I croak pulling off the nice lace apron my grandmother had given me for my birthday a few years before (she always had this vision of me being a homemaker, but I digress) and begin wiping his face with it. They're going to hospitalize me for this. The men with butterfly nets and straightjackets can't be far away. I know I should stop touching the Adonis, but my hands have a mind of their own and they don't have any interest in stopping.

The incredibly cute boy reaches up and grabs my hand and I realize that he's been laughing at me. I look into that amazing face and see that he has perfect teeth, not like the creepy veneer kind, but legit pretty teeth. I'm suddenly aware of the presence of my tongue in my mouth. I can't possibly speak. Luckily, he talks for me. "Relax," he says with a laugh, oh God, even his voice is beautiful. "It's just pie." And then he does something rather unexpected, at least it is to me. He reaches up with his free hand, the other still holding onto my wrist, and drags a finger along his face, scooping up a bit of the remnants of what I guess used to be peach and blueberry pie and runs the same finger down my cheek. He leans back on his elbows, releasing my hand. He seems quite proud of himself, judging by the cocky look on his face. "There, now we're even." His lopsided smile kind of makes my heart flip, but only a little.

I smile back and reach up to the counter and grab a towel to toss over to him. Let him clean himself up so I look like less of a insane person. "I am sorry, are you all right?"

He rubs the towel across his thick mass of hair and winces when he sees how many colors are left behind. It's hard to see on straight black hair. "I told you it's just pie. No harm done."

I roll my eyes. "I meant because you fell. I didn't hurt you did I?"

Now he appears a bit offended. He presses his palm against his chest and bows his head toward me with a goofy look plastered on his face. "Woman, are you kidding? I'm a big brawny man. You couldn't hurt me if you tried." His lopsided smile makes me a bit dizzy, but I feel the need to play along with his macho act.

I rock back on my heels and tuck my knees under my chin. "Oh, is that so?"

He wraps his arms around his syrup covered knees and continues, "Yeah, that's so." After a long moment of staring and silence we both break into laughter. He rakes a hand through his goopy hair, momentarily forgetting that anything is amiss about it. He winces at the sensation of pie filling, clearly he didn't get it all, but just continues to smile. "So, is there anything that I'm wearing that you'd recommend?"

I feel myself blushing now. Really? This makes me blush? Talking about pie? God I'm a loser, but I can't let him see that. "I like the pumpkin," I say simply, motioning to the glob of orange on his shoulder.

He nods slowly, still smiling, always smiling and his big eyes locked on mine. I don't think I've ever had anyone hold such intense eye contact with me before. "Pumpkin, all right I like pumpkin." We're quiet again for a long moment and I've completely forgotten about the crazy crowd of people in the shop. He sticks his hand out to me. God, even his arms are beautiful. "Well it's nice to meet you Pumpkin Pie, I'm-" but he can't complete his introduction, someone else so desperately wants to do it for him.

"Finn!" A high pitched and squeaky voice screams from behind him. I glance back at the attractive boy and he grimaces with a slow blink of his eyes. I take a giant leap and assume that he is in fact Finn. I look up at the owner of the squeak and she's everything I hate dressed in her white and blue New Shiloh High School cheerleading uniform. Her bouncy blonde curls are tied back in a tight ponytail so I can clearly see her angry brown eyes burning holes into me. "Oh my God baby, what did she do to you?" the girl yelps as she rushes to Finn's side, but not close enough to risk getting anything on her.

Finn sighs and rolls over onto his knees. "Mal, I'm fine, can you just go and get me a tee-shirt from the truck?" he requests calmly. Captain nonchalant this guy. Madame High Maintenance is not so easy though.

She stomps her foot, yes stomps, and shouts, "I will not. You're covered in crap. And oh my God, don't even think about touching me until you've gotten it all off you. I mean like three showers' worth." Then she puts her attention on me, "And you," that was a little scary. "I want to talk to your manager now!"

Beattie's ears must have been burning because she emerges from the kitchen at just that moment, Blanche right behind her. My best friend's eyes shoot from Finn then to me and then back again, a question in her eyes that I'll have to wait to answer. "Is there a problem out here?" Beattie questions, wiping the back of her hands on her apron. It amazes me how fast Beattie can go from casual to business professional.

The girl identified as Mal looked scoffs at Beattie's question, her stance aggressive with her fists cemented on her narrow hips. She points down at her boyfriend and barks, "I don't know lady, do you think there's a problem?"

Beattie extends a hand down to Finn and helps him the rest of the way to his feet. "Are you okay?" she asks, nabbing the towel from his hand and starts doing the same thing I had originally done, wiping him like a crazy person.

Finn takes the towel from her, the same smile he'd given me plastered across his face. "Really it's fine. Don't worry about it. I insist."

"Um, it is not fine!" the witch known as Mal exclaims with a wiggle of her index finger all up in my boss's face. "I want to know what you're going to do about it, lady?"

Beattie, ever the professional, did not punch this chick in the face. Clearly why she's in charge and I'm not. "Well, I obviously will comp your bill with us today." She reaches under the counter pulls out the largest "Hap-PIE-ly" tee shirt that we sell and hands it to him. He holds his hands up to try and refuse, but Beattie's having none of it. He takes off his royal blue New Shiloh letterman jacket revealing a pair of jacked, tan arms. That alone could have been enough to make me swoon, but in the next breath he pulls he pulls his heather gray tee shirt over his head to show off a body unnatural for any teenage boy to have. Mix that with the smell manly shampoo and the scents of various freshly made pies and it's just unfair. No mere mortal stands a chance. He slips on the white shirt Beattie gave him and it's clearly a size too small which only makes it cling to him in all the right places. All eyes in the shop glue to him, male and female alike. It's impossible to look away.

"You don't have to do that. Really, it was just an accident." Finn says earnestly, doing everything in his power to push his girlfriend away from us.

"Accident, my eye!" Mal exclaims making everyone stare a little harder. It feels like I'm in that nightmare where you're giving the vale-dictorian speech at your high school and you look down to see you're completely naked and then someone punches you in the face. "You're going to fire her aren't you?" Mal demands of Beattie.

Finn looks up at me in a panic and I think he can gauge how up-set this is making me. "Mallory, please drop it. Please." She opens her mouth to argue, but Finn's not having it. "Go. Now. I don't care if it's to the truck or to the table, but go." And with that she pouts and turns on the heel of her perfectly white sneakers back to the table. Finn sighs and devotes his attention back to Beattie and me. "I'm incredibly sorry about her. Don't worry about the bill or anything, it was just an accident. No harm done."

Beattie smiles and rubs my shoulder, a reassuring gesture for sure. "Thank you for that, but I'm still taking care of your bill, and no argu-ments." she says sweetly, holding up her hand to ward off any protests.

Finn nods and kindly asks of Beattie, "Well ma'am I will not disagree, but I will ask you to point me in the direction of your bathroom." She chuckles and points the way to the far side of the shop. I crouch down to start piling the dirty broken plates on my tray, ignoring the irreversible damage I've done to my apron when I heard Finn say something from behind me. "Hey Pumpkin Pie," I twist to look at him, realizing I haven't told him my name. He looked so ridiculous it takes everything in me not to laugh, bright red cherries in his black hair and blueberries stain his white Tee shirt. He shoots me that lopsided grin and says, "Smile, don't sweat it. I'll expect a piece of that pumpkin when I come back." My heart flips a little and then settles somewhere in my stomach as he heads around the corner to the bathroom. Maybe Rosie's right, a boy in reality is probably better than a boy on paper.

The shop lays in ruins by the time we close at nine. Bella sits in the middle of the checkered floor counting the stack of cash in front of her over and over. Rosie lingers behind her for about three solid minutes shouting out random numbers, messing up her count until Bella finally has enough and chases her through the kitchen. When they both emerge again, Bella exits with a victorious spring in her step as Rosie's covered from head to toe in flour. Serves her right if you ask me.

The delivery girls, who we don't see much of since they're a good deal younger than us, unroll their folds of money and rest their bike helmets in a row on the counter. There have been many trips to the opposite side of town to Harpersgrove's one hotel that can only possibly house 40 or so people. Where all the Arbies find to stay every year is anyone's guess and one of those local mysteries I never expect to be discovered.

Goldie comes up behind me and taps me on the shoulder. In her hand are two quarters and there's a smile on her face. She gestures towards the juke box and says, "It's your turn." We rotate when it comes to picking the song we listen to during clean up. I thank my lucky stars that it's my night because, as much as I love them both, I'm not sure I can handle either a show tune from Rosie or anything heavy metal from Blanche. I'm in a much mellower mood than that. I insert the quarters into the machine and select my personal favorite. G4. "House is Not a Home". I love it! The other girls, not so much. Of course their disdain for it probably has something to do with the fact that I choose it every time it's my turn. Hey when you have perfection why mess with it? That's my philosophy.

I begin to spin in circles and drink in the soft melody as I wipe down my tables and sweep up my area. I hear the others laughing at me, but I don't care. As crazy as it had been that day I'm pleasantly surprised at my good mood. Of course it's all my own and has nothing at all to do with a boy on whose head I may or may not have dropped pie. Nothing at all. Normally I don't get this way over a boy. One in reality anyway, but there's something about the way he smiled at me that I can't get out of my mind. Something about the way he spoke to me and even the way he called me "Pumpkin Pie" when I hate any and all cutesy nicknames. He makes my stomach flip, and not in the bad way it normally would. He has a girlfriend, I know, but in my momentary fantasy I'm willing to overlook that. I'm all about pushing away reality recently. I know he was just being nice and trying to make me feel better about my klutzy ways. I mean why else would a boy like that ever even look twice at a girl like me? I'm not unfortunate looking. It's true I have nothing on Rosie or Goldie in the looks department, but I'm pretty by normal standards. I'm six feet tall and slim with long brown hair and a pretty face, normal and basic. I suppose my insecurities in myself truly stem from being surrounded by supermodels all the time. Even the twins are strikingly gorgeous. They got all the best genes in the womb. Part of my brain always assumes that's why Eleanor prefers them, because they're so much prettier than me and look so much like her. My entire makeup is really nothing more than a hodgepodge of insecurities held together with self-doubt and duct tape.

When Blanche drops me off after we're done I'm overwhelmed with this feeling that I should get back in the car and go to Blanche's house of chaos for the night. I'll find some way home in the morning. Blatantly ignoring this instinct, I open the front door and desperately want to collapse on the doormat and sleep, curled up like a kitten. I'm so ungodly tired. But alas, I remember that I have in fact come to my house and not some fairy tale land, so what I want is always irrelevant. Tyler's my first encounter and she's far from her normal chipper self and that's even before she notices me. Usually, I go out of my way in every creative avenue I can find to NOT talk to my sisters, but there's something about her look now that makes me reach out to her. "Ty, are you okay?"

She throws the lip gloss in her hand back into her purse with more force than is necessary and looks up at me with a snarl, but it doesn't seem to be directed at me. Again straying from the norm. "No, and you won't be either." Crap now I'm involved.

As if exemplifying this point, Megan comes clopping down the stairs, her expensive shoes making her presence overwhelmingly known. "Are you ready yet?" she yells at her twin. She seems to be ignoring my existence which I normally would like, but now find unsettling.

"Are we going somewhere?" I ask, willingly interjecting myself into a conversation with not one, but both of my sisters.

Megan looks again to Tyler. "You didn't tell her yet?"

Tyler shrugs. "Waiting for you I guess." They fall into this deep, intense stare with one another. They're known for having this psychic twin conversations. I'm always the sibling left out.

I wave my hands in between them, actually wanting their attention. "Would someone like to clue me in now?"

"We're going to Dad's girlfriend's place for dinner." Tyler grimaces, trying like crazy to not break her teeth.

"No we are not!" I shout as I stomp around to find my mother. She has to be hiding here somewhere. I'd rather jump into a pit of needles than go to Becky's. God, the mere thought of her name makes me want to vomit. "Does this girl live in Harpersgrove?" I demand of the twins as I run through my head every Becky, Becca or Rebecca I've ever met in my life. Considering my father said she isn't much older than me I guess I probably went to school with her at some point. I swallow the bile rising up the back of my throat at the thought.

Tyler shakes her head. "No, she's in New Shiloh. Dad got her an apartment."

"How do you know that?" I ask as I again search for our mother. There aren't too many places she can hide.

Megan answers me. "Mom told us. She's been a little drunk all day since dad called her and told her that he wanted us to come, even though it wasn't really a request."

"Speaking of Mom, where is she?" I need to rip someone's head off and I've always wanted to do it to her.

"Aunt Wilma came and picked her up a few hours ago. They're going to Baltimore until tomorrow. Aunt Wilma called it the divorcees' night out. That made mom want to drink more."

I huff, now there's no one to yell at. "It's ten o'clock, why would we be going to dinner now?"

"Dad wants us all to be there to meet Becky together so he said that we'd wait until you got off work." Megan whines as she slumps into one of the chairs as the breakfast bar.

I lean defiantly against the fridge. "Well, forget him. I'm not going." I cross my arms over my chest and hug my hands around my body.

The twins look at each other and shared a little smile. Damn psychic connection. "He thought you might react that way. He said he'll bring you by force, if necessary."

I kick my heel into the fridge. I really hate this. I want to be rid of my father and this whole damn situation. "How are we even supposed to get there? Hitchhike?" I don't drive after all.

Megan bites her bottom lip. "Well, if you would just get your driver's license this wouldn't even be an issue."

"I live in a small town where pretty much everything is within walking distance!" I honestly didn't want to have to sit in a car with one of my parents as they taught me to drive. "So how are we getting there?"

The timing is impeccable, because at that moment I hear a shrill beep from outside. I open the shutters on the kitchen window and peer outside where a little yellow Jetta idles in front of our house. A thin arm, so obviously not belonging to my father, pokes out of the driver's window and waves. I chew hard on my lip and mutter, attempting to suppress the expletives that so desperately want to spill from my lips, "Son of a motherless goat."

We decide to wait as long as humanly possible before acknowledging Becky's existence. For the Conner girls to form a united front, the enemy has to be pretty major. Maybe she'll think she has the wrong house or think maybe we left. Alas, she doesn't go anywhere. Ten minutes go by before she finally puts the car into park and gets out. I grab the twins by their arms and lug them to the door. I hold my breath as I observe Becky for the first time. From the lack of sound on either side of me I know my sisters are doing the same thing. The only bit of relief I have is that I most definitely have never seen her before. She was not a girl you could forget. She stands about six three, seriously tall, which isn't a surprise since that's exactly my father's type. She's about seven inches around the waist with big boobs that make her look like she should break in half just like a living doll with impossible beauty standards. Her yellow blonde hair bobs around her fake tan shoulders and her highlighter yellow sundress nearly blinds me. I tighten my grip on the twins' arms and pull them toward the door. "Ow, what are you doing" Megan cries.

"I wanted to make her get out of the car, but I am by no means letting her into this house." I say, swinging the door open. Becky's so startled that she nearly falls off her white hooker heels. Someone should really tell her summer is over.

She flashes her bright white teeth at us and gushes, "Wow, what a reception!" Too cheery. "You must be Tony's girls-" I hate her already.

"Anthony, my father's name is Anthony. And judging by your age shouldn't you be calling him Mr. Conner?" I interrupt, not skipping a beat to let her finish her thought.

She doesn't blink, I'm not sure if that made her tough or stupid. I'm going with stupid. "You must be Elle."

"Very good, you were able to pick out the non identical twin. Would you like a reward?" The tone flies out of my mouth a lot meaner than I usually am, but this girl is a very large part of the break up of my already dysfunctional family. She doesn't deserve my kindness.

She swallows a little, her first sign of any weakness. Maybe there is a human down in there somewhere. "Um, well your dad's waiting for us. We should get going."

I pay Tyler twenty of my hard earned tip dollars to sit in front with Malibu Barbie and talk to her. No way in hell am I going to do it and the twins always sit in the back seat together. Becky and Tyler chat mindlessly about nails and Ariana Grande and such things that make me want to jump from the car or stab myself in the face. All the while Megan types feverishly on her phone. I'm left to sit in my own in silence and count the trees that fly by my window. I wish I could grab hold of one and slingshot myself back home.

It takes nearly an hour to drive to Becky's apartment. She most definitely does not live in New Shiloh like the twins had said. No, she's far out in Baltimore. I'm tired. I'm sweaty. I just want to go to sleep in my own bed. But that's not going to happen, at least not for a while.

We finally pull into a really nice condo development. Each residence has to cost at least twice what our house did. This is what my father buys for his mistress? Does he really think that bringing us here to see it will make us feel any better about his total and complete abandonment of us?

"Home sweet home," Becky whistles with an ear piercing giggle as we reach her front door. It makes me want to punch her in the throat, but I avoid the impulse.

Becky turns the lock and we walk into a child's play room. She has Hello Kitty pillows on her black leather couch and ridiculous colorful wallpaper with some frilly curtains. A crap ton of pastels. It's like a rainbow threw up in the living room. The conflicting smell of cinnamon and lavender chokes me as a I cross the threshold. She tosses her keys aimlessly onto a table beside the door and shouts into in open condo,

"Babe, we're here." A simultaneous cringe runs through my siblings and me. She's talking about our father after all.

My dad emerges from the adjoining kitchen, docked in a frilly purple apron and ridiculous smile. He's wearing a black Tee shirt and jeans and lost his glasses. Who the hell is this guy? "Did you have a nice trip girls?"

I cross my arms over my chest and bite the inside of my cheek. I can not express how much I don't want to be here. "Oh, it was lovely," I crow as dryly as possible.

His face falls instantly. "Michelle, could you at least be civil tonight? Please?"

I shake my head. "Nope, sorry can't do that. See I'm tired and I'm hungry. I really want to go to bed because I have to get up and go to school tomorrow morning. Oh, and then there's the fact that I really don't want to be here with you and your mistress." I bite harder on the inside of my cheek before I say something I can't take back and ignore the metallic taste of blood in my mouth.

He completely ignores me and exclaims, "Well, I can take care of the hungry part." And then he disappears around the corner, Becky close in step. Bastard! How dare he be all "silver-lining" when I'm so mad.

Tyler comes up beside me and shrugs. "Well, we're here. We might as well eat." Girl has a point, I guess.

It's the worst spaghetti I have ever eaten and I doubt seriously that it's just because I'm in a bad mood. My father has never cooked anything for us in our lives and the Victoria Secret model doesn't exactly remind me of Julia Child. The noodles are both overcooked and crunchy. The sauce is cold and I'm pretty sure some of the ground beef is still frozen. If I hadn't been so hungry I would have tossed it straight in the trash. Damn the Arbies, they'd taken my dinner break!

Becky pours herself a glass of wine and I can't hold back the snort. "What's funny?" she asks with a smile. She's so stupid.

I motion to the glass cemented in her hand. "Are you even old enough to drink that?"

She puts the glass back down, flushed with embarrassment and my father is mad. "Michelle Antoinette, stop it. Be nice to Becky."

My defiance kicks in and the sweet Elle checks out for good. "I don't have to be nice to her and I'm not going to be. She's your girlfriend. She's nothing to me."

I can see that I'm hurting Becky's feelings, but I can't bring myself to stop. I personally think that if you're going to sleep with a married man, especially one that's old enough to be your father, you should be willing to accept the consequences. That includes a little bit of loathing from your sugar daddy's nearly grown children.

My father chomps down on his lower lip, not in anger, more like he's nervous. I think that scares me more. He reaches over and takes Becky's hand and she smiles coyly. I begin to swallow my tongue. "That's not exactly true Elle, she is going to be something to you, to all of you. That's kind of why I asked you girls to come here to dinner tonight." Oh, my God. Oh, my God, please no. Becky's grinning like a freakin' idiot and I really want to hurt her. "This morning I asked Becky to marry me and she said yes."

"We're going to be a family!" Becky squeaks with delight.

The twins burst into tears, the one thing they're really good at. I do my best to recover my voice and hiss, "You've got to be kidding me! Jesus dad, why don't you just adopt her, that's probably more appropriate. And you're still married to mom! You can't even wait until you're divorced to get engaged to someone else? I can't believe this."

"You're being extremely rude young lady," my father says sharply as his eyes narrow at me. Ugh, what is with parents and the whole "young lady" thing?

"Now Elle," Becky begins, her valley girl voice making me want to die. "I don't expect you to see me as your mother-"

"Oh, good God, please stop! If you have any self-respect you will not finish that sentence." I stand and grab the hands of the twins. "Come on girls, we're going home."

"But Elle, I really want you to be my maid of honor. I'm sure you and I can become friends. Can't we try?" she requests so sweetly it gives me a toothache.

"No! Stay away from me!" I storm out of the condo, my sisters close behind.

It's a ridiculously expensive ride back home, but necessary. I was not going to be stuck in a car with that woman or with my father. How can he do this to us? How can he continue to hurt us and not care?

I head to school early the next morning. Sleep didn't happen for me that night, it didn't happen for Tyler and Megan either. We're all a little shook up about my father's announcement the night before. He's going to marry a toddler and for some reason he can't see how that might upset us.

Goldie, being the great friend she is, comes to pick me up early. I've had enough bonding for one lifetime with the twins. "Is everything okay?" Goldie asks as I get in the car.

And that's when I finally let it go. I start to cry. I can't cry to my dad, my sisters or my mom. I have to cry to my friends, they're my true family after all. "He's going to marry her. Oh, God, he's going to marry her!"

Goldie's frantic, like a sweet little puppy, to help me in any way she can. She runs her long pale fingers along my hairline, almost like she's petting me. "Sweetie you're going to have to pare that down for me a little. I don't know what you're talking about."

I bang my head against the padded headrest and wipe the stupid tears away. I know it's normal to cry at something like this, but I don't want him to have that kind of power over me. "My dad is marrying the girl. He's leaving us for her," I squeak out before the tears return.

Goldie appears even more shocked than when I'd told her my parents were splitting up. Goldie's always known for her little bits of sunny wisdom. I think it stems from the sunny color of her hair, but I'm not in the mood for one today. So imagine my surprise when she exclaims, "What a bitch!"

I start laughing so hard I'm not sure if the tears that come are from sadness or laughter. I roll over to my side and grip my rib cage, the skin of my forehead cooling against the passenger side window. She's the best. "Thank you for that, Goldie."

"I'm serious!" she squeals, a little disappointed that I'm laughing at her.

"I know, and that makes it so much better, but God stop or I'm going to pee," I laugh out as I swipe the rest of the tears from under my eyes. It's true, if Rosie or even Blanche had said those same words to me it wouldn't have meant nearly as much, mainly because they're things they already said to me normally. It's quite out of character for Goldie and that's what makes it special and meaningful. I know she cares that much. "You're sweet, Goldie." I lean across the seat and kiss my friend on the cheek.

She still seems a little peeved that I'm not taking her seriousness, well, seriously. She pouts, her chin jutting far forward and asks, "Are you okay?"

"I don't know, maybe, maybe not. I'm hoping soon I might be able to see okay on the horizon," I mumble, not sure I believe it myself, but it's the best I've got.

She smiles and turns the key in the ignition. "Because you know I can kill a person three different ways with my thumb," she says in her best spy voice which only makes me laugh harder. I feel better when she cracks a little smile too.

She chuckles as she throws her arm over my seat and backs out of my driveway. "Well, the offer remains on the table lady."

I snuggle down in my seat, really wishing I had a blanket or a teddy bear to cuddle. My eyelids are heavy and falling. I'm exhausted. "Good to know Gold, good to know."

Riding down the street about five minutes Goldie's laughing as hard as me. "She actually said she wasn't going to try to be your mother? How old is this girl?" she asks as she made a tight right turn too fast, nearly toppling us and the car over on its side.

I wipe the tears away again, thank God I've given up the mascara faze. "Like 21, it was ridiculous."

"And she wants you to be her maid of honor?" Goldie repeats in disbelief as we round another sharp corner. It only takes us a few minutes to get to school. I wish she didn't treat it like the cops were always hot on her tail.

I roll my eyes and nod. "Yeah, like that's ever going to happen."

"I don't know, it was nice that she asked."

"She's a monster that broke up my family. I'm not going to be her right hand on her super special day." I try to sound as cynical as I feel, but I can't make my words match.

Goldie sighs, tapping into her hidden wisdom, "Look, I'm not condoning her or anything. What she did was rather crappy, but wasn't your family already kind of broken?"

I know a part of what she's saying is right, but I don't want to hear it right now. "Broken or not, in wasn't hers to rip apart. I don't want any part of her."

Goldie nods, her massive ballerina bun bobbing like a bowie atop her head, understanding my side as well. "Okay, Elle, okay, I'm just saying think about it." I keep my mouth shut. I don't want to think about it, and it's not okay.

I need a pick-me-up. I had told myself to set aside my delusions about the boy in my locker, try to stick to reality. That is until my father's announcement of nuptials to a kindergartner. Now, I feel like a drug addict desperately in need of another fix. I turn my combination quickly, 6-13-23 and sigh in relief and general happiness as a new note flutters down to the ground. I pick it up as I close my locker, sliding down the cool metal to sit on the floor. I flip the letter open and my eyes hurry over the text inside:

"Dear 3788," I read to myself, feeling as though I can hear his voice as he wrote these words. "I guess it's a good question for you to ask, how did I get your locker number, or at least the locker of the girl I thought I had and not her name. Otherwise, I'm sure I just come off as some creepy stalker and we can't have that." I smile. "Anyway, I know it seems strange, but there was another kid at that party, a boy, probably a freshman, who goes to your school and he was so sure that he knew this girl, but only by face. He said that he saw her every morning from his homeroom as he waited for school to start. I asked him if he could be sure, and his answer was simple. 'Dude, you saw her, would you forget where she stood?' Of course, apparently he had forgotten, or just been wrong all together and maybe that's a good thing. I mean, it did lead me to you- of course, I'm not getting creepy or stalkerish, just making that clear." Again I smile, my heart swelling a little. "I know that we've only just begun to talk and don't really know anything about each other, but I feel like I can talk to you. Like we could really be friends and I could say anything. Of course, I'm sure that has something to do with the fact that I've never seen you, I don't even know your name. Might keep me from feeling any rejection, but I don't care. I like it, I like waiting for a letter from that pimply kid they call The Ghost. He freaks me out, does he do the same for you? I'm sure he does, I think you're only human if he scares you. But I don't want to go through him anymore. It takes too long so I want to give you my e-mail, because I really want to get to talk to you more. NewShilohFB33@nshs.edu, please e-mail me 3788, I want to talk to you. Sincerely yours, the mystery guy."

I shoot up instantly from the floor, in a near gallop to the library, the only place I can think of with internet access. The school doesn't have wi-fi and if I use any more of the family's data on my phone, my mother will turn me over to social services. I head to the quickest e-mail to set up. Considering my own e-mail is MichelleConnor@hhs.edu, I can't exactly use that, too obvious. I grin and pick the only username I deem appropriate. Locker3788.

Chapter Six

Have you ever torn a leaf at its veins? One that's fresh, just off the tree at the start of fall? It doesn't tear in straight lines or in any particular pattern. They have a mind of their own. I scoop up a pile of them on my walk home from work that night and rip each one apart slowly as I tightrope walk the curbs down the streets of Harpersgrove. Is anything predictable anymore? Does anything move in a linear fashion? Why does it seem like I can never see destination B from A anymore? Why does the world need to take me down a thousand different avenues, like a leaf ripping to pieces, for me to get where I'm going?

Mom's car was in the driveway when I finally get myself home and finish the last leaf in my handful. I really wished she wouldn't be there, but alas she is. I turn my key in the door. Mom's a stickler for locking it after nine o'clock, even when she knows I'm coming home. Part of me think that she hopes I'll be stuck sleeping on the front porch like a forgotten cat.

She's sitting in the living room, a glass of wine in hand and the television on mute. She's probably only looking at the colors. "Good night?" she asks kind of absently as she swirls the red liquid in her glass.

I remove my jacket and hang it on the hook inside the door. My mother never speaks to me on my way in the door. "It was good, pretty good. I made some decent tips." I don't know how to make small talk with Eleanor.

"Your father left a little while ago." Well that's to the point isn't it? I knew something had to be up. She'd never want to talk to me about my day, but vent about my father? That could take over conversations for years!

I flop down on the couch beside her. I'm in for a long conversation, may as well be comfortable. "Why?"

She takes a long sip, two gulps worth. "He wanted to talk," She's quiet for a moment. I know there's something she she's not saying. "The girl was with him."

"Becky was here?" I question, completely unable to hide my disgust.

She nods, swallowing hard. "Yep, I got to meet her."

"And?" I ask knowing my mother will think the same of her as I did. It's one thing we could have in common.

She seems to have aged ten years in a week. Her floral perfume is the only thing familiar about her right now. "Well, she was as much of a disaster as I thought she'd be, but she seems nice."

I nearly choke on my own tongue. "Nice? She seems nice?"

"Yes, Elle, the girl seemed nice. Terrified to be in my presence, but nice," she grumbles with a sigh. I'm still staring, and she doesn't like that. "What? I'm allowed to talk to the girl."

"Dad left us for her, why would you want to talk to her!" I shout. This is the issue. He's leaving us. He's leaving her for this toddler.

"Your dad left us a long, long time ago and I'm stupid. I knew that there had been other women. Becky's just the one that stuck," she says with a shrug, like we're talking about the weather and not her husband's abandonment of his family.

"I can't believe what I'm hearing! Aren't you the same woman who was freaking out and crying over this a few days ago? Now you're best friends with her?" I demand.

She rolls her big Bette Davis eyes at me. I HATE that! "Don't be dramatic, Michelle. I'll never like her, but I think she actually makes him happy. He seems, happier. Happier than he's ever been with me."

"Seriously, who are you?" I mutter with a blank expression. I'm beyond confused.

She takes the last sip of her wine and licks the drops from her lips. She spins the stem of the glass between her fingers and looks up at me with tears at the edges of her eyes. "I'm the middle-aged first wife trying not to be cliche and bitter." Of course. Everything is about her.

As I make my way down the hall to my attic stairs my sister Megan pops her head out from the room she shares with Tyler. "What's your major mal?" she asks as she twirls her hair around her index finger. For those of you who don't speak annoying teenager, mal is short for malfunction.

"Shut up, moron." I mumble as I hurry by her, the puppy barrelling around Megan to follow me down the hall in clumsy steps. At least someone in this family prefers me.

I reach the end of the hallway and pull the string that lowers the stairs. They're creaky and loud, something straight out of a horror movie. This is where my parents put me. Megan and Tyler get to split the master bedroom, my parents in the other and Poor Little Elle gets stuck in the attic. I hear the stairs lock into place and I lift the struggling puppy into my arms before trudging up them. Each step becomes more and more difficult. I strongly begin to consider turning around and sitting on them to take a break. I'm completely exhausted.

I toss my bag on my pink desk chair and flop down on my massive water bed with the Disney princess sheets. I know it's childish, but they are SO comfortable and I like them. I sigh deeply, breathing in the fresh scent of fabric softener and rub my hands over my eyes. Family is unbearably frustrating. I look across the room at the large glass cabinet on the far side. It's filled from top to bottom with my favorite salt and pepper shakers from my years of collecting. There's everything from

Darth Vader and Luke Skywalker to Marilyn Monroe and JFK; Mr. Salt and Mrs. Pepper from "Blue's Clues" to the Statue of Liberty and Mount Rushmore. They're my prized collection, my favorite things in the world. Right now I want nothing more than to break every single one of them. The yard sales, the flea markets, the hunting for the new and unique salt and pepper shakers is the only thing I really had with my dad and it feels ruined now.

I remember him waking me up at the crack of dawn on a Saturday morning and I didn't care because I knew it meant that he and I would have the whole morning together. No nagging mom, no irritating baby sisters, no work getting in his way, just me. I was his only focus. I remember the omelets we would eat at the diner at 5:30 in the morning when most our town was still asleep. I swiped a set of shakers from there once, but he'd later made me return them, because you know, stealing is wrong and stuff. We'd sit there and talk about my week at school, about the TV shows I was watching, or the books I was reading and he always seemed generally interested. I would write down points and discussion topics all week so I was ready with things to address. I didn't want a second of our time together was to be wasted. Those Saturday mornings were mine.

We'd drive the twenty minutes or so to New Shiloh and follow the homemade signs of poster board and permanent marker leading us to the quaint neighborhood sales where there was always the possibility of finding a hidden treasure. Of course they were our warm-ups to lead to the New Shiloh Flea Market. It was held every Saturday morning between April and November in the parking lot of one of those megachurches that can fit more people than an NFL stadium. You could find anyone there, from the family table who thought it better to join a big crowd then schlep it out at home, to the indie artists and jewelry designers, to personalized dog bowls and homemade fudge. When I was very young, like four or five, my dad would keep my hand cemented in his everywhere we went through the seas of people, but when I was nine we designated a meeting place, always in front of Miss Nancy's Candied Apples where we'd meet back for our celebratory treat before heading home. Our interests were too varied, he wanted to go off and find his vintage vinyls and I desperately needed to find the perfect shakers for my collection. Letting me go off on my own instilled in me this sense of trust that I knew he didn't have in my sisters. I loved my dad back then in those days. I thought I'd love him like that forever, but now I'm not sure I'll ever love him again.

I'm distracted by a blinking on my computer screen at the edge of my bed. I reach out and pull the Mac onto my lap. The e-mail icon is what I saw blinking. I have mail.

I open the message left for me and my day instantly brightens. It's of course from my mystery man.

I click to open the message, but as I do a new image beeps on my screen. An instant message from none other than my mystery man.

Hi there, it reads simply.

I take a deep breath and let my fingers linger above the keys a moment before I begin to type.

You're not stalking me are you? I ask, a playful thought in my mind.

His response is so quick that I barely notice it.

Oh God, is that how I'm coming off? Even his typing seems panicked. *I'm sorry. I don't mean to be weird.*

Ha ha, I can't help laughing, even in type. *I was just trying to make a joke, don't be so sensitive.*

Oh good, I'd hope you wouldn't think that way, but you never know, right? he asked. *So, how was your day?*

I instantly feel sad and exhausted again. If I can tell anyone it's him, right?

I have to say, I've had better.

Lay it on me, he writes with an added smiley face on the end. *I'm your sounding board.*

I crack the thumb knuckles on both my hands.

My parents are getting a divorce and my dad's already getting remarried.
Ouch, that sucks something awful, he types in response.

He's the first person that night to not make me feel like I should be in love with the idea.

My dad got remarried a few years back and it's a pretty crappy feeling all ways around.

I appreciate that he takes the time to use proper grammar. Nothing drives me more crazy than millennials that can't take time to text full words.

My fingers start to fly as I let the anger flow out of me, *And the girl's only a few years older than I am. Everyone in my family seems to think I should be happy for him, even my mother whom he left, but I just don't want to. It's not even that I can't do it, I just don't want to.*

You don't have to, he types back, I can hear the sincerity in the voice that's not audible. *I think it's completely understandable that you don't want to be happy when it comes to the thought of the woman you think broke up your family. I get it.*

Finally, someone does.

Thanks, that means a lot to me. And it's the truth. It does mean a lot to have someone on my side.

No problem, it's reality, he says, adding another smiley face. *I wanted to ask you something, if that's okay?*

Sure, I respond instantly, even though I feel a little resistance in the pit of my stomach. I'm worried he'll ask me something personal, something I don't want to answer. And this edge of mystery that I've had for the first time in my life will end. In this digital age where everyone knows everything about you all the time, it was nice for just once to be able to hold something back.

I think we should meet, not like tomorrow or anything, but in the near future...

I nearly swallow my tongue.

...I mean we don't have to if you don't want to... he types back at lightening speed when I don't answer after two seconds.

I think about you a lot and I feel like I want to talk to you face to face, actually get to know you. It drives me crazy that I don't know what you look like, or what your voice sounds like.

I know we live in this world of instant connection, but something appeals to me that he can't snap, tweet or Facebook me. I get to have this mystery that's reserved for an older time of love letters.

I have to think very hard about how to word my next message. In all honesty, I'm not sure I know what to say. My fingers flex back and forth over the keys before I can bring myself to type,

Where would you want to meet? I mean, that makes a difference. You could be a serial killer so I'd prefer it be somewhere open and public, you know, with a lot of witnesses.

I'm only half joking.

He pauses for a moment, the longest he has in our whole conversation.

I had a thought about that.

He goes silent again, longer than the last time. It makes my chest ache a little.

Well, you know I go to New Shiloh? He doesn't pause for an answer, so I assume the question's rhetorical. He continues,

There's this big Halloween dance every year, it's like a masquerade. We could meet there. It'll be a big room of people and we'll both be in costume so if we both want to forget it we can just walk away like it never happened.

Well, that's appealing.

What do you think? And just as a side note, I promise that I am not a serial killer.

I take another long moment to consider my words, pushing my hair away from my face. I bite down on my bottom lip and let my fingers do the talking.

Can I consider it and get back to you? It's the only honest thing I could think to say. *I just don't want to give you a decision until I'm sure.*

He doesn't pause this time.

Of course, take all the time you need.

And with that I click and sign off. I spin in my chair until I'm facing away from my bed and computer. I smile, only slightly, to myself and muse over the thought that the mystery man wanted to meet me. A boy wants me for the first time.

...

"A masquerade?" Goldie questions at lunch the next day as she raids my brown paper bag for snacks. "What a wussy move."

"What?" I call out in disbelief as I snap my phone out of her hand. "What about it is a wussy move?"

Goldie looks bored and extremely underwhelmed from behind her long black lashes. "A masquerade? I mean-well-isn't that kind of... lame?" Rosie snorts as she twirls the straw around in her coke can.

"And what are you laughing at, Chuckles?" I demand of her.

She shrugs and continues to giggle as she pushes her perfectly curled blonde ponytail away from her shoulders. "I mean a masquerade is rather cliché, don't you think?"

"What's cliché about it?" I whine as I clutched the phone to my chest, protecting the conversation from their scrutiny. All three sets of their eyes settle on me. "What?"

Nixie nibbles on the inside of her cheek. Her red hair's slicked up in a ponytail, only dripping down a little on the table. We're used to living in a puddle around Nix. "Sweetie, a masquerade ball is like the oldest story there is. It's kind of corny."

I can't resist the need to pout and my bottom lip juts out, causing them to snicker at me. "Shut up." I mumble, resting my chin on the table as Goldie bogarts my corn chips. "I think it's kind of romantic."

Rosie pats my head, it's completely patronizing, and I really want to punch her. "Okay sweetie, whatever you say," she singsongs to me and continues to mess with my hair.

"Stop calling me sweetie," I mutter over my pouted lower lip.

Goldie shakes her head and asks through a mouthful of chips, "What is it you'd like us to say, Michelle?"

I narrow my eyes at her. "You know I hate it when you call me that, Gwendolyn." They all offer a grumble of understanding and Goldie looks like an angry kitten at my use of her full name. I sigh and continue, guarding my pudding cup from Goldie's grabby hands, "Well, you are my friends and I guess I just want to know what I should do. I mean, I want your advice on what I should do."

Rosie, my constant adversary in this area, opens her mouth to speak. This should be good. "I think you should go for it."

I swallow my gum and start to choke on it. "What? You thought this whole thing was a bad idea!"

She twirls her lip ring around in her mouth. "I still do think it's a bad idea."

"Is this a trick?" I ask, cocking my head to the side in question. The girl is the queen of ulterior motives.

She smirks and responds, "Because I don't think you'll get this out of your system until you actually meet the guy. Either you'll love him and we'll all be really happy for you or you'll think he's a creep and we'll all be there for you and it'll be done." Her smugness overwhelms.

"Plus," Nixie continues for her. "It's a big event, not somewhere all alone. And it's at Blanche's school so you'll have a wing man if things go awry."

I look at Goldie for her wisdom and input and she points a thumb in the direction of our friends. "I'm with them." The three of them sit on the other side of the table in front of me, balancing their chins in their hands. They wait.

I can hear him breathing before he even reached us. The Ghost walking into our cafeteria, making a beeline in our exact direction. He hands me an envelope and I smile up at him, the best I can anyway. He's an extremely unpleasant human being, both in smell and demeanor. "Oh, and I thought we might never meet again." He casts me a menacing stare and walks away. "Whoa-whoa, wait, where you going? Don't you need a letter from me?" I ask as I pop up out of my seat to follow him.

He shakes his head. "He said you wouldn't need one." Then he's gone, disappearing once again.

"What is it?" Goldie eagerly demands, pulling my attention back. She's hopping up and down on her plastic blue chair and Nixie looks just as excited. Rosie, who sits in between them, looks ready to punch them both.

I shrug and flip the envelope over, tearing the seal. I pull out a note and something on a gold, shiny card. I unfold the note, reading it aloud to the trio before me, "Hey 3788, I figured I'd take a leap of faith and send you a ticket. The dance is Saturday and I really want you to be there. I'll be waiting for you." I pick up the card. It's the ticket and a small thrill sends a tingle down my spine. "Guys, what am I going to wear?"

"Well what kind of dresses do you have?" Bella asks me later that afternoon at the pie shop. Her eyes never leave the pile of books scattered around her at the counter. The girl is a pro at multitasking.

When in need of fashion advice, my friends are my only solace. To be totally honest I'm somewhat inept in the area of fashion and being trendy. I think leg warmers are cool.

I throw my hands over my face in defeat and scream back to Rosie, "Seriously woman, am I going to get my food any time in the perceivable future?"

Her little eyes peer over the kitchen window and she hisses, "You want to switch jobs for a while and see what I deal with back here? Because I'd be more than happy to see if you could do any better than me!"

"Go back to your hole and get my pie!" I yell back at her. Bella's still buried in her applied physics textbook. I'm needy, vulnerable, and throw my face across her text so she has no choice but to deal with me. "I don't dress up that much. I think the only dress I own is the one I wore to my grandmother's funeral..."

Bella's horrified and shakes her head back and forth with vigor. "I don't think that's going to work." She removes her glasses from her eyes and places them atop her smoothed back brown hair.

I slam my head against my folded arm on the counter, my forehead barely missing the lip of the register. "What the am I going to do? I don't do this kind of thing. I'm not a girly girl. This is a big mistake."

"What's a mistake?" I hear Blanche's voice ask. I tear my face away from arm to see her coming through the door. She removes her denim jacket and places on the coat rack, simultaneously running a hand through her bobbed black hair.

"She's going to a masquerade with the mystery man," Rosie calls from the back. Apparently, Rosie has time to announce my personal business to the world, but not to get my pie!

"New Shiloh's masquerade?" she questions, trying to hide her smile. She fails miserably. She can be such a child sometimes.

I plant my forehead back onto the cool marble counter. Bella grunts, my weight is still crushing her and keeping her from studying. Clearly she's uncomfortable, but do I move? What do you think? "I can't do this, I can't do this. I officially resign from my life." The carousel ride is over. I'm ready to get off.

Suddenly, I feel a hand clutch a clump of hair and lift my head up. My best friend of course, here to encourage me. "You can do this. I'll help you," Blanche says with a smile. It's a reminder of why I love her. When I need her, she's there. No questions asked, never an argument. "Now, what are we trying to do?"

"Find a dress for her that she didn't wear to a funeral," Bella absentmindedly mutters as she places a glass of frothy milk in front of a lady seated at the counter whose dining experience is only slightly impeded by Bella's mega amounts of studying.

"Well that's oddly specific, but okay. Let me think," Blanche proclaims as she takes a seat at the counter next to the lady with the milk, deep in thought.

"Aren't you on the clock?" I ask her.

She waves me off like an annoying buzzing bee. "Please, this is much more important-" Then she glances around me. "Beattie's not here, is she?" I shake my head and sigh. "Okay then this is much more important," she repeats, confident and reassured in the stance she takes like a politician at a podium.

I grab a rag and start wiping down the counter, at least I can pretend to be productive. "Okay, what do you suggest?"

"Well you don't own anything that could possibly work and you're too tall and skinny to fit in any of my stuff," Blanche says to the universe and no one in particular. I don't even need to be here for this conversation.

Her eyes dart to Bella. Who scoffs and slams her textbook shut, "I'm at least six sizes bigger than her and that's probably understating." I would kill for Bella's curves. I'm a popsicle stick with nothing to me and she's an hourglass. The world is cosmically unfair. Blanche purses her lips, processing this.

"Damn, and we know that Rosie's never even seen a dress that isn't black or leather before-" We take the angry grumble from the kitchen as Rosie's affirming response to this. "What to do, what to do?" We sit there and ponder for what seems like forever. I have no ideas at all. I can honestly only think about how much I want a taco, but I want to look like I'm part of the group. All of a sudden a light bulb in Blanche's mind goes off, "I've got it, I've got it."

"Care to share Obi Wan?" I request. I'm certain that her idea has to be better than the nothing I've come up with.

"Don't your sisters have like seven thousand dresses that they don't wear anymore? I'm sure we can get something out of that," Blanche resolves, quite proud of herself. This plan is less than nothing, definitely not better.

I sigh and shake my head. "That won't work." I let my body fall listlessly back across Bella. Much to her displeasure of course and that of the nice couple trying to pay for their pie.

"Why not?" Blanche demands, slamming her hands on her hips.

"Are you kidding Blanche?" I ask with a laugh. "They would never, ever let me borrow anything they ever owned."

My soul sister grins in a way that makes my stomach flip. It's a devious, evil smile, reminiscent of a certain cat from Wonderland. She leans in close and whispers, "What they don't know, won't hurt them."

Chapter Seven

66 Were your sisters drag queens in another life?" Blanche chuckles as we open another garbage bag full of old dresses.

I laugh too, "Something like that." I pull out one dress that literally lights up like a disco ball. "This one still has a price tag. I don't think either one of them ever wore it." Not that I can blame them, it's pretty damn ugly. I inspect it thoroughly for some type of warning label. There's no way this thing doesn't induce seizures.

"How much did they pay?" Blanche asks as she rips open yet another black trash bag.

I lift the price tag to examine it and then drop it again. "I think I'd rather not know," I grumble, frustrated with my family more than ever for the unequal treatment between the twins and me. I didn't have access to my father's black Amex card after all. I shove the dress back in the bag and whinny like a horse, sitting back on my feet. "I think this is hopeless. My sisters wear some pretty trashy crap." I see street corners in their probable futures if the clothes we're finding are any indication. "I've never even seen most of these."

"Don't lose hope grasshopper," Blanche gasps with an expression that makes me nervous. "I think I might have found something that's not terrible." Promising, everything up to this point has been quite tragic.

I move over in her direction and squat down to the open bag in her lap. She takes out the dress of which she speaks and she's right. It's not terrible. In fact, it seems pretty good. It's a hot pink knee length dress that flares out like a bell at the bottom with a simple pink bow at the top. It's subtle. It's simple. It's completely anti- Tyler and Megan. It's perfect. "Wow, this is really nice."

"Yea, why was it with you sisters' stuff?" Blanche wonders, reading my mind as she so often does.

"That's a good question. Is there anything else in the bag?" I ask as I sit down beside her, cradling the dress in my lap.

Blanche rips the bag open a little further and reaches inside. She finds a blonde wig and long pink gloves with connected diamond (cubic zirconia of course) bracelets. "Mean anything to you?" she inquires with a puzzled look.

I smile as my mind drifts back to movie marathons with Rosie and Goldie when we were little girls. We had such dreams of being Hollywood starlets. "It's Marilyn Monroe. 'Diamonds Are a Girl's Best Friend'!" I exclaim with a laugh. This explains why my sisters would have something even close to simple. They're trying to copy the greatest sex symbol of all time. It's all clear now.

Blanche nudges me with her shoulder. "Well, what are you waiting for? Try it on!"

I ripped off my sweatpants and tee shirt. I'm never afraid to be less than modest in front of Blanche, and wiggle myself into the bright pink silk. "Do I look stupid?" I ask as I twirled around in the pink dress. I'm not girly in the slightest, but no one can deny the power of Monroe.

My best friend flashes me a toothy grin, pushing her short black hair out of her eyes. "Not at all, you have channeled the Marilyn quite well. You have to wear it."

"Well, what are you wearing?" I ask as I examine myself in the basement mirror. "I mean I wouldn't want us to clash too much."

"What am I wearing to what?" she says absently as she stuffs the mess we've made into new trash bags. We're nothing if not tidy.

"To the masquerade?" I say matter-of-factly, imagining the look complete with a drawn on mole on the left side of my face. She begins to laugh so hysterically that I'm sure she'll be sick. I whip around to look at her and she's collapsed onto her side. "What's so funny?" I demand with my hands firmly on my hips.

"You think I'm going to that stupid thing? Are you insane!" she shouts through her bubbly giggles. The only time anyone has ever laughed this hard at me was when I told my mother I wanted to cut my hair my short. According to her my "masculine" features couldn't tolerate it.

"Well, it is at your school," I defend. I mean she has to go with me. There's just no two ways about that. She has to.

"So?! I've never been to dance in my life, and I have no intention to start now," she continues as she straightens, returning to her work of cleaning up our mess.

"But you're like the most popular girl at your school, how can you not go!" I exclaim, beginning to freak out. I can't do this by myself. Having Blanche with me is the only thread holding me to my sanity and it's starting to fray.

"It keeps me mysterious and revered," she says only with a hint of sarcasm.

"But I need you to go with me. I can't do this alone!" I squeal. I feel a panicked heat rushing up my neck and I'm sure my pale skin is blushing a bright tomatoey red. Fainting was the next item on the menu.

Blanche grumbles and buries her head in a pile of clothes. "I don't wanna. Do you really want to make me do something I genuinely don't want to do? Is that the kind of friend you are?"

"Yes!" I yelp before she can even get the last word out.

"Well damn, at least think about it woman!" she shouts, snapping her head around to look at me. She throws a bright yellow tutu at my head. The material scratches at my face and does nothing for my growing anxiety.

"I have thought about it. You're my best friend I need you," I push on with the best pout I can muster. My big puppy dog eyes fill with real tears and I doubt she'll be able to handle me crying.

Blanche furrows her brow and throws her face back in dresses. "You cannot call the best friend card for the rest of our lives if I do this."

I shrug, "I can live with that." I doubt I'll ever need it as much as I do right now.

She flops back into a sea of abandoned outfits and flips her head to look at me. "I have nothing to wear to a masquerade," she hisses, hating me only a little.

I reach down and pick up the silver, sparkly dress. "Want to be a disco ball?"

...

After Blanche and I clean up the sea of clothing in the basement, I secure my outfit to the safety of my attic. I venture down into the kitchen to find sustenance. I open the fridge as my sisters come through the door. I wish I was starving again in my room. They walk straight past me to the basement door. "What are you two doing?" I ask, my heart leaping into my throat and that nervous heat working it's way back up my neck.

Tyler looks annoyed, shocker. "We need outfits for this weekend."

My heart jumps a little further and it's hard to swallow. "What's this weekend?" I ask, hoping that I don't already know.

Megan laughs, pitying my social ignorance. "God, do you live under a rock or something! It's the New Shiloh Halloween Dance." Damn! "We're going down to look for clothes to wear." Double damn!

"You're not buying new clothes?" I coldly respond. After going through the hoards and hoards of stuff they have it's surprising that they wouldn't go for new.

Tyler looks like she might cry. "Mom took our credit card. She said that until the divorce is final we have to make due with what we already have. It's like living in a third world country or something! It sucks in epic proportion!" I need to sit them down in front a Netflix documentary or two about Africa to really show them the third world.

"Yeah, major suckage," I agree, trying not to swallow my tongue at the thought of my sisters going to the dance. The same dance that I'll be at meeting a guy that I don't know, that they have no idea about and that they will surely tell my mother about when they see me. This is not good! Not good at all! "You guys don't even go to New Shiloh. Why are you going to the dance?"

Megan rolls her eyes so far that I'm surprised they don't spin around inside her head. "You're such a loser Elle, do you know that? These two majorly-" apparently this is the word of the day, "-hot guys on their JV football team asked us to go."

I slither in front of them, blocking their path to the basement. "And now you're going downstairs? To look for dresses?" I ask, trying to the hide the panic and stall them a little longer. My knuckles turn white against my grip on the door frame, I'm surprised I don't break a piece of it away.

Tyler pushes me aside, not hard to do considering I can't really feel my legs. "Yeah, you freak, get out of the way!" she exclaims as Megan laughs. They brush past me down the stairs. God, I really hope neither one of them wants to be Marilyn Monroe.

...

"Good evening, beautiful!" I say to Bella later that night when I hear the bell of the cash register as I come through the door of the shop later that night.

She smiles, but it's not the cheerful grin I've come to know from my faithful Bella. "Hey," she mumbles, her voice trailing off at the end.

"What's the matter?" I ask as I hang up my jacket and tie on my apron. I can't handle any bad news or unfortunate situations. I just need a night of chaotic peace in my pie shop. I need something to be normal.

She closes the cover of the book she's currently lost in, it must be serious business to pull her away from a text. "There's someone who came in about two hours and insisted on waiting until you got here. She said it's really important that she talks to you."

"She? She who?" I wonder, huffing with exasperation. In my current life I dread it could be anyone.

Becky, my father's new fiancé, sits in a booth near the back of the diner. I look to Bella for help and she just shrugs, back to Charlotte Bronte and drifting away from me. "She said she won't leave until she talks to you."

"Bah," I mutter as I schlep toward the back. Better to get it over with quickly and with as little pain as possible. Like ripping off a band-aid.

I collapse down in the seat. "What?" I snap, crossing my arms over my chest. I pull out my phone and place it on the table in front of us. I want her to know that she holds none of my attention. I need her to know that she matters less than my social media accounts.

She's dressed much more modestly than she had been the last time I'd seen her. Wearing a pair of jeans and a simple cream colored sweater, with her blonde hair pulled back in a long ponytail. She wrings her hands together on top of the table. "Your dad is really upset about how things went the other night. I wanted a chance to talk to you about it."

"There's nothing to talk about Becky. I'm not going to be in your wedding and you can't make me," I said like a petulant child.

She looks disappointed, but not surprised and says, "I understand that, and I'm not going to make you. I wouldn't want you to do something you're so opposed to doing. That's not what I want to talk to you about."

"Then, what is it?" I don't want to talk to her. I HATE her. She's ruining my family.

"I know you don't like me. I know that you blame me in some way for breaking up your family-" Wow, maybe she's not as stupid as she looks. "But I think you know that's not true. Your dad told me that he's been thinking about leaving your mother for a long time. They're not in love anymore."

"Please don't explain my family to me. What the hell do you know about it?" I roar, fire and angry heat burning at the corners of my eyes. How dare she! She isn't a member of my family. She doesn't belong with us. How dare she stick her nose into my family's business.

She doesn't blink. If not for being so hard pressed on hating her I'd probably respect her. "You don't know me kiddo-"

"Whoa, whoa, whoa, you're four years older than me, Becky. Why don't we avoid the cutesy names," I shout at her. One of the tears escapes and I curse at the betrayal of my own body.

"Okay, okay, I'm sorry," she continues, avoiding my level of anger. Maybe those four years make more of a difference than I realized. "Something you don't know about me Elle, is that my father left my mother for a much younger woman too."

"What?" I ask. She had completely knocked me off my bearings. Even the anger dissipates for a moment with my confusion.

She nods, taking a sip of the water I was sure Bella had provided her. "I was a little younger than you, fourteen. He left my mom after twenty years of marriage for a nineteen year old and I hated her. So, I get why you don't like me." I want to speak, but I opt to let her speak. Truly, I have nothing of use to say. I'm still trying to digest.

"Her name is Ingrid. She emigrated here from Bosnia. She wanted a rich husband and she didn't care if it meant taking one from someone else."

"What happened? I mean, you were 14 eight years ago, do you like her now?" My throat's suddenly dry as the Sahara and my voice cracks a bit.

She laughs without smiling and says, "Oh no, I haven't seen my father since his wedding, but our situation was a little different from yours."

"How so?"

Her expression goes blank, like she's recalling a memory. "My mom was still in love with my dad when they got divorced. Is your mother still in love with Anthony?"

I desperately want to say she is. I want to say that their lives are like one of the cheesy romance novels that so often I catch Goldie reading on her breaks. But if there's one thing Anthony and Eleanor have raised me not to be, it's a liar. I shake my head and fiddle with the edge of my phone case where a piece of the plastic has broken off. "I doubt my mother is capable of love, but especially not with my father."

She nods, understanding, and I actually believe that she does. "Plus, my father didn't just drop my mom when he left, he dropped me too. I told you that I hadn't seen my father since his wedding, that's wasn't completely my choice. Ingrid decided that she was going to start a new family with my father and that he needed to let go of me. And he did."

"I'm sorry," I whisper, unable to keep hating her. I mean, how can I when she says something like that?

"It's okay, this isn't about me. What I'm getting at is that your father is not going to do that to you. I would never let him. I know all too well what that feels like. He will never abandon you like my father abandoned me," she promises, her hand tapping the table for emphasis as I try to ignore the sound her engagement ring makes.

I feel tears return to my eyes, but they don't feel like a betrayal now. "My dad doesn't care about me." I know this to be the truth. I know that's the way it is. He hasn't cared in a long time.

She reaches out and touches my hand and shockingly I don't pull away from her. "You're wrong Elle, your father loves you."

"Then why has he always been away? He hasn't chosen to spend any-time with me in a long time, a really long time. He never chooses me." I always try to pretend like I don't miss him. Like losing our days at the flea markets doesn't affect me, but it does. It hurts my heart so badly that some days I can barely breathe.

"That wasn't because of you. It's your mother. Your father wants to spend time with you again. He knows that he might be too late, but he really wants it," she says with a genuine smile.

My heart floods with anger. "Then why isn't he here telling me this himself?" I yell at her. Right now I know she's not the one I'm mad at, but she's the only one here.

Again, she doesn't back down from me, and this time I respect it. "Because he doesn't want to push you. He hopes that you'll come around in your own time, but he's not going to force you. He doesn't even know I'm here, but he's hoping that he can start to mend your relationship and I want that too. I just hope you can come to like me, or at least tolerate me."

"Why would you marry an older guy with a family if you had your family destroyed by a woman who did the same thing?" I have to ask. It seems to me that with her past this is the kind of relationship she'd avoid.

"I have serious daddy issues, I know that. I don't want you to go through what I've gone through. I want you and your father to fix this while you still can, and maybe come to know that I'm not the Wicked Witch of the West." I appreciate the honesty. At the rate she's going I'll have no choice but to respect her

"I can try that," I say softly. "But I can't say I'm going to be in your wedding, or even that I'll go."

"Will you think about it?" she requests.

I nod. "Yeah, I'll think about it." Maybe she isn't as backwards as I'd thought. People are constantly surprising me these days.

She gets up from the booth and shifts her purse to her shoulder. "That's all I ask." I stand up too and I wipe my hands on my apron, unsure of what I'm supposed to do next. We stand eye to eye, not something I can do with many people at my height, and she reaches out to shake my hand. The formal gesture seems alien to me, but I play along. "I hope you'll take the chance to get to know me. I think we can be friends."

I doubt that it's possible, but I don't have to hate her. "Tell my dad I said hi," I offer as I dodge her request.

She smiles and slips on her jacket. "Maybe you and the girls can come over for dinner sometime. Give it another try?" she asks.

"Sure, why not?" And the thought really didn't repulse me.

Every Saturday my mother has an insane list of chores for me to do before I even consider anything for myself. My sisters are, of course, exempt from this. Saturday mornings they drool over the cheer squad and wish they were on it. That takes precedence over everything!

With my father gone the list has gotten longer. My mother's pretty much unwilling to do anything around the house. So, it was all left for me. Of course it's the day of the dance, so my superhuman abilities in the world of housework come in mighty handy to get everything done in time.

Around two o'clock the twins trudge through the door looking exhausted, as though they actually practiced with the cheer team. Scrubbing the kitchen floor on my hands and knees, it takes everything in me not to strangle them both with their long hair as they track mud across the already clean floor. "You guys really suck, you know that right?" I hiss.

They roll their eyes in tandem and it makes me nauseous. "Oh, shut up, you big baby. It's just a little dirt," Tyler mutters, dropping her designer purse on the floor by my face.

"Then, why don't you clean it up?" I demand rocking back on my heels, tossing the brush into the bucket of dirty, soapy water.

"Because it's your job, freak," Megan says and Tyler giggles. At least they have each other for amusement.

"Besides," Tyler chimes in. "We have to start getting ready for the New Shiloh dance tonight."

"That's not for hours," I mumble to the floor as I begin to scrub up the new dirt. It's like starting all over and I still have so much to do after this. I have to be getting ready too. I still need to figure out a game plan for avoiding them. I'll cross that bridge when I come to it. Too many other things to worry about in the moment.

Tyler looks at me like I'm some kind of alien. "You know absolutely nothing about being a girl, do you Elle?" I recognize the look on her face. She's pitying me!

I take my aggression out on the floor and scrub harder. "You're probably right, Ty. I wouldn't know a thing about it." I'm sweaty and gross and pretty unfeminine. There's not much room for argument.

I hurry through the rest of my chores and listen to the bickering up above me as my sisters fight over hair care products, glittery eye-shadows and nail polish. And then suddenly, for a good ten minutes, I don't hear a sound. I find that more disturbing and terrifying than anything. I put the vacuum back in the hall closet and investigate. I climb the stairs to the second floor and still hear nothing. I glance in their room, they're not there. I look in the bathroom, not there. I check my parent's room. Nothing. I feel an uncomfortable sensation rise up the back of my throat, like I'm going to be sick. There's only one other place they can be, but I hope that they've jumped out the window to their deaths instead. I turn the corner and peer down the end of the hall. Sure enough the stairs to the attic, my bedroom, are pulled down. I run full speed up the stairs, taking them two at a time. My heart beats in my ears as the panic rises.

Tyler and Megan sit beside each other on my narrow bed. They spot the one thing I don't want them to see. Tyler has the dress in her lap and Megan holds the blonde wig in her hands. My fingers ball into fists at my sides and I feel the nails dig into the skin of my palms. "What are you two doing in my room!" I shout.

"What are you doing with my dress!" Tyler shouts back.

"I got it from a bag in the basement. You know all the stuff you guys buy but never wear. But what are you doing up here? You know you're not supposed to be up here." I hiss again, my jaw clenched so tight my teeth might shatter.

"You have a hair straightener and we didn't want to share ours." Megan explains as though that excuses everything.

"Then you ask for permission, you idiot!" I yell, yelling was the only way they ever hear anything. I extend my hand out to Tyler and say, "Now give me the dress."

She actually laughs at me. "Um, no, it's not yours."

I feel my skin begin to burn.

"You're kidding me, right? Give it to me."

Megan takes the dress in her own hands, away from her twin, "No, I don't think so. Anyway, I've kind of decided that I want to be Marilyn Monroe at the party tonight. It's not like a freak like you would have any use for it."

Tyler snatches the dress back, "No Meg, I'm going to wear it. Maybe if it had been down where it was supposed to be, I would have been able to get it." The last comment is directed at me.

For a few moments they snarl back and forth, grabbing the dress from each other and screaming that they each want to wear it. Finally the inevitable moment happens, and the sound of the ripping fabric burns my ears. They split the dress completely in two. Hot tears sting my eyes at the overwhelming selfishness. I really shouldn't expect better, but for some reason, I do.

"You two really don't care about anyone but yourselves, do you?" I mumble, my eyes settling on the ripped sections of what was supposed to be my happy night, resting on sisters' laps.

The twins let the two halves of the dress drop and hit the floor. I swear I can hear the pink fabric slam into the white carpet. Megan shrugs, her face nothing less than purely mean.

"Well, maybe you should have asked to use the dress."

"Yeah, because you would have let me?" I say sourly, biting back the tears that desperately want to spill over the edge.

Tyler tweaks her shoulders, sharing the same look of cruelty as her other half. "Well, now you'll never know."

I want to hit them, hurt them, destroy them. Do something to make them miserable. But I don't get the chance to do anything. Below I hear the front door close and my mother's voice calls up, "Girls come down here, we have company."

Chapter Eight

I follow my sisters slowly down the stairs, my feet dragging. What am I going to do now? The twins will probably take inventory of all their clothes before leaving tonight so they can be sure I don't take anything. I doubt I'll have time to go buy something new. I don't know what to do or how to even go about it.

In the kitchen my mother stands with her back to us. In front of her stands her sister, Aunt Wilma. I don't like Aunt Wilma. The twins however are in love with her.

"Aunt Wil!!!" they shriek running down the stairs to wrap their arms around her, the three of them giggling and jumping up and down like the idiots they are.

Then Aunt Wilma catches sight of me and her attitude sobers. Our distaste is most definitely not one sided.

"Michelle," she says simply and coolly. On her hip my aunt balances my baby cousin, Anastasia. The baby's strawberry blonde hair stocks straight up in little fluffy wisps and her crossed eyes have gotten worse. It takes everything in me not to laugh at the awkward little child.

Aunt Wilma lifts Ana up and hoists the small boulder over to me. Ana squirms and kicks, unhappy with the exchange. I hesitate and that annoys everyone.

"Well, take her," Aunt Wilma demands and I do. "She's already been fed, but she might need another bottle around bedtime. Make sure she doesn't go to bed too late and that you dress her in the pink pajamas not the purple ones."

I look behind me, searching for who she was giving these directions to. Seeing no one I find the need to clarify, "Are you talking to me?"

In her classic nonchalant fashion, my mother hops in, "Oh yes Michelle, I nearly forgot. You need to watch your cousin tonight. Your aunt and I are going out."

I shake my head and try to pass the baby back.

"No, I have plans tonight."

No one takes her from me and she squirms and thrashes like a fish out water.

"Well, you'll have to push your plans aside for the evening. Your sisters are going to an important dance and your aunt is taking me clubbing. It's singles night after all."

"No, sorry, I have plans." I say again trying to hand the baby back, but still no one takes her. It's like being stuck with a bomb in an Adam West *Batman* movie. "Mother, you didn't even ask me if this was okay. Why do you always do this to me? I can't watch the baby."

My mother huffs, no real mystery where my sisters learn their pouting skills. "Well, young lady I'm sorry, but you're just going to have to give up one Saturday night for your family."

I want to argue further, yell and scream and stomp my feet, much like my sisters would, but she doesn't give me a chance. She kisses each of my sisters on the cheek and turns to me and says, "We'll be back at midnight young lady and there's a whole load of laundry you skipped over this morning."

With that they're gone and my sisters are back upstairs getting ready for the dance to that I can't go. This is important, but they don't care. They don't care about me at all.

I pull my phone out of my pocket and dial Blanche's number. She's going to be mad.

...

It's been about an hour since my mother and aunt left for the evening. Leaving me alone with the Satan spawn that is my cousin Anastasia. My sisters left a half hour after that, and the dance is in full swing by now. It's just the two of us left, watching Peppa Pig and Ana having a jolly good time pulling out my hair. I want to cry.

After Ana's third temper tantrum over my not restarting her DVD fast enough a knock sounds at the door. Good, an axe murderer to finish me. Lovely. I look through the peep hole, having slightly psyched myself out for it to actually be a serial killer. Perhaps what's there is worse. Blanche. "I see your feet at the door, so you might as well open up."

I jump back from the door, making Ana scream out in a fit of rage. I roll my eyes and flip the deadbolt. I pull at the door to let Blanche inside. She looks amazing, donning a skin tight red dress on that swishes against the floor and a slit that comes up just above her knee. Her makeup's done to the nines, red lipstick showing off the pouty mouth she tries to hide and blue eye-shadow stretching up to her eyebrows. My mouth hangs open as I gawk at her. Where's my tomboy best friend?

"What!" she demands, sick of my staring.

"You look incredible! Who are you supposed to be?" I ask, shifting the massive baby to my other hip.

Blanche bites her lip and reaches down into the burlap bag in her hand and retrieves a long, bright red wig. She positions it on her head with ease and smiles. "Jessica Rabbit darling. I'm not bad, I'm just drawn that way."

I laugh, much to Ana's displeasure. "Well you look great. I hope you have a great time."

"Oh no, no, no, you're not getting away from me that easy. I had to buy a ticket, go shopping for a dress, do my makeup and tell everyone I was going to this stupid thing. Let me remind you that I didn't want to go at all." Blanche and Ana trade some psychic look of distrust that I don't understand. With so many siblings, Blanche speaks baby better than anyone I know.

"I'm sorry, but I don't have much of a choice," I groan as I point to the child attempting to rip my sweater open. "Unless you think I should bring her as an accessory."

"Oh, ye of little faith. You think I would have come all the way over here without a plan?" Another car pull up next to Blanche's magic pumpkin in front of my house. "See and I was beginning to think she was going to be late."

I feel instantly calmer as Beattie gets out of the car, looking a little frustrated, but no more than usual really. "Could your house possibly be harder to find?" she grumbles as she makes her way up the sidewalk. It's a ridiculous question of course because everything in Harpersgrove is no more than a ten minute drive from anything. You can't get lost if you try.

"What are you doing here?" I ask as she finally approaches the front door.

"I'm going to watch the baby while you and Blanche go to this dance thing." She reaches out to take Ana, but I pull away.

"No Beattie, I can't ask you to do that."

Beattie shrugs, her arms still extended for the child. "Well, then it's a good thing that you're not asking and that I'm telling you. Now, give me the baby."

"But, but-" I babble knowing that there's something holding me back, but I can't remember what. Then it hits me. "I don't have anything to wear, the twins wrecked my dress."

Beattie rolls her eyes and jogs back to her car. She emerges again with a tan garment bag that seems to be stuffed to its limits. She extends the hanger to me and motions for the baby. I'm curious enough to hand Ana over. The baby doesn't fuss in Beattie's arms. Perhaps she instinctively knows that Beattie is not one for shenanigans.

"What is it?" I ask, staring at the plain tan material of the bag like it's a venomous snake ready to attack.

Beattie balances Ana on her hip. "Open it and see."

I hand the hanger to Blanche so it can be held steady as I open it. I pull the zipper down slowly and let the beautiful contents spill out over the edges. It's a long white ball gown with a skirt completely made of flowing crinoline and a bejeweled top made of satin. "Beattie, this is beautiful." I shriek when I see it in it's entirety.

She seems less than impressed. "Just something I had lying around," she says as she swats at the baby for pulling on her black Metallica tee shirt.

"But I can't take this!"

"Well you're not taking it. I expect it back tomorrow, but for tonight just consider me your fairy godmother." she said with a grin. As cold as Beattie sometimes pretends to be I know how sweet she really is. This is all the proof I need.

Blanche starts pulling on my arm. "Come on you, we've got to get you ready. We're already ridiculously behind."

So I let Blanche drag me up the stairs, the frilly dress flopping behind me. We leave Beattie to fend for herself with the baby. I'm more worried for Ana.

Over the next twenty minutes I let Blanche pluck and prod and curl and twirl to her little heart's desire. I'm in agony, but at least she's appeased. She piles my long brown hair in loose curls up on top of my head and lets them spill down my back. She whips out a huge container of makeup and I fear what she'll come up with next. Makeup always makes me look like a clown. She buttons the seven thousand clasps down my back to put me in the dress and I don a pair of black Converse that no one will see under the six miles of tulle.

"Voila!" she finally proclaims as she flops on my bed, exhausted. I turn to my full length mirror and barely recognize myself. Blanche hands me a decorative silver masquerade mask and I slide it gingerly over my well done hair and the look's complete. I'm a princess. It's a bit daunting and wholly unfamiliar. I hover normally in the middle of this place between girly and tomboy that's mainly blasé and boring so no one notices me. I never sway to either extreme so I don't stand out. But this is definitely an extreme. I like it.

My best friend beams at me, pleased with herself. "Thanks, Blanche," I giggle as I twirl around on my bedroom floor.

"Aw shucks, it's nothing. Now, let's get going before your prince charming thinks you're not showing up."

She grabs my hand and together we scurry down the stairs, careful of course with our respective dresses. Beattie waits for us at the bottom, "Well," she begins when she sees me, "don't you clean up nice?"

"Thanks, Beattie," I gush, swooshing the dress from side to side.

"Now, you said your mother will be back at midnight, so don't forget to be back before then. I really hate your mother, and don't feel like killing her tonight. Plus, I'd prefer you not be in trouble," Beattie sighs slumping forward. She herself is in for a long evening with the little monster.

I kiss her on the cheek and Anastasia tries to pull at my hair. "I won't be late, I promise."

"Okay, now get going or you'll miss the whole thing."

I grab Blanche's hand and we rush out to her ugly orange VW bug. It's so rightly named the magic pumpkin, due to its shade and the fact that Blanche keeps the poor thing running with rubber bands, paper-clips, and her hopes and dreams.

The car roars to life and we're off to the dance. I'm going to meet my mystery man. I feel sick.

Blanche parks the magic pumpkin and we make our way into her school. It takes everything in me not to run screaming the other way. This is a big, terrible, ugly mistake.

The school has been temporarily transformed to something out of a fairytale book. That is, if you don't look too hard. The crepe paper and streamers coat the graffiti covered lockers and balloons bounce against fluorescent lights in the ceiling. It's nice nonetheless. "It looks great," I mention casually to Blanche who hikes up her red beaded skirt that makes it so hard for her to walk.

"Why don't you just kill me now?" she grumbles while fumbling on her too high heels that have her stumbling like a newborn baby deer.

I smile to myself, she acts morose, but I know that it's not completely killing her to be here. One, she's my best friend and I know she'd do anything for me. Two, she looks so good, even with her unfeminine walk, that every guy in her school can barely keep his jaw off the floor. Blanche very much likes to be looked at, even when she tries to hide it. I pat her on the shoulder. "Keep it together champ, it's only one night. And you know I love you for this. I just couldn't have come here on my own."

She sighs and flings her arm over my shoulder, mainly for balance. "Yeah, yeah, I know. You're helpless without the wonder that is me," she says with a grin flashed over her shoulder.

A stocky guy in an ill-fitting Batman suit passes us and lifts his mask. His mouth falls slack and his bug from their sockets. "Woah, Summers, is that you under there?" he catcalls to Blanche with a whistle. I'm disgusted.

Blanche snarls, "Careful Peter, you might start drooling." She acts outraged, but I see the extra swagger in her walk. Oh yeah, she's loving this.

We reach the doors of the auditorium and hand our shiny, gold tickets to Santa Claus and the Mad Hatter and they return a ripped half to each of us (both staring at Blanche all the while). I stop dead at the doors, my feet cemented to the floor. Blanche reaches out and squeezes my hand. She's got me. I pull the mask over my eyes, disguising me entirely. She rests her hands softly on my shoulders and smiles. "You're going to be great kid."

"What if he doesn't like me?" I blurt out, suddenly realizing this is what I'm afraid of most. I don't have any experience with boys. Literally, none to speak of except for a disastrous kiss here or there that I'd rather forget. I desperately want this boy to like me and a part of me hates feeling that way. I'm a strong, independent woman, damn it!

She chuckles softly, her hands gripping my shoulders keeping me centered. "Then forget him! You don't want him, but I don't think that's going to happen. You look amazing and you are amazing. He'd been insane not to fall in love with you right away."

I take a deep breath and slip out of Blanche's grasp and into the crowded auditorium, before I lose my nerve. The room's dark and swirling with colored spotlights. Some loud music I've never heard pounds in my ears and nervous stomach. I swish in and out of people looking for who my mystery man might be. I think about getting some punch, but have horrible visions of red streaks running down the front of my dress, reminiscent of *Carrie* and decide strongly against it.

I link my fingers behind my back and wade through the sea of people, all bumping and grinding to a rap song that moves so fast I have no idea what the words even are. I take a deep breath and try to push the oxygen all the way down to my toes so I don't pass out. I really wish the Mystery Man and I had worked out some way of recognizing each other. I mean what am I supposed to do, go around and ask everyone if they're my Mystery Man. I'll be escorted from the premise, or end up with some perv in the making. Crap!

I survey the faces as the song changes to something slower, a poppy romantic ballad that would be right up Rosie's alley. My eyes keep scanning the crowd, now breaking up two by two like a high school Noah's ark for the slow song. There are a few guys who occasionally look at me, but their eyes pass quickly. I can't know for certain if any of them are mine. I blow a rogue curl out of my face, feeling embarrassed even though I know no one here is aware of my secret. I can only stand a few moments more of it before I bolt for the door, run straight home and forgot about this disaster all together-

Then I see him and he's my guy. I know it. He's tall, which of course I always notice first, being that I'm so tall myself. He has coal black hair that flips up in a few curls, and a perfect chiseled face. He's dressed in a dark brown Prince Charming costume. He's my guy. Of course the only surefire way I know is that covering his bright blue eyes is a mask, much like the ones people wear at New Year's. The only difference to this one is that it doesn't read the numbers of the year, but rather four numbers that I have come to know quite well. 3788. I focus on my breathing so I don't faint. He's incredibly beautiful, my fears of him looking like a sideshow attraction are now diminished. It's not that I'm stuck up or anything, but I think every girl hopes the man of her dreams will be beautiful. And he is.

I stop in front of him and he beams at me. "Hello Mystery Man," I yell over the booming sound of the music, not sure of what else could give me away.

He grins and points to his mask. "Yeah, I realized you'd have no way of knowing it was me. Poor planning on my part." His voice is smooth and musical, as beautiful as he is. He doesn't say anything else, but takes my hand and we start to dance. It's like something straight out of a fairytale, except for the fact that it's so hard to take him seriously in that mask. I do my best to ignore it.

I'd been terrified at the notion of dancing tonight. I'm a rather ungraceful and klutzy excuse for a human being. Something like an epileptic piece of asparagus, but dancing with him seems effortless. It's like we're floating.

"I was getting worried you might not come," he confesses after we'd danced for a few moments. He has to lean down to my ear so I can hear him. The warm feeling of his breath on my neck makes my hair stand on end.

"I'm sorry about that. A slight obstacle came up, but I wouldn't have missed it." I try not to see this as a lie, but if Blanche and Beattie hadn't shown up I most certainly would not have made it.

"Well, I'm really glad you're here," he answers with a lopsided grin.

I blush, trying to hide my face in my shoulder. "Me too."

We continue to dance to the song that seems to last forever, and I catch sight of the people on the peripheral. Blanche is being wooed by a group of superheroes, acting uninterested as always, but soaking it all up. I do see my sisters both with their JV football players, bickering about something, probably someone else with their dress. Tyler ended up in the horrendous disco ball dress with platform shoes and white lipstick and Megan's dressed like Little Bo Peep. They're absolutely laughable. I avert my eyes and act like I don't see them at all. The last thing I need is for my sisters to discover I'm here.

The impossibly long song finally fades into an ending and moves into another obscure rap song. The crowd starts to the thrash, knocking me into him and he pulls me gently by the hand out of harm's way. He leans down close to my ear again and whispers, "You want to go somewhere a little quieter?" I nod and allow him to lead the way.

We walk just outside the door of the auditorium onto a pavilion that I'm sure is used for a cafeteria in the warm Maryland springs. It's surprisingly cold that night, especially for October. He notices my discomfort and removes his jacket to put it around my shoulders. "Thanks." I say with a smile.

He leans against a pole in the middle of the pavilion and crosses his arms over his chest. His eyes are still blocked by the stupid mask. "So, are you disappointed?" he asks. He fiddles with the buttons on the bottom of his shirt and avoids eye contact with me. Is he nervous? I don't understand. How can boring ole me intimidate someone this perfect?

"No, not at all. You?" I dread his answer. I mean, I know that Blanche is right. If he doesn't like me he can go to hell, but I desperately want him to see me that way. I'm never the pretty Conner woman, the leading lady of the story. That's an honor held by my sisters and mother. God, I want one person to see me like that. I want it to be him.

To answer me he steps in and does something I didn't expect. He put his arms around my waist and leans into me. And then he kisses me.

I don't know what to do! The last time I'd been kissed had been by Freddy Michaels in sixth grade behind the jungle gym. Our braces got stuck together and they had to call an ambulance to separate us. It was humiliating. But the Mystery Man is nothing like Freddy Michaels. His strong hands support my back, pulling me into him. I cup my own hands behind his head of coal black hair, so different from Freddy's ginger cowlicks. His mouth is warm and comforting; familiar, like a memory I'd forgotten. He pulls back slightly, catching his breath and moves a hand to my cheek. It's rough, like it's worn from work, but I want to nuzzle up into it. His blue eyes cut through his mask and into my own eyes and I can't break the gaze. He gives me that lopsided smile and asks, "What do you think?"

My mouth hangs open and I can't close it. I know I look like a freak, but I can't do anything about it. "Thank you," I'm finally able to blurt, and I do mean blurt, out. I practically scream at the poor man. I want to crawl into a hole and die.

A bright grin spreads across his lovely face and I blush a deeper shade. Damn it, I don't want to be a stupid tomato! But he doesn't seem to mind. "Well 3788, you are more than welcome." And then he kisses me again. I feel like I'm melting into a puddle at his feet, but I can get used to it.

From off in the distance the song changes once more, but this time it's a tune I know. I smile at the memories it brings me, but tears still sting my eyes. "What is it?" he questions, sensing my mixed emotions, the tips of his fingers brushing gently at the apples of my cheeks just below my eyes.

I point to air, to the music. "The song. Stevie Wonder, 'Isn't She Lovely'. My dad has told me since I was a kid that it's the song he wants to dance to with me at my wedding." My cheeks blush at the feeling of his fingers and the embarrassment of my own memories. It's a stupid thing to get me so emotional.

"Well, that's nice," he replies with a goofy smile, lopsided and perfect. Of course, he only says that because he doesn't know.

I shake my head at the searing heat behind my eyes and protectively wrap my arms around my torso. "Yeah, you're only saying that because you're not acquainted with my father."

I expect for him to throw back something clever. Something like, "How bad could he be if he made you?" or equally cheesy like I'd expect guys to do when confronted with feminine emotions, but he doesn't. He doesn't say anything. Instead he leans down and kisses me again, harder than before and I embrace it. When he finally pulls away his eyes remain on my face as he releases me and reaches up to the mask covering his own eyes. There's a question in his eyes, but I can only hold my breath in answer, moment of truth.

When the mask flies up past his beautiful black hair I choke on the breath I've been holding. It's a face I've seen before. Of course the last time I had seen him, he'd been covered in pie. "Finn," I breathe, so quiet I don't think he can hear me.

But he does.

"You know me?" he asks, a curious smile curling on his lips.

This can't be. It's not possible. Finn! The hot guy covered in pie is my Mystery Man. I want to rip my mask off and reveal myself, but I can't do it. There's a nagging thought that holds me back and sits heavy in my stomach.

"Don't you have a girlfriend?"

He sighs and shakes his head. "No, Mal is a crazy person. We broke up a few days ago, I promise. That's completely over. But how do you know me?"

I open my mouth to speak, even though I'm not sure what, but I don't get the chance. The door to the pavilion behind us flies open and my half Chinese Jessica Rabbit sticks her head out. "Sorry to interrupt princess, but it's 11:45." Crap! Where had the time gone? Hadn't we just gotten here? I whip back to Finn who looks at me with the strangest expression. It reminds me of the look I have when I burn my tongue on something tasty. "I'm sorry Finn, I have to go." I desperately want to stay, but it's going to take much longer than fifteen minutes to get home in the magic pumpkin and explaining all of this to my mother was going to be an impossible feat.

I start off in Blanche's direction. Upon reaching her she pushes me in front of her to act at my shield. She always knows what I need before I do. "Wait!" I hear him shout from behind, but I keep moving, bobbing in between the people. The urge to get away overwhelms and I grip Blanches hand so hard her knuckles crack. I'm sure he's following after me, but I know Blanche and I can get away quicker.

And we do. We make it to the magic pumpkin before Finn even reaches the door. I pile the miles of fabric up onto my lap and into my face, all the while screaming for Blanche to hit the gas.

As we peel out of our parking spot I glance back to see him standing in the doorway looking hurt and confused. His tall, muscular frame fills the doorway and his chest rises and falls with heavy breaths from running after me. His eyes are narrowed and his jaw clenched, he doesn't know why I'm running. I have to, I'm doing him a favor. There's no way a guy like Finn will want a girl like me. We're from two different worlds. It will never work.

In Blanche's rearview mirror I see him hold up something his hand and it jingles from his hand. I search down the front of my dress where I'd put my keys for "safe" keeping like a deep sea diver spelunking for pearls. They're not here. He has them. I turn in my seat and take a final look back at him, my mask still blocking any recognizable part of my face, and the expression of hurt in his eyes nearly kills me. Hurting him is the last thing I want to do, but a little pain now is worth a shattered and disappointed heart in the future.

"What happened?" Blanche demands as she rips off her Crayola red wig revealing her sweat slicked black hair.

I take off my mask and rubbed my face. "It was Finn!" I shout, ignoring the streaks of mascara and eye shadow on my fingers. "You know the guy from your track team? The ridiculously gorgeous and athletic and popular guy? He's the mystery man!"

Blanche takes a turn too fast and smacks me into the window. I should really put on my seat belt. "Yes Michelle, I saw that it was him, but what happened? You just ran from him."

"It was Finn! I can't date a guy like Finn!"

"Why not?" she asks as she runs a stop sign, a shrill blast of a horn following behind us. Getting arrested or in an accident will not get me home any faster.

I brace myself against the door and continue, "Think about it Blanche. Just for a good long second. Do I strike you as the kind of girl who dates Johnny High School? No, if anything, I date Freddy Michaels." He's still parasitically present in my brain.

"Who the hell is Freddy Michaels?" she shouts, running another stop sign. I'm going to die in the damn pumpkin.

I bury my face in my knees and mumble, "A kid I knew in middle school."

"What does Freddy Michaels have to do with this? You're making no sense, you psycho!"

"Don't yell at me! It's just not meant to be." I pull the scratchy fabric of my skirt up to let my legs breathe, they're sweating like Niagara Falls!

"Oh, so the swapping of spit you two had going was just your idea of parting ways?" she accuses as she blows through a red light, flipping off someone who honks at her.

"You saw that?" I shriek, my head snapping up to catch her eyes.

She nods, makeup streaking her face. When the evening started she looked like a movie star. Now she's more like a cheap hooker after a hard night. "Yeah, sweetie, everyone did."

I plop my head back on my knees. This really is a disaster. "No, no, no, that's not what I wanted."

"Well what exactly was the purpose of this little escapade then? You met the guy, you like the guy, the guy likes you, but you're not happy?"

"He doesn't like me Blanche. He likes 3788, the girl he's been writing secret notes to all this time. No way a guy like that would ever like a girl like me," I mumble to my knees, avoiding all eye contact and the judgment I'm sure is spilling from her.

"Oh, my God, please get over yourself and quit the pity party. You're being an idiot," she growls as she hit the accelerator a little harder. I'm not sure if she's trying to get me home faster or if this is just some manifestation of her anger toward me.

"No, I'm not!" I shout, pulling the pins out of my hair, letting the curls fall loosely down my back. "He likes 3788, he likes this beautiful princess. I'm sorry, but who wouldn't like that? It's a fantasy, but you know me, the real me. When was the last time you saw me do my hair or put on makeup or wear something nice? I'm not that girl, but he is totally that guy. You go to school with him, you've seen his girlfriend. Do I in any way remind you of that girl, Mal?"

She pulls the car over, the breaks protest with a screech. She knows we don't have time for this and it makes me want to kill her, but she's stopping anyway. She turns off the ignition and flips in her seat to glare at me. "He's not with Mal anymore, you moron! Did it ever strike you that maybe he's looking for something different, that maybe he's looking for you! God, you're so stupid sometimes." She slams her hand down on the steering wheel and her knuckles turn white in her grasp.

"Shut up! I'm not stupid, just get me home. I don't want to talk about this anymore. We don't have time for this." I turn on my side toward the window the pressed my forehead against the cool glass and wait.

Nothing happens.

I peer over at Blanche. She's biting hard on her lip, staring at the steering wheel and mumbling something to herself as she tries to the turn the ignition over again. "Um," she says simply as she peeks over at me. "It won't start?"

"Is that a question?" I hiss through a clenched jaw.

"I'm sorry Elle, it won't start," she repeats, trying to turn it over again. It makes a sad clinking sound that fizzles into nothing.

"No, no, no!" I bark, unbuckling my seat belt and throwing open the door. Stupid pumpkin!

"Where are you going?" Blanche demands as she leans across her seat.

I crouch down to her eye level and inform her, "Well, I've got about ten minutes to be home and you obviously aren't going to be able to get me there."

"It's two miles, what're you going to do? Run?" she exclaims out the window.

I pull up my skirt to reveal my Converse and sigh, "Yep." And off I go.

I run as fast as my feet can carry me, which trust me isn't all that fast, but quick enough to get me home. Halfway through I lose one of my shoes, but don't have the time to stop for it. There's no time for anything.

Just as I turn the corner onto my street, my aunt's car pulls up in front. "Damn," I mumble. My being out in a ball gown without the baby and Beattie in the house is all just a little too much for me to explain. I have to think of something.

My master plan is nothing all too ingenious. I scoot around to my neighbor's back yard. There's a loose board in the fence that separates our houses that I can possibly squish through into our yard. The crinoline in my skirt could be a problem, but I'll have to work passed it. My mother keeps our back gate padlocked from the inside so the "hoodlums" can't get into our yard. The closest thing Harpersgrove has to a "hoodlum" is the kid with ink black hair who skateboards in the corner store parking lot and insists we call him "Skye". The lock makes it kind of impossible for me to get in through my own backyard. I reach over the top of the neighbor's fence and unlatch the door. My skirt swishes against the spiky grass, making more noise than I want, so I have to move fast. I wish that my dress wasn't such a bright white. I stick out like a sore thumb against the landscape. I can't wait to crawl into my bed and forget this night ever happe-

I hear an unexpected sound behind me. I forgot about Precious. I rotate around to see my neighbor's terrifying German shepherd growling at me, her teeth bared, ready to pounce. I push myself up against the fence and start feeling for the loose board. "Nice Precious, good Precious, pretty Precious," I sing to the vicious, rabid creature. My voice breathy and high, reminiscent of a fairy in a children's movie, but it seems to make the stupid dog mad. She crouches lower, her shoulders narrowing together over her head, and I know she's about to come after me. Luckily, in the same moment I find the board. I push it aside and squeeze through the tiny hole as fast as I can, but as I feared my huge skirt gets caught in the boards and I'm stuck. "Fudge!" I hiss, as I feel Precious's teeth pull on the end of the skirt. Scares the daylights out of me, feeling her tugging my body back toward her, but luckily it also sets me free from being stuck. I stagger to my feet as the board slams itself shut. There's a whimper from the other side, Precious must have been hit in the face by the swinging board. Serves her right. I've made it home, but in how many pieces? I take a deep breath and take a look down at the damage. The skirt's covered in grass stains and mud and behind a good foot and a half of fluff is missing. Hopefully Precious enjoys her treat. Beattie will not be pleased with what I've done to her dress. I hustle to the door and before I can touch the handle the sliding glass swings open. I nearly swallow my tongue at the thought that it could be my mother. Thank the Lord, it's not.

"What did you do to my dress!" Beattie barks, her hand on the baby's ears. I wouldn't have expected Beattie to protect anyone from harsh words, even the little Satan Spawn.

"I'll pay you back for it, I promise, Beattie. It was a long night," I say, breathless, as I drag my disheveled self through the doors. Upstairs the door closes and again I feel my tongue sliding down my throat. The dress is in shambles, she can't see me like this. There's no way I can talk my way out of this one. "Switch clothes with me?" I plead, my hands clasped together in prayer. I'll get down on my knees and beg if that's what she needs.

"Oh you've got to be kidding me," Beattie sighs with a roll of her eyes.

"Please Beat, it's the last thing I'll ever ask you, please!" I'll give her my first born, all the money I ever make, my virginity as sacrifice to the gods if that's what it takes. I cannot take the wrath of Eleanor and the loss of my mystery man in one night.

"Michelle where are you?" my mother shouts from upstairs.

"I'll be right up mom, give me one second!" I call up, a pout spreading across my face to my employer. Last ditch effort.

Beattie snarls, "You owe me so big."

I zip up Beattie's orange hoodie and watch as my boss scurries across my backyard in a stained and tattered ball gown. She's displeased to say the least, but I know she'll forgive me. Beattie's good that way.

As she runs out of sight, my mother and aunt emerge down the stairs.

"Why weren't you answering?" my mother demands as she looks me over. Her face is bright and pink from either alcohol or over activity. I'm hoping for the booze. Her white blouse is cut too low for a woman of her age and she's wearing far too much makeup, but there's a glimmer in her eyes that I've never seen before. I suppose "singles night" was a success.

"Sorry," I mumble as I hand the baby over to Aunt Wilma. Ana is surprisingly complacent, much more so than she'd been when I'd left. That Beattie is truly a wizard.

"I thought I told you to put her in the pink pajamas" Aunt Wilma groans as she shifts Ana to her hip. The baby immediately tries to reach back to me and I try not let the smugness overwhelm me. Nobody likes Aunt Wilma.

"Sorry," I half-heartedly apologize, trying to catch my breath. I still can't believe I got away with this crazy night and my mother is none the wiser.

"Why are you wearing makeup? And why is your hair so curly?" my mother asks scrutinizing every aspect of me as she so loves to do. Okay, so maybe she's a bit the wiser.

I shrug, trying to be cool, but I'm letting my weight bounce back and forth between my feet so it just looks like I have to pee. "Got bored, figured I do a little something to myself."

She inspects each side of my face, holding my chin in her hand, and says, "You could do more."

Classic Eleanor Conner, at least she doesn't seem to suspect anything. Honestly, I could probably tell her the truth because there's no way she'd ever believe me.

"Did you guys have fun?" I ask, crossing my arms over my chest, wishing to get away to that bed of mine.

Aunt Wilma narrows her overly plucked eyebrows at me, "You don't care."

"You're right, I don't, but it's nice to make conversation," I say, swishing past her. "I'm going to bed." I'm too exhausted for any of this. My heart is full and my soul is a little cracked. Sleep is the only fix.

But the good times keep coming. The front door opens and closes again and followed by the bickering of my two sisters. If I make a run for it I think I can get up the stairs before they see me.

I try.

I fail.

"God, if you weren't such a loser, Elle, you totally would have been at an awesome party!" Tyler proclaims with a laugh, making Megan giggle as well. There's only one brain between the two of them I swear.

"Oh well, I so wish I weren't a loser," I said as I rub the back of my neck, scratching more glitter into my skin. How do girls do this on a regular basis?

"You totally missed some drama with the coolest guy at New Shiloh," Megan gossips as she takes a bottle of expensive Swedish water from the fridge.

That stops me. "What drama?" I hope of course that they aren't talking about Finn and, subsequently, me.

"Finn Wise, he's like the king of that school, met some girl and she like ran out on him and he spent the rest of the time asking everyone if they knew who she was," Tyler says with a roll of her eyes. "I mean, seriously, who runs out on something that delicious?"

"I know right," Megan adds. "That girl was such an idiot. I would have done him right there in the middle of the dance floor."

"Good to know you set your sights so high," I criticize, doing my best to keep my dinner in my stomach. I stupidly hoped that Finn had just forgotten me and would go on with his life. That would have been too easy.

"You're just jealous that it wasn't you," Tyler huffs as she tosses her purse on the counter. She hops on one of the stools at the breakfast bar and pulls off her platform silver shoes. The smell that radiates from her feet could take down a fleet of strong men. It takes everything I have not to gag.

The irony strikes me that my sister has no idea what actually happened. "Yeah, Ty, you're right, totally jealous."

...

The next morning I'm supposed to be at the pie shop bright and early for a shift, but I can't do it. I call Beattie and lie to her that I'm a little under the weather and I'd try to come in later. She's not been super pleased, but it ends with a sigh and a reminder about the dress I'd ruined. That only made me want to cry. I've ruined a lot more than the dress.

I lay on my bed staring at the unicorn poster I'd hung on the ceiling when I was twelve and think about what I can possibly do now. I don't know who to trust or who to believe. How can Finn possibly want someone like me? It doesn't seem probable. I'm too basic, too plain Jane, and he's an Adonis in a track uniform. Stories like these never work out.

Beside me, my computer pings for the thousandth time. Yet another message from Finn to 3788, asking what he'd done wrong, where I'd gone, what he could do to fix it. I hug my arms around myself as my gaze drifts to the glass cabinet filled with the trinkets of my childhood and I know there's only one place that can make me feel any better. I bite down hard on my lip and pick up my laptop, taking a deep breath before I type the only response I intend to give Finn.

I'm so sorry, I type, fighting hard against my tears. I can only be honest, guarded but honest. That's all I have for him. *You didn't do anything wrong, it's all me. It would never work between us. I'm not right for you. Work on finding the real 3788, whoever she is. I'm sure she'll make you happier than I can. Goodbye, Finn.*

With that I click the sign-off button and exit the account, never to return to it, I'm sure. I hug my arms back around myself and settle against my comfy and familiar princess sheets and let my tears roll off my face and down to my pillow. Sometimes you just have to close doors, I guess.

The New Shiloh community flea market is in full force late on a Sunday morning, and by late I mean nine thirty in the morning. Their busiest time is around six thirty or seven, but with the season winding down for the year, everyone soaks up every single second that they're able. All around me people are bustling, haggling, and making deals. Children scream, parents chastise, and everything is pure chaos. It's so loud I can't hear myself think. It's exactly what I need.

I stroll aimlessly from table to table, betraying my natural instincts to shop with a purpose and only look for my coveted salt and pepper shakers. For once, I want to take in everything. I hike my old vinyl PowerPuff Girls bag, that had become the Yard Sale Bag when I was little, up my shoulder. True, I had better and sturdier bags at home now, but it would be wrong to travel with anything else. There's comfort in the familiar and I need a little bit of it.

I pause at a table filled with boxes and boxes of glass beads, the light catching them and my eye so that I have to stop. In the far corner sits a little old Asian woman on white wicker chair, fanning herself with a full blown, Spanish flamenco dancer style fan. She has a neon green visor that covers her perfectly coiffed grey hair and simple round face. She sports a fanny pack that cuts her lemon yellow jumpsuit in half and she keeps smiling and nodding at me. I smile back and try not to feel uncomfortable as she follows me with her eyes as my fingers roam the cool smooth glass of the beads.

"These are beautiful," I mention to the little old woman, raising my voice more than necessary.

She smiles a little brighter, her eyes disappearing into slits and her musical voice responds, "Thank you, I make them all myself. Three for five dollars, any ones you want."

For a flea market that cost almost kills me. I've never spent more than a dollar fifty on anything in my entire life. Besides, what am I going to do with three random glass beads? It's completely impractical, or at least that's what I try to convince myself. But truth be told, I don't need a reason, I want them. I reach into the pocket of my dark blue jeans and take out a crumpled old Lincoln and hand it to the old Asian woman. She motions around to her two tables on either side of us.

"Any three you want."

It seems like the most daunting task in world considering there are literally thousands of beads scattered amongst the boxes, each one completely different from its neighbor. My eye catches a burnt orange triangle shaped bead sitting on top of the box of yellow beads. It reminds me a lot of a piece of pumpkin pie. In the box next to it are all these white iridescent beads, one of which is rippled on the edges and has silver specks inside that reminds me of my mask and dress. I know what I'm looking for to complete the triad. I search the boxes for something brown, anything brown that will match the color of Finn's costume, but even amongst the thousands of beads there's nothing that comes close. I huff aloud and shift my weight from foot to foot, so much for finding closure in inanimate objects. On a whim I search the bucket of blue and I reach in to snatch one in particular as though someone might try to take it from me. It's simple and round and the exact color of Finn's eyes. As long I live, I'll never forget those eyes peering back at me from behind that ridiculous mask that he wore. I bite hard on the inside of my cheek, I'm not going to cry. I hold my hand up to the little old woman to show her I've picked my three and she smiles back and gives me a little drawstring bag to keep my purchase safe. She pats me softly on the arm, a mothering gesture that I'm sure will break me and she says, "You come see me again, and you bring your friends." Always looking for a sale, how typical.

I wander around a little while longer, trying my best to avoid any and all family stands so that I won't find any salt and pepper shakers.

My fragile psyche can't take it. I try to convince myself that I'm far more interested in handmade wood carvings of bears or old football and baseball memorabilia, but it's not working. I'm about to just give up and leave when a familiar sight enters my line of vision. I'm fairly certain that Miss Nancy, of Miss Nancy's Candied Apples, spots me before I do her, and she's a sight for sore eyes. Her stand is bright and vibrant against the chaos that surrounds her. She has the same sign behind her table that has been there since my childhood with two crossed bright red candied apples, "Miss Nancy's Candied Apples" above it in hunter green letters. She wears her signature yellow apron with the white lace around its edge that she folds in half so it only covers her legs and ties in the back around her slender frame. Her pin straight salt and pepper hair is cropped at her chin and she wears her half glasses on the edge of her nose with a pearl beaded chain that wraps from ear to ear. She smiles brightly and raises her arms to me in a welcoming gesture. The overwhelming need for some type of mothering energy is too much for me to resist. I rush through the crowd of people, nearly knocking over a small child and a dog that cross my path, but I can't stop. I almost knock her over I run into her so hard. The musical laughter that springs from her ears warms my heart all the way down to my shoes.

"Well, well, well," she begins, the air whistling through the sizable gap between her front teeth. "My eyes must deceive me because Ms. Conner doesn't come out this way to see Miss Nancy no more." I grin at the thick southern accent that I'm fairly certain is fake, but it's so warm, crisp, and comforting. She's like the human embodiment of a peach cobbler.

"Good lord, girl! I think you've grown two feet since the last time you were here."

I have to bend down to hug her short, five foot tall frame. I bury my nose in the comforting smell of her neck and wipe away the sudden surprised tears that spring to my eyes.

"It's good to see you, Miss Nancy," I murmur, trying my best not to blubber.

She leans away from me, concern etched on her perfectly weathered face.

"What's with the water works?" she gently pushes as she shoos away a pesky child trying to grab an apple off her table. Miss Nancy has no patience for shenanigans.

I shrug and sniffle dramatically as I stuff my hands into my pockets.

"Everything's so messed up," I admit with an orphan sob, looking up at the sky as though it can make my tears stop. "My parents split up, my dad's getting remarried. I've pretty much destroyed my first and probably only shot at romance. It's all just so screwed up."

Miss Nancy sucks her cheek into her mouth and takes a deep breath in through her nose. She's ready to instill some grand wisdom. She leans over to her right and picks up a shiny red candied apple wrapped in yellow cellophane and hands it to me saying, "My mama taught me two things that I hold dear to this day. One is that there's nothing a good homemade candied apple can't fix."

"And the second thing?" I ask, crinkling the apple's wrapper around my fingers. I can smell the sugary goodness through the plastic.

She winks and rubs her hands down my arms. "The second thing is that hiding from your problems doesn't make them go away," she adds giving me a knowing smile.

"Who says I'm hiding?" I ask as I chomp down into the crunchy exterior of the heavenly apple. It's sure to pull out all my fillings, but it's totally worth it.

She juts her hip to the side and planted her fists squarely on her waist. She is small, but she is mighty.

"Child, I haven't seen you here in years and all of a sudden you show up talking about how your life's falling apart? Sounds like you're avoiding something to me."

Of course, she's right and I'm in no place to argue. I shift my sad little PowerPuff Girls bag, with only my three glass beads inside up my shoulder. "Do I have to face it?"

She smiles again and touches my cheek before being pulled away by another customer.

"Face it or not, it's your choice, but it's real. It's there no matter what you do."

I take another bite from my apple and know Miss Nancy's right. She's always right. I pulled my phone from my back pocket and text Beattie to let her know I'm on my way and hightailed it across the street to wait for the lone bus that will get me close to Harpersgrove. The smell of diesel signals my journey home to my adult problems.

Normally, Sundays are the busiest and most fun days at the shop, but I'm not in the mood to be happy today. I drag my feet down the street, stalling as long as possible before I have to go inside. I knew for a fact that I'll be bombarded with people wanting to know how it went. Who the guy was, what happened, when the wedding would be, and all that jazz. Having no interest in revealing any of those things, I stall. Plus I really don't want to hear any crap from Blanche, Beattie, or especially Rosie. If our faithful pie baker knows how much of a disaster the night before had been, I'll definitely be in store for a big ole helping of "I-told-you-so" and I don't want to hear it.

A group of people wait on the hard wooden bench I forced Beattie to bring in for people to sit on while they waited for tables to become available. Every neon colored stool is filled with a person waiting for their pie to be delivered at the counter. They sip on coffee and read the New York Times, happy to be left alone. The counter's for loners. The booths are full of elderly couples and families with children or groups of friends, all waiting for pie. Business is as usual, but nothing feels usual to me.

"Well, it sure took you long enough," Bella says from beside me as she hands Mrs. Bederman her change. The middle aged mother experiences that familiar consumer panic as she tries to shove the change back in her wallet and get out of the way of the line that's formed behind her.

"What?"

Bella laughs, "I don't move too much from this spot, as you well know, and I've been watching you walk down the street for the last ten minutes. It's cold out there, what took you so long."

"Just enjoying the glory that is autumn." My skin flushes as I press my palms to my face to clench my embarrassment.

She rolls her eyes. "Whatever, I'm glad you're here. You're on counter duty."

I give her a salute. "Aye, aye, captain." She doesn't ask, strange. I thought that it would be the first thing on everyone's mind.

The day goes on and I fill orders, interact with Bella at the counter, Rosie in the kitchen, Nixie and Goldie working out on the floor. Not once does anyone ever ask me. I'm getting paranoid. Do they know something I don't? Was it all really a dream? Have I finally lost it?

When the lunch shift rolls around, I can't take it anymore. "Okay," I demand as I trap Nixie on her way to the kitchen with a pile of orders for Rosie. "Is nobody here going to ask me about last night?"

Nixie exchanges quick eye contact with Bella before looking back at me. "What're you talking about?"

"Are you kidding me?" I exclaim, making the seven year old sitting in front of me giggle. "Eat your pie." I hiss at him and his mouth digs down inside the flaky crust and apple filling.

"Um," Nixie begins before scurrying away quicker than I've ever seen her legs carry her out of water. She passes Goldie who looked confused.

"What's the matter?" she asks as she drops off her own order for Rosie before replacing her pen to the safety of the mountain of hair on her head.

"Why aren't any of you asking me about what happened last night?" I'm a little hurt now that none of them have asked. Do they just not care?

"Oh, well, that's because of Blanche's text message." Goldie says simply, making Bella shake her head and press her palm against her forehead.

"What text message?" I ask as I hand the seven year old a stack of napkins to clean his face.

"The one telling us not to ask you about last night because you were upset about it and probably wouldn't want to talk about it." Goldie continues frankly.

"My dear, sweet, simple Goldie," Bella adds. "Do you remember what the end of the text message said?" I can see Rosie's eyes shooting daggers at her simple best friend from the kitchen and Nixie looks like she has a headache.

She ponders this a moment and then her lips turn down a little at the corners. "Oh, right, not to tell Elle about the text message. Whoops." Goldie remembers with a shrug, not overly affected by her mistake.

"It's okay Gold, don't worry about it. Thanks for the consideration, but I'm okay." I say with a smile to all of them, returning to my work. Once again, my best friend comes through for my feelings. Blanche might have seemed mad at me the night before for the way I'd handled things with Finn, but at the end of the day she protects me. She always protects me. I love her for it.

The ringing of the bell on the front door pulls my attention. I look up and fight the urge to hit the ground when I see who it is. Standing at over six feet tall with his brawny chest and chiseled face and perfect hair is my Mystery man. And in his hand, he holds my keys.

Chapter Nine

I need to act fast. I grab Bella hard by the arm and harshly whisper, "Listen to me and listen good." I have her thoroughly freaked out and therefore also have her attention. "Whatever he says, no matter what, they are not my keys. Do you understand?" She has absolutely no idea what I'm talking about but she nods in agreement.

Finn walks up to the counter I and collapse to my knees, making an effort to look like I'm doing something important on the floor. "Can I help you?" Bella asks, the confusion still in her voice. I pinch her ankle with my sticky fingers to stress that she needs to be cool. Not Bella's strong suit.

"Yeah," Finn's voice answers. He sounds tired, like he'd been up all night or something. Of course I know he had been up e-mailing me. That makes me feel worse. "I found these keys last night and there's a key chain on them to this place. I thought maybe you'd know if some-one lost their keys." There's more in his voice than just the attitude of a Good Samaritan. For some reason that makes me smile.

"Um," Bella stumbles, fighting the urge to look down at me. "I mean, I haven't heard anything, we do sell a lot of those key chains-" Total lie, only the girls who work at Hap-PIE-ly even bother to purchase one. "But I'd be happy to hold onto them for you in case anyone comes look-ing for them."

She extends her hand for the keys, but he pulled back quickly, pushing them protectively into his pocket. "No," Finn stands firm, taking a seat at the counter, my counter, where I have to work. Damn. "No thank you, I'll hold onto them."

Bella shrugs. "Suit yourself. I'm going to restock napkins." And with that she disappears into the back. In her mind she's handled the situation. Bella doesn't function well in awkward situations. Much more the sheltered wallflower is she, not one for drama.

I take a deep cleansing breath, the pungent sweet smell of the sticky floor makes me dizzy. My hair's sloppy and pulled up in a messy ponytail. I have no sweeping beautiful curls like the night before. My face is covered in flour and sweat forming quite an interesting paste on my forehead and I'm pretty sure there's some toothpaste crusted in the corner of my mouth. No beautiful makeup and flawless skin. I don a grey sweater and dark blue jeans with my Crocs. Nothing in comparison to the epic ball gown I'd worn yesterday. I remind myself of all this for a simple reason. There was no way he'll know who I am. I mean above everything else I'd worn a mask. So imagine my total surprise when I rise to my feet and his downtrodden expression turns to a happy smile and he muses, "Hey, it's you."

My heart's in my shoes and my stomach catapults to my throat. I'm going to drop dead right here. He waits for me to make some sign of recognition before finally saying, "Pumpkin Pie right, you dropped a whole tray of pie on my head." I'm still trying to remember how to breathe, not purposely ignoring him, but he keeps talking, "Aw, so I guess you do that to all the guys. Maybe I should talk to your boss, you know, just for the safety of the public." He gives me that glorious and oh so paralyzing lopsided grin and I have to restart my heart.

His smile turns to a frown as he reaches out to touch my hand. "Hey, are you okay?"

I have to pull myself out of this!

"Yes! Fine!" I shout, yep shouted, at him. He looks a little terrified as he leans an arm's length away from the counter. Not like I can blame him or anything, I am acting like a crazy person. I sigh and try again, in a normal, human voice, "Yes I'm fine and yes of course I remember you. Sorry, it's been a bit of a nutty morning." Understatement of the century for sure.

He sighs in his own relief. "Don't worry about it, it's cool." I stand there, wiping and re-wiping the same place on the counter for like five minutes, waiting for him to say something else. I really don't want to speak first. He pulls the keys out of his pocket. "You wouldn't happen to know of anyone who lost a set of keys would you?" They jingle together and sound echoes through my ears.

I look at the keys as though they're unfamiliar and do not in fact hold my house key, store keys, and my variety of witty and visually appealing key chains. I shake my head and say, "Nope, sorry, but Bella made a good point. Maybe you should leave them here in case anyone comes in to claim them." And so my mother can't lock me out of my house.

He frowns, placing my keys once again back in his pocket. Damn. "No thanks, I think I'll hold onto them."

I obviously have an out. The guy clearly has no idea that I am, in fact, 3788, but I can't keep my mouth shut. "So, why won't you give them up?" I prod, smoothing a placemat in front of him along with silverware. I'm not letting him go without pie.

"What do you mean?" he asks, shifting his weight uncomfortably on the neon yellow stool that's far too small for him. It reminds me of an adult sitting on a piece of children's plastic furniture.

I balance my elbows on the counter and bring my eyes to his level. "Well, I think it's obvious that you didn't just find a set of keys." I continue as I place a piece of pumpkin pie in front of him.

"Why is that obvious?" he questions as he picks up his fork. He shovels half the piece into his mouth in a single bite. Boys are so classy.

"Well, because if you just found a random set of keys and people were offering to take them off your hands you'd get your good deed for the day without any of the follow up responsibilities. You would jump at the chance. However, you're holding on to them like they're diamonds or something."

MICHELLE ANTOINETTE CONNER, SHUT UP!!!! But even the screaming in my head can't silence the word vomit. "It seems a little strange."

He sighs and runs a hand through his perfect, curly black hair.

"Well, I guess you caught me." He finished the pie off in a second bite. It's actually rather fascinating to watch.

I cut him another piece and replace the empty plate. "I have a knack for spotting this kind of thing." Okay, so apparently I'm a pompous ass now too.

He laughs, "Yea, I guess you do."

I extend a hand to him. For the sake of my own sanity I need to re-move at least one level of mystery from this equation. "I'm Elle."

"Aw, see and I was beginning to like calling you Pumpkin Pie," he laughs taking my hand. He squeezes it a little and provides me with in-formation I already know, "I'm Finn."

Now would be a great time to walk away from the counter. Introductions are out of the way, but of course the word vomit let's me do no such thing. So, I pour him a cup of coffee and lean against the counter. "Now, why don't you tell me all about it?"

It's quite an interesting ordeal to hear about yourself from the per-spective of another person. The way in which Finn describes his bud-ding relationship with me is in no way how I saw it. Of course I have all the information and he doesn't, so clearly I'm right.

"I don't know what it is. I just can't get her out of my head," he mum-bles into his fourth piece of pie, sticking with the pumpkin, a man after my own heart. On the third piece he'd forced me to get a fork and join him. I'm powerless to the pie.

This is my chance to discourage his affections. You know in case he does ever figure out that I'm his fantasy girl. At least then he might not be so disappointed. "She seems too good to be true," I add as I swallow some pumpkin deliciousness. Rosie has truly outdone herself today.

He shakes his head. "No, she's amazing, I can tell. I've always gone out with these girls who have been so, so..." he tries to find the right word. "Plastic."

I laugh, a mouthful of pie going up the back of my nose. Totally worth is. "You date a lot girls with boob implants and nose jobs, do ya? Or are we talking sex dolls?" I ask as I pour him another cup of coffee and give a piece of cherry pie to the woman sitting at the end of the counter.

He rolls his eyes, throwing his straw wrapper in my face. "No, you know what I mean. They're fake, no personality. Plastic."

"Yeah, I remember your girlfriend from our last little encounter here. She seemed like a peach to me," I respond as sarcastically as I can muster.

He rubs the back of his neck, most likely remembering Mal's behavior as well as I have. "Yeah, I'm sorry about that. She's a bit unbalanced." The apples of his cheeks flush a bright red under his creamy pale skin and I can tell he's embarrassed.

I shake my head and choke back the acidic feeling at the back of my throat. "Then why would you date a person like that in the first place? I'm sure you had some idea that she was like that when you started dating her."

He bites the inside of his cheek as his eyes dart to the nosy preteen who's intently watching us back and forth like a tennis match. "Yeah, I did. She doesn't exactly hide it well."

"Then, why?" I push, giving the nosy little chunker beside Finn his third piece of pie.

He picks up a fork and digs into the kid's pie. The sound that erupts from deep inside the boy's chest is some mix of a gasp and cackle with a dash of outrage. Finn ignores it and tousles the boy's floppy amber locks before handing him another fork so they can both enjoy. "I don't know, I guess when you're like me you're supposed to date girls like that."

Whatever's about to come out of his mouth I'm certain I'm not going to like. I cross my arms and narrow my eyes to slits. "What exactly does that mean?"

"Well, I mean, when you're considered popular, you're supposed to date the popular girl. I don't like it sometimes, but that's just the way it goes." He's reminding me of Molly Ringwald in the Breakfast Club, and I've never wanted to punch Molly Ringwald so much in my life.

I pull the plate away, his fork screeches against the lament counter making all of us cringe. "Oh, boo-freaking-hoo. It must be so hard being so damn popular. I feel so bad for you."

I drop the plate, with the last bite still atop, in the dirty dishes. "What the hell is your problem?" he demands, throwing his hands back as the child beside him hurries away to find his mother. I guess he's not interested anymore.

"Nothing, I have no problem." Apparently, I'm making the right choice in not telling him who I am. Clearly, he's too snobby for me.

Pushing his stool back to stand, he stalks around the counter only to be pounced on by Bella, who appears from nowhere. "No customers behind the counter!" she shouts and he hops away walking his way back to where he came.

"Obviously, there's something wrong." he says, his massive muscular form towering over the yellow stool.

I grab his silverware away from him. "You know, life's hard for those of us on the other side of popularity. I don't really feel like hearing how hard it is to have everyone love you." I know why I'm so furious. He's unknowingly defining our problem. Literally, explaining to me why we can never work. High school is a class system. The beautiful and popular stick together at the top while the rest of us scrape the bottom of barrel, landing ones like Freddy Michaels if we're lucky. I know all of this on my own, but hearing him inadvertently tell me the same is killing me.

He shakes his head, his eyes big and sad. "Maybe it's not that simple. Did you ever think of that?"

I pretend to ponder this a moment before saying, "Nope, it's really just that easy." I have very little interest in hearing the woes of this beautiful boy in regards to his perfect life.

"Wow," he breathes as he grabs his coat and throws a rumpled ten dollar bill on the counter, not even close to covering what he owes. "That's really interesting."

"What?" I demand, kicking myself for not keeping my mouth shut for once.

He smile is cold and his eyes are dead as his voice loses all its warmth and kindness. "Pumpkin Pie, you're no different than anyone else." And he turns and leaves, his loud footsteps booming all the way out the door.

"My name is Elle!" I shout at his back, but he's already gone.

I'm fuming, what a jerk. How could I ever be attracted to someone like that? I scrub the counter with a fury unlike any other, taking all my aggression out on the marble.

Rosie pops her head up in the kitchen window. "What was that Michelle?" she yells at me, the judgement spilling over her words.

"I know! He's a total jerk, right?" I hiss.

I look up, after a too long moment of silence, to see Bella and Rosie exchange looks. "No honey," Bella begins. "He's not."

"Then what are you talking about?" My attention focuses back on Rosie as she emerges from the kitchen with an industrial sized bag of coffee.

Rosie bites her lip, as though she's unsure about how to answer. "Um, angel, you were kind of the jerk."

"How was I a jerk?" I exclaim, waiting for an answer from either of them. One of my customers taps her coffee cup on the counter, passively demanding a refill, which I ignore.

"The guy opened up to you and you kind of just shoved his face in the sand," Goldie states as she brings back a tray of dirty dishes. "That was rather jerky of you."

"But, but-" I said try to find my justification that seemed so clear to me only moments before, but it's lost now. I plop my elbows on the counter and mumble, "Damn."

"Can I ask a question now?" Bella asks sheepishly she raises her hand up to the level of her eyes like a child in school

"Sure, why not?" I respond absently as I stare off in the distance, continuing to ignore my customer with the coffee cup.

"Why did he have your keys?" she asks, and that grabs everyone's attention.

"He had your keys?" Nixie inquires as she too joins the conversation.

"Holy crow, Mr. Good-body is the Mystery Man?" Rosie shrieks as she jumps in the air, spilling half the bag of coffee on the ground. The aroma is amazing. The view is a mess.

I sigh and rest my head against the now very clean counter. "Yes." I mumble into the marble.

They break into a cackle of questions and shrieks, so loud I can't tell one from the other. They're a mush of annoyance. "Leave her alone," I finally hear a kind voice say as the bell on the door rings. I peer up through my blurred vision, I didn't realize I'd begun to cry. Blanche takes off her jacket and waves the others away from me. She sits on the stool Finn abandoned and lowers her chin to my level. "You okay?"

I shake my head, my chin rubbing against the cold counter. "No, I'm not."

She smiles in understanding and smoothes her hand over the chaos of my hair. "I just saw Finn leave and he didn't seem too happy. What happened when you told him?"

I furrow my brow. "I didn't tell him."

"What?" Blanche insists, snapping upright and taking my ponytail with her. "Why not?"

"Because I couldn't, I don't want him to know." I sob, biting my cheek, trying to keep myself from crying any more.

"Well, you're being stupid," she chastises with a click of her tongue. I put my forehead back down and focus on ignoring the the tapping of the coffee cup down the counter.

"What a piece of work is man, how noble in reason," my English teacher quotes from Hamlet in class the next day. I had barely slept the night before; so my brain is fuzzy and my hair is greasy. I'm not a happy girl.

Lost in my daydreams I didn't realize Mr. Peters was standing at my desk staring at me. Crap! Had he asked a question? I hate being the center of attention in any circumstance, but especially when it comes to something negative. I hear Lucy snicker behind me and I flush a deep red. Damn. "I'm sorry, Mr. Peters. What did you say?"

He looks at me crossly, his furry caterpillar eyebrows meeting in the middle. "Young lady, I said that it is your turn to pick your partner for your project."

He "young lady'd" me. I feel like crawling under my desk and dying. "Oh," I say simply, surveying the room. My eyes land on Nixie who's desperately trying to sink down in her seat. "I pick Nixie." Everyone laughs. I flush a little deeper.

His large stomach inflates and deflates in frustrated breaths as the giggles dissolve into a hum. "Ms. Conner, are you feeling all right?" He places a glass fishbowl full of slips of paper on my desk that I hadn't noticed before. "I just finished explaining this."

I reach forward and pull a slip out of the bowl. "Sorry, Mr. Peters, I didn't sleep well last night."

He nods and motions for me to open my paper. I stare down at the little white slip. When I read what's written on the inside, I'm sure I'm going to die. Or that I'm cursed. Fate once again twists against me in a cruel, cruel way, as it always seems to do. I swallow, though my mouth's completely dry. "Lucy Wilcox," I mumble.

The room falls into a silent hush and I swear a tumbleweed blows across the room. There are no secrets in a town as small as Harpersgrove, so the fact that Lucy insists on making me as miserable as she can isn't a secret. I peek back and she's staring at me, smiling like the cat who ate the canary. This will be great.

I try to sneak out of class quickly without talking to Lucy. The project isn't due for at least two weeks so I don't need to talk to her yet. In fact, there was probably still a chance I can get out of being partners with her. Mr. Peters likes me after all, I'm sure he'll understand-

Lucy interrupts my thoughts by stepping into my path. I almost fall into her. She looks annoyed. I blush. Damn. "Hey loser," she hisses flashing me her shiny veneers. She smells of the same expensive floral perfume my mother wears. Must be a witch's staple.

I shimmy around her. "What do you want?" I mumble, squeezing through the little space she leaves me in the doorway to get away from her.

"Look," she says, keeping pace with me as we walk down the hall. "I'm no happier about this than you are. Trust me. Working with a freak like you is at the bottom of my list, but we have to do it. I'm a candidate for val-"valedictorian, for those of you who don't speak prom queen. "And I'm not letting you screw that up."

"You know I'm a candidate for that too," I add with a smile, reminding her that she's not the most perfect human the world has ever known.

She just waves me off, like the concept of me beating her in anything is ridiculous. Of course, what am I thinking? "We need to plan how we're going to do this."

"Can we talk about this later? I have class," I request as I open my locker to exchange my books.

She slams it shut, my fingers barely escaping in time. Such an angel. "Well, I want to talk about it now."

"I don't have time for this," I state firmly as I grab the books I need for my next class.

She snaps her cinnamon gum in my ear as she continues, "Fine, I'll just have to come by that precious pie shop of yours after school."

She disappears before I can whip around and inform her I'd rather skip a whole week of classes than have her come anywhere near my sanctuary. But it's too late and she's already gone.

I hope sincerely that she's kidding. Hap-PIE-ly Ever After isn't the kind of place that Lucy and her drones frequent, ever. Of course, I still walk a little slower on my way into work that day.

I hang my jacket up on the coat rack and smile to Bella who motions for me to come over to her. "What's up?" I ask as I secure my apron behind me, pushing a pen behind my ear.

Her eyes shine brightly as she leans over the counter. "You already have someone waiting for you in your section." Considering Bella's home schooled and has never actually met Lucy I'm sure that was who it has to be. I take a deep breath and head to my tables.

It isn't Lucy.

Finn smiles up at me with his bright blue eyes and lopsided grin. "I think I'll have peach today."

I slide across from him in the booth. "What're you doing here?" I demand, my eyebrows knitted together. I don't know what I'm feeling.

He leans back a bit, a playful look spreads across his face. "The sign on the door did say open, didn't it?"

I roll my eyes. "That's not what I meant. I just figured that after yesterday you wouldn't want to come back." He's so stupidly beautiful that I have to focus on organizing the sugar packets not to gawk.

He chuckles, taking the sweetener container from my hands. "Oh Pumpkin Pie, one little tiff and you think I'm going to run for the hills?"

"It wasn't exactly a little tiff." He may take my sugar, but I always have my salt and pepper.

He shrugs. "Was to me. I'm not going anywhere." There's an awkward silence. I hate those. "Now how about that pie?"

"Peach?" I swallow against a dry mouth.

"With a little piece of pumpkin," he adds with a coy smile. He's learned the way to my heart.

I laugh without sound and get up from the booth, my joints creak and pop as I stand. My body's as exhausted as my mind. "Coming right up."

He doesn't leave. The entire afternoon through my shift he sits at that table and whenever I have a break I sit and talk to him. "So, you have two sisters?" he ask as he sips his water. He's already gone through four cups of coffee before I insist on the switch.

I nod, my hands under my chin. "Yup, identical twins. They're awful, awful people." I figure why beat around the bush?

He lets his head fall back and laughs. "Well you just put it out there, don't you?"

I shrug. "Life's too short not to, don't you think?"

"I don't know, I think life's too short to live in the negative." His phone buzzes next to his hand, but he ignores it. He hasn't reached for it once any time I've come to sit with him.

My turn to think it over. "Well, I suppose I could understand that too. But my sisters do suck." He laughs. I laugh too. It seems so normal. "If you met them, you'd see what I meant."

Rookie mistake, for as soon as you speak of the devil, he is bound to appear. And over my shoulder at that moment I hear the squawking of two similar devils, identical voices. I glance at Finn who was looking up at the door. "Hmm," he hums as he smiles playfully, enjoying the pained expression on my face. "Identical twins, seem to be annoying. Friends of yours?"

I snarl, not really at Finn or at my sisters. If the twins are here probably means they aren't alone. I raise the level of my glance to just above the booth's ledge and sure enough there's Lucy, leading my sisters into the shop. I groan and slink down further in the booth. Maybe if I slide under the table they won't find me.

They find me anyway.

"Hey, freak." Lucy snaps she slaps her hand on the top of my seat. Megan and Tyler snicker behind her and she rolls her eyes slowly to the back of her head. I have to suck my lips into my mouth to keep from laughing. The rejection of my sisters by anyone they so admire pleases me, even if that person is Lucy Wilcox.

Finn's jaw hangs slack and his eyes are wide and shocked. I suppose, not everyone is used to being called names as a term of endearment. Especially when you're at the height of popularity like Finn is. I offer Lucy my cheesiest smile and say, "So good to see you as always." Then to my sisters, "and who let you two out of the tanning bed?" The stare at each other with appalled looks on their orange faces and the giggle inside bubbles over and overwhelms me. Finn chuckles too and I feel better having someone on my side.

It seems to take until that moment for Lucy to realize that Finn is even there. She pushes her dark straight hair behind her shoulder and shifts her weight to her left hip to extenuate her figure. She's quite good at being noticed. "Well hello there," she coos, actually coos. "You're Finn Wise, aren't you? From New Shiloh?"

He smiles politely, but barely steals a glance at her before turning all his attention back to me. He's not interested in her at all. "Yeah, that's my name." He's trying to focus on me, show Lucy he's not interested. She doesn't get the hint. How could anyone not be interested in her?

"Say, didn't you just break up with Mallory McDonald?" she asks, shifting her weight again, the lip of her Tee shirt rises up to reveal the skin of her midriff and small heart tattoo on her hip that she'd gotten over the summer. The girl's shameless.

"Yes I did," he answers, his eyes still locked on me. I bite my bottom lip to keep from smiling or laughing anymore. Lucy already makes me miserable enough, I don't need her thinking I'm laughing at her.

She cocks her head to the side and pouts her lips, faking sincerity as she says, "I was so sorry to hear about that. I've met Mallory a bunch of times at cheer competitions. Poor thing and those fat ankles. It's a wonder she hung onto a stud like you for this long."

I can't hold it in, a snort escapes, Finn laughs too, but Lucy does anything but. "Don't people need water and forks and things?" she demands. That's the traditional Wilcox diet I'm sure.

I nod slowly and let out a breath as I start to get up. "I'm sure you're right, Lucinda." Lucy hates being called by her full first name even more than I do. So, of course, I use it every chance I get.

Before I can rise all the way, Finn grabs my hand. "Hey, you don't have to go anywhere." His skin is warm and soft over mine. I can feel my cheeks flushing and my ankles are weak. I dart my eyes toward the floor. The last thing I need is for him to see me swoon.

"As much as I hate to say it, she has a point. I should probably get back to work." I admit as I tap his hand in mine with my free hand.

He reluctantly lets go of my hand. "Well, I'll be sitting right here when you get another break."

I pick up his empty plate and promise a replacement and return to my work. Unfortunately, Lucy and the twins decide to follow me rather than stay with Finn. As I reach across the counter to grab a set of plates from Bella, Lucy leans in close to my ear and harshly whispers, "I told you I was going to make your life miserable, Conner," she glances back at Finn. "And maybe now, I've found a way."

In all honesty, Lucy Wilcox doesn't scare me, not much anyway. She's like a housefly, annoying as all hell, but basically harmless. I mean, what's she really capable of doing? Telling Finn that I'm some kind of crazy freak? She already did that and he ignored her. Besides, what do I care what Finn Wise thinks of me? Nothing, I'm not his mystery girl in reality. He doesn't mean a thing. At least that's what I'm trying to convince myself.

Lucy doesn't stick around after her threat. She sashays out of the shop like a model on a catwalk with my sisters trailing behind her. Probably off to plan my demise. Fantastic.

Finn however, stays planted in the same spot that he's been all afternoon and into the evening. There's something fishy about it and I'm sure I know the tuna responsible.

I plop down in my seat in his booth, three empty plates in front of him. The boy does like pie. He flashes me his brilliant smile, but I refuse to be distracted. I snap my fingers and extend out my hand. "Give 'em to me."

He cocks his head to the side, trying to convince me he's confused. It won't work. "I don't know what you're talking about," he lies, smiling a little brighter, but I cannot be swayed.

"Give me the keys, Finn." I command, my hand still extended, waiting.

His smile turns down to a frown and he leans back against the booth, getting as much distance from me as possible. "Why do you want them?"

"Because I know that you're not just hanging around here to talk to me and it's beginning to get a little sad." Well, that and the fact that my mother apparently changed the location of the hide-a-key and I'd had to climb in the house through the broken basement window the night before. I really don't want to do that again.

He removes a huge wad of keys from his jacket pocket and detaches mine from the set. "Good lord," I judge in a tone harsher than I'd intend. "You put them on your own keys."

He shoves them back in his pocket. Damn! Another night through the window for me. "I just didn't want to lose them. Why do you even care so much?"

I try to be super cool about it. "I don't. Not about the keys, but about your mental state. And your jock physique, all this pie cannot be good for it." I motion to the empty plate that scatter the table.

He runs a hand through his thick dark hair and starts stacking the plates on top of one another. "Look," he begins, scooping up the last morsel of whipped cream off one of the orphaned plates. "I'm not completely insane, or a stalker for that matter. I know that the chances of this girl coming in here looking for her keys and me sweeping her off her feet because I possess them are slim to none."

I probably should get up before I let him go any further, but I can't help myself. I want to hear. "Then what are you doing?" I ask.

"I don't know Pumpkin Pie-" I have told him my actual name, haven't I? "I guess some part of me is hoping that'll happen. That she'll come in here and see me and we'll ride off together into the sunset on a white horse."

It's the most romantic thing I've ever heard. My overwhelming teen instinct is to wrap my arms around him and confess that I'm the one, the girl he's been looking for. But I my lips are cemented together. I can't speak those words. "A white horse? How gay are you exactly?" I say instead. Real romantic, right?

His laugh is infectious and hearty, all the way through his body. Whew, I was worried he'd get mad. As much I want to fight it, I really like talking to Finn. He's a pretty great guy, as great as I'd imagined him. It's so unfortunate. "Hey, I told you I knew it was stupid, but a guy can dream."

I try to make it seem like it's nothing. Mainly so I can deny the warmth running through my blood and the feelings I need to deny. "I suppose." But there's something bothering me about all this, something

I need to know. "I have a question." I raise my hand like a little girl in class.

"Shoot," he says, taking a long sip of his water.

I lick my lips, trying to think of how to start. "How do you not know who she is?" He seem confused and I know I hadn't been clear. "What I mean, is she didn't have a full set of body armor on did she? It was just a costume. How do you not know exactly what she looks like?" Because honestly, I'm not sure if he's just messing with me or not. Does he know it's me and that's why he's paying so much attention to me? It seems probably enough to me, otherwise why is he sticking around?

He rips open a sugar packet and absently pours the contents into his palm and moves them around with his thumb. "I mean she's a brunette and tall, but that's about all I got. Geez, do you know how many women that describes?" I do, four live in my house as a matter of fact. "I mean she was in a big dress, her face was covered by a mask and her hair was piled ten feet up off her head. I have no idea what she actually looks like. Who knows?"

He makes a valid point. I myself had made a big deal to Blanche that I'm not the same girl as I was that night. She looked nothing like me. So, I guess it makes sense that he doesn't recognize me now. I sigh and balance the weight of my head on my hand. "Still, for the sake of your mental health I think I need to ask you one more time. Sure you don't want to relinquish the keys and start anew?" He'll say no, but I really don't want to sneak in through that window again.

He smiles and shakes his head. "Nope, I think I'm going to hold onto them just a bit longer." Well, trying never killed anyone.

"Suit yourself. I'm just here for your well being." I rub my side where I squeezed through the window. I'll be ever sorer tomorrow.

He reaches out and takes my hand again, sending a shiver through my body. Control yourself Michelle! I shout at myself inside. "Thanks, Pumpkin Pie, I appreciate it."

The front door jingles open, but I don't pay it any mind. That's until the person who entered ends up beside me. "Becky!" I shriek, so surprised to see her that I scare her, and myself.

"Hi Elle," she says with a sunny smile. Her blonde hair twists back in a messy bun and she's wearing shorts and a sweatshirt. An outfit that on me would've looked sloppy, but on Becky looks like a damn supermodel.

"Becky?" I'm surprised to hear Finn's voice say.

My future stepmother hops back and puts her hands on Finn's face. I have to sit on my own hands to keep from punching her.

"Oh my god, Finn! How are you!" she yelps as Finn gets up to hug her. They stand nearly eye to eye, Becky can pull off the supermodel height so much better than I can.

Okay. So either I've had a stroke or I'm stuck in the twilight zone. Kind of hoping for the stroke. How do these two random people in my life know each other? They are not from Harpersgrove. There is no six degrees of Kevin Bacon!

"How's your family?" she asks after finally breaking apart from a hug that lasts just a little too long for my jealous heart.

"They're good. My brother Pat and his wife just had a baby," Finn answers with a smile, so warm for Becky. I'm beginning to freak out a little. It's not a stroke. They really know each other.

Becky's hands fly to her mouth as the hopping resumes. "Oh, my God, that's awesome. Boy or girl?"

Before Finn can answer her I jump into the conversation. "Timeout, timeout, how do you two know each other?"

Finn seems to only now remember that I'm here. "Oh, sorry, um, Becky dated my brother Pat in high school." And Becky nods in agreement. Oh, isn't that just perfect.

"But how do you two know each other?" he asks, his eyes flicking back and forth between us.

I laugh even though there's nothing funny about this and settle back into my seat. Becky looks to me to answer, but there's no way that's happening.

"Oh no, I'm going to let you field this one."

Becky pulls on the knot of hair on top of her head and runs her hands over her flawless skin. "Well, I'm actually getting married myself."

"Oh Beck, that's great." Finn says sincerely. It warms my heart a bit. He's not patronizing her, he's generally happy for her. "Who's the lucky guy?" Oh this should be good.

Becky sighs and looks at me again there's an apology in her eyes that almost makes me feel bad. "Elle's father, actually."

Finn shoots me a panicked look, but I give him my brightest smile.

"That's right, welcome to the freak show. Rebecca is my future stepmother." And all this time I thought I was coping better with this. "What can I do for you, Becky?" I wish I could get over the anger, but clearly I'm not there yet.

She seems really uncomfortable. I feel a little worse. "Well, your dad wanted me to stop by and see if you wanted to come over to our place for dinner. You know, like we'd discussed." Damn, I had agreed to that.

I sigh and pull my phone out of my pocket to check the time. "Sure, um but I don't get off for another two hours."

Becky waves it off. "Oh of course, I just ran to the grocery store to get everything. I'll probably need two hours." She laughs and so does Finn, so I make myself too even though it's forced.

"Okay, I'll be there," I say, hoping she'll leave, but then I see something. No! Becky's looking at Finn. No!

"Hey, I've got a crazy idea!" Becky exclaims happily as she claps her hands together. No! "Finn, why don't you join us for dinner?"

NO!

"I'm sure he's got plans already." I interrupt frantically. I do not want Finn there in the messed up situation that is my family. It's just too twisted. Besides, I can't remember how much detail I've gone into about my crazy life givers in my e-mails and letters. I don't need him any closer to the real identity of 3788 than he already is.

"You don't want me to come?" he asks, throwing his hand over his heart as though I've wounded him.

I sigh. "No, of course I would like you to come, but-" He cuts me off before I can cite any further objection.

"Then, it's settled, I'd love to come Becky."

"How are you seventeen in America and not drive?" Finn asks me on the way to my dad and Becky's two hours later. He's been unable to drop this line of conversation since right after Becky had left the shop. He asked whether I wanted him to follow me or just take one car. I informed him that it was either go in his car or I'd take a cab and meet him there, which had been my plan if I'd been going alone.

"I live in Harpersgrove Finn, not Baltimore, not even New Shiloh. Everything I need is within walking distance and when it's not I take a cab or convince someone to drive me."

I can never understand why this concept is so hard for people. I don't get why all my friends seem so eager to get their licenses. I spend my money on what I want, they bought gas and paid for insurance. I think I get the better end of the deal.

Finn shakes his head as he skips through songs on his phone in search of the perfect beat. "Whenever you have off next, I'm teaching you to drive."

"Why?" I demand. I don't want to drive, haven't I made that clear by now? "I don't want to."

"It's not always about what you want, Pumpkin. Driving is an important rite of passage in life. You must complete it." He can tell I'm not sold. "Besides, you staying in Harpersgrove forever? Any plans to go to college or anything?"

"Of course." I say, flipping on the heat in his car. My skin has broken into goose bumps and I desperately want to be warm.

He pulls off his knit hat and tosses it in the backseat. Clearly he's not cold, but he's too polite to turn off the heat. "You plan on walking everywhere wherever you go to school?"

Actually I had planned on that, but something in his tone makes that seem stupid. I shrug. "I guess not."

He seems pleased enough with himself. "Good. Then it's settled, I'll teach you."

I grumble under my breath, I don't want to learn to stupid drive.

"It's that last building on the left," I say coldly, as we pull into the condo complex

He laughs at me. Jerk.

"Aw come on now, Pumpkin, don't pout."

I narrow my eyes at him.

"Elle, my name is Elle." Of course I don't really mind the pet name, it's kind of sweet. But right now I'm peeved, and don't like him so much and the Pumpkin business loses its cuteness.

"I'm so sorry, Elle," he apologizes with a grin. He knows my anger isn't genuine. "Can I ask why you were so opposed to me coming tonight?"

"If I can ask why you'd want to come?" I counter, my arms still crossed over my chest. I'm still freezing.

He tugs on his scarf and nods slowly. "I suppose that's fair. My dad and stepmom are out of town and I really don't like going back to a big empty house all alone. I'll take a dinner with other people when it's offered." Warmth floods my cold frozen heart. Damn. I can't stay mad at him.

"Do they do that a lot? Leave you alone, I mean?" I ask as he parks the car. The brakes squeak. He should probably get that checked.

He shrugs. "I don't know, I mean, my situation is a lot like yours. My dad also married someone who went to high school with my brother."

"Oh, that's gross!" I judge sharply, realizing how bad it probably sounds to say about the guy's family. "Sorry."

But Finn's not fazed. "No, it's okay. I would have to say that for at least a little while I agreed with you. The concept of my dad dating a girl so young, let alone marrying her, made me sick."

"How old were you when your parents split?" I ask pulling my knees up to my chest. It's not like I'm in a massive hurry to get in there anyway.

He looks down at the steering wheel and fiddles with the tips of his fingers. "Um no, actually, my mom died when I was thirteen."

I reach out and touch his arm, his a grin twitches at the corner of his lips.

"Finn, I'm so sorry."

He squeezes my hand. "It's okay Pumpkin, it was a long time ago and I'm glad my dad finally found someone to make him happy."

We're standing at the door to my father and Becky's apartment for a good long while. I refuse to knock. "Is there a problem?" Finn asks after too much time.

I chew on the inside of my cheek. "I'm debating how long it would take me to run home from here."

Finn rolls his eyes as he lifts his hand to knock. "You're silly." That results in my extremely mature reaction of sticking my tongue out. He only laughs more.

The door opens to my father on the other side. He wearing a black Ramones Tee shirt and faded jeans. He has new tortoise shell glasses and the remnants of his hair are slicked back. Who the hell is this man?

"Hey kids!" he exclaims excitedly as he crushes his arms around me. My father hasn't really hugged me since I was about nine. So I'm more than a little stunned. Finally, he releases me and he sticks his hand out to Finn.

"Glad to have you here tonight, young man." That sounds more like my father. Finn straightens his spine and takes my father's hand.

"It's my pleasure, sir." My dad makes some weird noise and waves off Finn's formality.

"Please, call me Tony."

I can't help the snort that erupts from my mouth. "Tony? When have you ever been Tony?"

My dad shrugs, messing up his famously perfect posture.

"What can I say kid? I'm a new man."

I bite down hard on my bottom lip and follow him inside. "You can say that again," I mutter to myself.

Finn and I hang our coats on the hooks right inside the door. There's some really poppy late nineties music blaring from the kitchen. Obviously Becky's choice considering my dad still listens to Miles Davis LPs. Becky bustles in from the kitchen. She has on a cute little sundress that it was really too cold to be wearing, but she looks so sweet that it doesn't matter.

"Hello kids-" Really? Kids? "I hope you're hungry."

I want to vomit all over her nice burgundy carpet, but Finn makes a move before I can. He puts his arms around her and hugs her briefly.

"Starving, thank you again for having me."

Becky blushes, I assume it's because she's playing the adoring house-wife. For all I know it's that Finn looks like his brother and she finds him attractive. It's all just too gross and creepy.

"Oh please, it's nothing. We're both happy to have you here." My father, who sits at the dining room table, looks at her adoringly, like the sun and moon rise and set for her. I've never seen that look before. He's definitely never looked at Eleanor that way.

My dad turns his attention back to us. "Yes, it's nice to meet Michelle's boyfriend."

"Dad!" I hiss as Finn bites back a chuckle. I'm so glad this amuses him. I shake my head feverishly. "No."

My dad slinks away to the kitchen. "My mistake," he mumbles on his way out of sight.

Becky too is smiling brightly. "Well, if you guys want to help me set the table, dinner's just about ready."

I sigh and we follow Becky into the kitchen where my dad whistles along to the bubble gum music. Holy crap, maybe it is his choice in music. I'm disturbed by this man posing as my father. I always knew the aliens would come for my family, but my hope had always been that they'd take my mother.

Becky prepares quite a spread. Roasted chicken, some type of cool, whipped sweet potato thing, green beans that are not from a can, and homemade cranberry sauce. It looks like something out of a Martha Stewart magazine. I feel the compulsion to compliment. A big step up from the spaghetti disaster.

"This looks really good, Becky." I tell her through a grumbled mouthful of food.

She brightens up entirely, like I'd told her I was giving her a million dollars and she gushes, "Oh, thank you, Elle. I hope you like it!"

I swallow hard before shoveling more food in my gullet. "I'm sure I will."

My father wastes no time digging into Finn. Apparently my subtle comment hadn't been heard. Dad's still on the boyfriend interrogation track.

"So Finn, what do your parents do?"

Finn swallows and says, "Well, my dad has his own law firm and my step-mom is actually in law school right now, but she works as his secretary for the time being."

"What about your mom?" dad asks as he sips his iced tea. He winces against the sugary taste. My dad is a black coffee or water kind of guy. It's a true testament to how he feels about Becky that he's even attempting to choke down the tinted sugar water. He'd never do that for Eleanor.

Becky kicks him hard under the table. Considering she had once dated Finn's brother, it's understandable that she knew about Finn's mom.

"We don't have to talk about that," Becky offers with a sympathetic smile, ignoring my father whimpers of pain.

Finn smiles and answers, "No, it's okay, Becky." Then turning to my father says, "Actually, my mom died about five years ago." The tone of his voice tells me that it's a sentence he's said so many times that it's practically prerecorded.

My dad puts his fork down, forgetting the growing pain in his shin.

"I'm truly sorry, Finn." My father steals a glance at me and his eyes are racked with guilt. I can't hold his gaze, burying myself back in my potatoes.

Finn smiles, oh so diplomatically and responds, "Don't worry about it sir, you didn't know. Besides, it was a long time ago." This voice doesn't sound like Finn's at all. I'm sure he's tired of talk about it.

"Do you like your stepmother?" Becky asks, slightly changing the subject.

Finn swallows and cuts sharply at his chicken, "Yeah, she's great. In fact I'm pretty sure you'd remember her. Kathy Phelps."

Becky chokes on her tea and coughs out, "Your father married Kat Phelps?"

My dad calls time out. "Who is this?"

"Well, she and I were actually in the same cheer squad in high school." Of course Becky had been a cheerleader.

"Oh," dad breathes as a hush settles over the room. Apparently he's not the only man to find comfort in the arms of a child.

I decide to end the awkwardness. "Finn, you told me that your dad and stepmom were away. Where did they go?"

He lets out the breath he's been holding, glad for my change in subject. "Aspen, they're skiing." In the distance Becky's Hello Kitty clock giggles to chime the time. We've already been here an hour.

"Well that's nice," Becky begins, scooping out more sweet potatoes for herself. "Any special occasion?"

Finn shakes his head, his tongue sweeps out over his lips and I have to grip the table to keep from fainting. The boy can make anything hot.

"No, after Pat got married and was gone, my dad married Kathy and they just started traveling all over the place." He quickly checks the ever buzzing phone beside his hands, but dismisses it just as fast. "Honestly, I know that Kathy wants to have a baby right away. I think my dad's trying to distract her for a while."

Finn and I laugh. Becky and my dad did not. I'm insanely grossed out that this is even an option for the two of them. That's probably stupid, Becky is after all only twenty-two and my dad's other children are all nearly grown and we don't need him for much. The sweet potatoes, that had been so delicious in my mouth only moment before, now churn in my stomach and I doubt they'll taste as good coming back up.

"Food's really great Becky," I interject with a bright and cheesy smile, distracting her in any way I can from the baby train. I'm not emotionally healthy enough to entertain the idea of a baby brother or sister that out in public everyone would assume is mine.

The corners of her mouth turn up slightly and she scoops up my plate and hers. "Thank you Elle," then she turns to our guest. "Finn, would you mind helping me clear the table?"

Finn seems surprised that she's asking. Frankly so am I, but grabs his plate and my dad's before following Becky to the modest kitchen.

As the conversation in the next room turns into a soft hum, I'm absorbed in the uncomfortable silence lingering between my estranged father and me.

"What's up?" I ask, straightening in my chair, full defense mode.

He stares at me so intently his eyes may pop out and bounce against his new glasses and says, "Becky wanted me to ask if you'd reconsider being her maid of honor." I groan, but my dad speaks again before I can outright refuse.

"Just hear me out, Ellie," he hasn't called me that in an eternity. I feel obliged to listen.

"I know that this has been really tough on you, probably even more than your sisters. I know you don't really blend well with your mom and the twins-" Understatement of the freakin' century. "And I'm sorry that I haven't been there for you that much. It was selfish and wrong. I see that now. I miss our days at the flea markets. I'm sure you barely remember, but they were the best times of my life. You've always been such an amazing kid and I missed so much. I know it's hard for you to believe, but it's been Becky that's made me see a lot of that. She told me that I have to fix things with you, work on the twins too of course, but really mend the bridge with you."

"How would she know anything about it? She doesn't even know me." I say softly, crossing my arms over my chest. I feel the need to form a barrier between him and my frail emotions.

He smiles at me, as if he'd known I'd say this.

"Becky's been my assistant for four years now, ever since she graduated high school. Whenever your mom would call to tell me anything that was going on, or if you'd call, anything, it was Becky who handled it. I hate to say this, as your father it's shameful, but I can't lie to you. Becky knows you better now than I do."

I look at my father like he's a stranger, because that's who he is. I truly don't know him. When I'd been growing up he was cold and stiff. Always in a suit and tie, even on a Saturday. His face always pinched and angry, looking all too much like Mr. Potter from *It's a Wonderful Life*. But this guy, the man sitting across from me, is so different. He's at ease, he's smiling, he's calm. And then it hits me. My father didn't leave my sisters and me, we would always be his. He left an unhappy marriage and I knew why.

"Becky makes you happy, doesn't she?" I ask, staring at him so deeply he begins to blush. We have that in common. "I mean not just because she's young, but who she is."

His entire expression softens as he settles back against his chair. He removes his glasses and rubs his eyes with his thumb and forefinger like this is the first time he's been able to relax in quite a while. He hoped I'd come to this conclusion on my own and I did.

"Absolutely, my dear. I wish I could have found a more tactful way of ending things with your mother, been more direct or something, but the heart wants what it wants and my heart wants Becky."

I look down at my folded hands on the table and know I'll regret my next words as soon as they leave my lips. I say them anyway.

"Fine, I'll be her damn maid of honor."

Chapter Ten

Becky cries, profusely, when I agree to be her maid of honor. Apparently she'd been waiting on the other side of the kitchen door eagerly hoping I'd take the position, shushing Finn every time he tried to speak and impede her snooping abilities. When I do agree, she bursts out into the dining room all aflutter. She crushes me in her arms and tells me how fun it will be. We'd pick the flowers, the dresses, and just everything. The need to vomit rises up in me again. What Becky sees as fun I see as cruel and unusual torture. My father eases her off of me. I think he knows I'm about ready to take back my answer. I know she's excited, but I don't want to do any of those things. I barely even want to show up on the day. What have I gotten myself into?

Finn's nice enough to drive me home even though Becky practically insists on doing it herself. She probably wants to talk my ear off about roses and centerpieces and, oh, God just thinking of it makes me nauseated!

I say my good-byes to Finn and he tells me he'll be by the diner the next day, and apparently for every day for the rest of his life. The lights are on inside the house, so I hope the front door's unlocked, which thankfully it is. Ha-ha! Score! No basement window for me!

My mother's sitting at the dining room table, a glass of wine in her hand and the bottle at her elbow.

"And where, may I ask, have you been?" she asks coolly as the wine gurgles out of the bottle and into her glass.

I hang my jacket up on the rack by the door.

"Dad and Becky invited me over for dinner." It sounds so normal coming from my mouth, like something I do on the regular.

She growls. Yep, growls, just like an angry cat.

"I didn't want to believe it, my own daughter." The wine sloshes in her glass and I know it's not her first or even third helping of the night.

I roll my eyes.

"And what did I do this time, Mother?" I ask with a sigh as I flop down in the chair across from her. This could take a while, may as well be comfortable. She recently had the dining room chairs redone in a soft blue velvet, so comfort is one thing I can achieve.

"Megan and Tyler told me that you'd been cavorting with that harlot, but I just did not want to believe it," she hisses as she took a long swig of her wine.

I scoff and kick the mahogany leg of the expensive table, which just seems to tick her off more.

"I was having dinner with my dad. Whether you like it or not Eleanor, he is still my father and always will be my father. And that "harlot" as you call her is going to be my stepmother."

"You don't speak to me like this," she snarls as she refills her glass with again, this time with a shaky hand. I take a deep breath and snatch the bottle from her and hurry into the kitchen. "Hey! Give that back!" she slurs.

I tip the bottle over and pour its contents down the drain, the sound of the liquid gushing from the bottle echoes in the otherwise silent house and I know she's going to be mad. "You know what, Mom," I clip sharply through a clamped jaw. "Maybe, just maybe, if you put a little effort into making yourself happy, you wouldn't have to make dad miserable."

She grabs the bottle from my hand, but it's already empty. There hadn't been much in it to begin with. "Young lady, I don't know what's gotten into you, but you need an attitude adjustment!"

"You put everything on him," I yell, unable to stop myself. It needs to be said. "And I'm not saying he's right. Cheating on you was wrong. Leaving the way he did was wrong, but at least he owns up and says it was. You make it seem like you're such a treasure to live with, like none of this was your fault. I've got to tell you, as much as you want Megan and Tyler and me to believe it, he didn't leave us, he left you. He still wants us, he doesn't want you!"

And with that I leave her standing speechless in the kitchen, her glass of wine spilling on the floor. Maybe it's harsh. I mean, she isn't exactly in the state of mind to absorb what I'm saying, but I don't care. She makes me so mad I could spit. It's an impossible situation to not stand your our mother.

I hustle up the stairs, ready to take a nice long shower and go to bed, putting this day behind me. But on my way to the bathroom, something stops me. Down the end of the hall, the stairs to my attic are down. I can tell you for a fact, beyond a shadow of a doubt, I had not left them that way.

I creep upstairs as quietly as I can to pounce on my trespasser(s). My heartbeat pulses in my ears as I crest the top step. Tyler sits at my computer doing God knows what and Megan rifles through a box of papers I hide under my bed.

Suddenly, I hop up and scare the daylights out of them both. Their brunette twin messy buns snap back in shock. They look at me like deer caught in the headlights.

"What are you two doing up here?" I demand, my voice shrieking above a normally audible level. The puppy sitting next to Tyler flinches at the sound.

"Um, well, um," Tyler babbles, looks like she might pee her pants. I've always known she's scared of me. "Tell her what we're doing, Meg."

"Well," Megan begins, more coherently than her carbon copy, but still an edge of fear in her voice. "You're such a nerd and all, we figured you'd have that math textbook for that class we're taking." Really?

That's what she's going with? Apparently, since Ty's head bounces up and down like a bobblehead at that answer.

I cross my arms over my chest and shift my weight from side to side.

"Oh that explains it, you were looking for a textbook?" They both nod at hyper speed. My fake smile drops from my face.

"You were looking for a textbook in my computer and a shoebox under my bed?"

They don't seem so happy anymore. I bite down hard on the inside of my cheek to keep from screaming and hiss, "Okay, neither one of you is leaving this room until you tell me what's going on."

They trade nervous looks, trying to gage if I'm serious or not. I stare down Tyler. She's the weak link after all.

"Okay, okay," she caves finally, even though Megan hits her relentless in the leg to shut her up. "Lucy."

What a horrible way to start any conversation, and make me nervous.

"What about Lucy?" I bite harshly.

Tyler swallows hard. "W-Well, Lucy asked us to come and snoop through your stuff."

"Oh my God, Tyler, shut up!" Megan squeals, stomping her foot on the ground.

"Oh no, Tyler, for the first time in your life, do not shut up," I crow, narrowing my eyes at my little sister. "What are you looking for?"

Tyler scratches the back of her head, picking the puppy up off the to distract herself. He whines in protest. "Something having to do with you and Finn Wise?" she says as though it's a question.

My heart might explode out of my mouth.

"There is nothing going on with me and Finn Wise. That's what you can tell Lucy Wilcox." I hiss, reaching forward and grabbing them both by their hair. Tyler releases the puppy back onto my floor and he takes comfort curled up in an abandoned sweater on my floor. Just before I pushed the twins to the stairs I hiss in their ears. "If I ever, ever, catch one of you in here ever again I promise, I swear, you will regret it." They hurry down the stairs, tripping over their own feet and clutching the backs of their heads.

I feel sick. I fall down onto my bed, picking up the shoebox Megan had been going through. In the box, all of my letters from Finn are out of their envelopes and laying open. On my computer is the e-mail that Finn had sent me about the dance and about meeting me there.

I can't breathe. The twins know. I'm aware that it doesn't say his name anywhere in any letter or e-mail, but the twins aren't as stupid as they look and Lucy Wilcox is certainly anything but dumb. They know, but what bothers me the most is fretting over what they can possibly do with the knowledge.

I throw up in my trash can.

The next morning I wait in the driveway for a half hour for Goldie to pick me up. I awoke nearly an hour earlier than necessary to avoid seeing my sisters. I'm panicky and pacing, and, God I want to die. I have never been more thankful to hear Goldie's Pinto clunking down the street. I rush to the end of the driveway, barely letting her stop before I jump in the backseat of the car, overtop of a confused Rosie.

"Where's the fire?" Rosie asks with a laugh as she turns around in the passenger seat to look at me. I'd nearly crushed her to get into the seat behind her, putting a dent in her barrel rolled hair.

"I'm in deep, girls." I mumble as I press my forehead into the back of the sparkly gold seat.

"How so?" Goldie asks as she pulls away from my house, the gravel stirs up in her wheels and I know I'm almost free.

"The twins know I'm 3788." I admit softly. "And they're going to tell Lucy Wilcox."

Goldie slams on her breaks, smashing my face into the back of the seat.

"Damn it, Gold! Ouch!" I clutch my throbbing cheeks and shoot daggers at her reflection in the rearview mirror.

Goldie completely ignores my pain. "How do they know about that?" she demands, Rosie seems just as eager to know.

I sigh and rub my forehead, sitting back against the seat. I lock my seat belt into place before Goldie can propel me through the windshield.

"Lucy came by the diner yesterday and saw me with Finn and told me she was going to ruin my life. And then last night I went up to my room and Tyler and Megan were snooping through my stuff. My letters and e-mails were all open."

Rosie runs her tongue around her lip ring and says, "This is why you always burn the evidence girl! That sucks something fierce. What do you think she's going to do?"

I've been trying like crazy NOT to obsess over this detail.

"Tell him, I guess. Then he can be crushed that I'm the girl and he'll never want to speak to me again." I say as I bite my tongue, surprised at the tears that form at the back of my eyes.

"And I'll never get my keys back," I add dramatically, tossing my head back into the headrest and throwing my arm over my eyes.

Rosie reaches back and runs her fingers through my hair, a lovely gesture. Very un-Rosie like. "You don't know that for sure. Maybe she won't say anything, I mean maybe she just wants to torment you with it and not say a word."

"Does that sound like the Lucy Wilcox we know?" Goldie asks with a confused glance.

"Goldie, shut up!" Rosie barks as she punches her best friend in the arm. "Can't you see she's upset? We're supposed to be comforting."

Goldie shrugs as she pulls into traffic. "Well, I see no point in lying to her." Then she turns to look back at me, her massive knot of blonde hair swinging around her shoulders. "I hope nothing happens. But you have to admit, it would be really out of character for Lucy not to do something sneaky."

"Thanks for the honesty, Goldie, it's refreshing," I said coolly.

"Don't think too much about it." Rosie encourages as Goldie fiddles with the radio station. She settles on something folksy that she knows I'll prefer and I love her for that.

"Easier said than done," I whine, pulling my knees up under my chin. Normally, Goldie would throw a hissy fit over my feet on her seat, but this time she keeps her mouth shut.

For the first time in my school career I sincerely consider cutting a class. The concept of having to sit through an excruciating hour with Lucy, God forbid having to talk to her, actually makes me ill. I hate what this is doing to me, but my educational ambitions win out in the end. I really want the opportunity to pull valedictorian right out from under Lucy's high heeled feet. I tuck my chin down to my chest and scurry into English class, taking a seat behind Nixie.

"Hey," she says when I was settled.

"Hey, Nix," I respond with a curt smile as it try to make myself as small as possible.

"I wanted to let you know that I'm your partner now for the Hamlet paper," she says quickly, turning back in her seat a spray of water cascades off her slicked up hair.

It should make me happy, less time with Lucy, but instead I panic. "Why?" I demand, pulling Nixie's shoulder so she's forced to face me.

Nixie narrows her eyes at me and puts her pen down to give me her full attention.

"Well, Lucy went to Mr. Peters and said that it would probably be better if she works on the paper with Anne because they're on the same schedule with cheerleading and with you and I both working at the pie shop. It's better, easier."

It's too simple, I can't stand it. Lucy's going to make me crazy. What's she planning? What's she up to? I must know!

And then as if she reads my mind Lucy bounces into the classroom. She looks right at me and again I feel sick.

"Hello, Elle," she singsongs with a smile as she passes my seat, her hand sweeping briefly over my shoulder. In all the years we've been adversaries, Lucy has never called me by my first name. There was always an insult thrown in, this is overwhelmingly disturbing. She eyes me coolly, as she saunters back to her seat and sits down, crossing her overly long legs.

What is she planning?!

I can't pay attention through the whole class. I feel Lucy's eyes burning through the back of my brain and it's making me nauseous and uneasy. And I most certianly did not want to hurl in the classroom! Maybe I have a stomach ulcer.

It takes her until the end to say anything to me. "Have a good day, Michelle," she calls in a bubbly voice as she walks past me again.

"What are you doing?" I demand grabbing her arm before she can get away from me, but my voice comes out all squeaky and weak.

"What do you mean, Elle?" she asks, fluttering her fake black eyelashes at me. They're perfectly plastic, just like her.

"That's what I mean," I yelp, my voice steadying a bit as I point my index finger into her face, and still she doesn't flinch. "You refer to me as freak or loser or something else mean! You don't ever call me by my first name."

Her smile changes, became colder, more devious. She takes a few steps toward me until she's only inches from my face and whispers in my ear, "I told you Conner, I'm going to make you miserable and you've given me every tool to do it."

I swallow the bile rising up the back of my throat, but I can't lose face in front of her. If I do that, she'll win.

"If you're trying to do something involving me and Finn, you're wasting your time. We're just friends."

She laughs loudly in my ear. "Oh that's rich, Michelle. Really, it almost sounds like you believe that." She smacks together her perfectly painted pink lips and the smell of her bubble gum lip gloss overwhelms.

"Then what? What are you doing?" I demand.

She rips her arm out of my grasp, casually swinging her backpack over her shoulder. "Aw, now you really don't think I'm going to tell you that, do you?" Her smile grows, she reminds me of a horror movie clown from my deepest and darkest nightmares. I doubt I'll sleep for a week. "You'll just have to wait and see."

Oh, God. I really don't want to.

The whole day I feel sick and dizzy and completely off my bearings. Normally going to pie shop makes everything better, it's my totem, my balance. Today I'm not getting that. It seems to be happening less and less frequently these days. That hurts me.

"He's back," Bella sings musically when I come inside.

I roll my eyes and throw my jacket to her, the rack's already full. I saunter back to my station, which is also rather full, but I don't care. They'll wait. I sit down across from him. The seat is wet and I really don't want to think about why.

"Do you have anything else to do with your time?"

"Good to see you too, Pumpkin," Finn says with a laugh as he puts his phone to the side. His homework is open on the table in front of him and he's buried in a calculus book.

I'm not in the mood. I've had a long day and I'm incredibly cranky.

"Seriously, are you going to come here every day?"

He shrugs.

"As long as the pie stays so good, I don't think I could possibly go away." The early setting autumn sun cuts through the blinds in slates and brightens his already sunny face.

I just roll my eyes, it's impossible to be mad at him, no matter how much I wanted to be. It's like staying mad at a cartoon character.

"What can I get you?" I ask, tapping my pen against the pad in my hand.

"Pumpkin, I'd like a piece of pumpkin," he winks, proud of his ability to incorporate his nickname for me into his order. Boys are stupid.

I pat his hand and stand up, heading to another one of my tables to take their order. It's cozy and uncomfortable at the same time knowing Finn's eyes are on me. I feel a little swagger added to my step for his benefit.

But just as I start to talk to my new customers, the bell on the front door jingles and I glance up on instinct to see who it is. My tongue slides down my throat and I choke on it. It's her. Beautiful, perfect Lucy Wilcox, followed closely again by my sisters. She grins and her hair swished against her back as she glides toward Finn's table. Her hair and her arm brush my back as she sits across from him. It sends an awful chill down my spine. My new table stares at me in uncomfortable silence as tears blur my vision. I can't move or speak or breath. I can only stand there and gawk at these poor people as my ears lock in on every word behind me.

"Hey, Finn." she begins in an overly sugary, sweet voice. Her gum snaps in her mouth and her floral perfume overwhelms the room.

"Lucinda," he snaps sharply as he sips his water, the ice clinking against the glass.

"Are you mad at me?" she asks her voice sad and sweet. Who the hell was this girl? Has everyone gone nuts?

"No, I don't know you well enough to be mad at you," he admits as he shifts his weight in the creaky seat.

I can hear the smile in her voice and it makes my stomach turn. I clutch the table before me for balance and my customers trade concerned looks.

"Oh, but Finn, you do know me. You know me too well."

"What're you talking about?" he asks, a confused edge to his tone. I feel like I'm going to pass out on the lovely family in front of me.

I turn around just enough so I can see them out of the corner of my eye. Lucy reaches out and touches his hand. A jealous chill ran through me. That's my hand!

"It's me, Finn," she says, still in that same fake tone. What a manipulator she is. She'll do anything to get what she wants, but I never expected what I hear next.

"I'm 3788."

My eyes slam shut as tears quickly flood them. I offer an apology to the family and scurry away like a beaten dog to the kitchen, sliding down the back of the door when I'm safely on the other side. I'm so stupid it hurts! How did I not see it? Lucy didn't have the twins investigate my relationship with Finn because she wanted to expose me. It's because she wants to be that person. She wants to be the one he desires. She wants to take me, from me.

"What's wrong?" Rosie worries, kneeling down next to my quivering mass of a body on the kitchen floor. "Honey, what happened?"

"Lucy, Lucy, Lucy," I stutter over and over again. "She...she...she," I can't complete a thought. I'm so distraught and off kilter, completely taken by surprise. I've known for such a long time how evil Lucy is, but this is a new low even for her.

Then I feel the door push against my back. I roll out of the way, now lying on my stomach, my face in the floor. I try to ignore the fact that I know how long it's been since Rosie really scrubbed it. Bella pokes her head in and urges, "Woman, get off the floor, you've got to see this."

"What?" I mumble into the cold linoleum. The floor feels amazing against my face, puffy from crying.

"It's the freakin' Spanish Inquisition!" she says with amusement.

I peer up at Rosie who shrugs and steps over me and out of the kitchen to see what's going on. I pull myself up to my knees and wipe my face clean. I don't need anyone to see me cry, especially not Lucy. Or Finn.

I rise to my feet and gingerly push the door open. Bella, Rosie and Beattie stand behind the counter, watching Finn's booth with the focus of an Olympic tennis match.

"What's going on?"

"Lucy's on trial," Rosie exclaims with a bright and happy smile. Being an outsider herself, Rosie hates Lucy too.

Finn and Lucy both have their hands folded on top of the table. It reminds me of an uncomfortable job interview.

"Well, why do I call you 3788?" he questions, his voice stern and even. His eyes flick up to find me and are gone just as fast. I like to think he wants to make sure I'm okay.

Lucy never breaks focus; the girl could win an Oscar with this talent.

"Well, because that's my locker number at school," she answers softly, tucking a curl behind her ear. Lucy's a pro at question and answer. She's beaten me at the Geography Bowl three years in a row after all. God, I'm going to throw up again.

"Okay, then who was I originally trying to talk to?" he asks, he voice unchanging. His posture is stiff and a piece of pie sits untouched in front of him.

"A girl you met at a party of mine, you mixed me up with her." Damn! Were my sisters taking notes off those letters?

Finn adjusts his weight in his seat and takes a deep breath.

"Well you sure seem to know a lot about it." His large frame fills up much of the booth and his gray Tee shirt stretches tight across his chest and the rising and falling of his breath. The veins in his neck bulge against his skin. I can tell he's upset.

She shakes her head, still smiling. I'll kill her.

"Finn, my mystery man, of course I know a lot about it, I know everything about it. It's me."

She looks so tiny sitting across from him, but her ego and superiority fill the whole shop.

Finn's quiet a moment before he slowly raises his hand and takes Lucy's. I'm going to cry again, I know it. It's all over, whatever this thing is between us. Lucy smiles like the stupid idiot she is, but I'm not really mad at her. I'm mad at him. How can he think that she's me? How he confuse that witch with me?

Suddenly Finn's eyes lock with mine and he pulls his hand away from her talons.

"I just have one more question."

"Anything," Lucy answers, interlocking her fingers under her chin. Her voice does actually sound a lot like mine right now. She's done her homework.

"What did you lose?" he asks, back to his stern voice. I can't breathe, he's not buying her charade.

"Excuse me?" Lucy stumbles, the sweet edge gone from her voice. He's thrown her off guard.

"At the dance, when we actually met. What did you leave behind?" he demands, the coldness increasing in his voice. A chill settles in the room as all the customers zero in and strain to her what's happening. The glories of the gossipy small town.

"W-well," Lucy flounders, trying to search for some way out of this. I glance back at my sisters who are in a full out panic. They left out a very important detail and Lucy will never let them into her precious circle now. "Well, if I forgot something how would I know what it was?" Weak answer.

Finn crosses his arms over his chest, his strong and burly chest.

"You would have noticed this." he says, a sly smile in his voice. He's only trying to embarrass her now.

Lucy bites down on her lip, her eyes darting back and forth, trying to recall the thing SHE hadn't actually lost.

"Of course," she proclaims suddenly, a smile of fake recognition on her face. "My cell phone, I've been looking for that everywhere. Do you have it?"

Finn laughs humorlessly, his shoulders slumping forward and I can't tell what he's thinking.

"It was a really good try Lucy. I don't know where you got all your information, but it was a good effort," he says as he shoots up from the booth and marches off to the bathroom, his fist tapping against the wall as he goes.

Lucy sits there dumbfounded like someone punched her in the face. Then, she catches me looking at her. She zips up from the booth and stomps over to me. My sisters keep a bit of distance behind her. Her wrath can reach quite far.

She points a stiff, well manicured finger in my face and threatens, "You think this is over? I promise you, freak, this is not over!"

"You can leave my establishment if you're going to speak to my employees that way," Beattie orders sternly, stepping in between Lucy and me. I'm grateful for her. I always am.

Tyler reaches forward and touches Lucy's arm. "Come on, Luce. Let's get out of here. We can go do something else."

Lucy's jaw tightens and she slaps my sister's hand away.

"Hey!" she grunts. "Mini freaks, get the hell away from me and stay away. God, you're no better than your loser sister. Stop trying." And with that she storms away, everyone in the shop watching her go. My sisters both seem like they're going to cry.

I take a step toward them, my face cold as a single tear lingers on the edge of my eye lid. I shake my head slowly.

"Why would you two do this to me?" I demand softly. We've never been close, but this is a brand new level of cruelty. Did their popularity really mean more to them than my life?

Megan rubs her arm, trying to act like she doesn't care. "Oh, come on, Elle," she starts to whine, but I can't let her finish.

I shake my head more feverishly.

"No, no, there will be none of that. I know we don't always see eye to eye and we don't get along so well, but this is the coldest, meanest, cruelest thing you've ever done. I'm your sister, whether you like that or not and you completely betrayed me." My bottom lip starts to quiver as the tear escapes. My sisters exchange shameful looks. "Maybe you belong with Lucy. She's a shark and so are you."

"Elle," Tyler's voice trails off strained and sad. Her hands clasped in front of her as her platform Mary Jane scuffs the floor. She looks like a little girl.

I stare down at my feet, my jaw locked and fists cemented on my hips. I'm done. I know I'll lose it completely if I try to say anything more. Rosie decides to help me out.

"You two need to leave." They don't move and the true hard-ass that is my Rosie emerges. "Hey, Barbies, are you deaf? Get the hell out. Now!" They shuffle out the door with their tails between their legs.

As they leave, Blanche holds the door open for them. As she enters her thumb juts in the direction of the door.

"What's wrong with Tweedles Dee and Dum?" she asks and then takes one look at me. "Sweetie, what's the matter?"

I've barely spoken to Blanche since the dance. She's training for the state finals and taking care of her brothers and I'm falling for a guy who doesn't know that he already knows me- Wait, falling for him? Was that really what I think? No, no I can't, oh God I can't!

I lean forward, across the counter and wrap my arms around her shoulders, pulling her to me and she hugs me back, hard.

"I'm glad you're here."

I breathe in the smell of clean sweat and powder fresh deodorant. It's so classically my best friend that I want to bury myself in its familiarity and stay there forever.

She rubs my back and I felt better right away. Rosie scurries past us, failing to be nonchalant and murmurs, "Ca-kaw, Ca-kaw. The eagle has landed." Of course I have no idea what on earth that's supposed to mean, but I pull away as Finn returns from the bathroom. For a split moment I forgot he was here. I turn away from him and Blanche blocks his view so I can wipe my face again with the back of my hand, but Finn doesn't seem all that interested in me at the moment.

"Blanche," he pleads, his voice desperate when he sees her. "Come on, you've got to talk to me." He puts his hands on her shoulders and squares her body to his. His knuckles are white he's gripping her so hard, but she doesn't pull herself away.

"Will you drop it please?" she urges, tying her apron on. What little interlude do these two have going? Another jealous chill runs through me, and this is my best friend.

"But you were there with her. Why won't you just tell me who it was?" he begs, his voice breaking. I know how hard and frustrating this has been on him. I hate that I'm the one doing it to him.

Blanche purses her lips and places her hands over his on her shoulders. She's fighting every instinct to look at me, I know.

"Because it's not my identity to give away. If she wants to tell you who she is, she will. I'm sorry but I can't betray my friend like that." She turns quickly to Bella. "What section do I have?"

"Back half," Bella answers softly, disappearing with Beattie and Rosie into the kitchen.

Finn drops onto one of the stools at the counter. I lay my arms on the marble in front of him, and bring my eyes down to his level.

"Are you okay?" I'm close enough that I can smell the peppermint of his shampoo and the warmth of his aftershave and it wraps around me like a hug.

He shakes his head, his skin rubbing against his arm.

"I don't know," he admits and then his piercing blue eyes meet mine and I swallow hard against the spark that flies between us. "That was really low of her."

I nod in agreement. "I know. I'm sorry." And I don't just mean for this.

He reaches into his pocket, pulling out the keys.

"What're you doing?" I ask, unable to breathe. Has he realized it's me? A part of me hopes.

He shrugs and says, with his eyes focused on the keys, "You're right, you've been right the whole time. I'm obsessing over it too much. Take them, it'll help my mental health right?" He's smiling now, but his eyes are still so sad. His heart breaks and that shatters mine.

I take them and cradle my keys in my hand. My pie shop key chain, my store key and house key, a little puff ball that's supposed to look like a penguin that Blanche had given me on my birthday. I smile at them. I've missed these inanimate objects. No more basement window for me.

He reaches out and grabs my hand and holds onto it. The tips of his fingers are calloused and rough. I still wonder how they got that way. But his palms are soft and smooth. The gentle caress makes me want to cry.

"Do you think you could get out of here for a while?" he asks of me. There's a "please" hidden under the words.

I glance around the shop, it's pretty dead. Blanche can probably handle it on her own until Nixie gets there and if not she can always call me and I can come back.

"I guess so, why?"

He smiles a little brighter, his eyes locks on our intertwined hands.

"Because, you're going to learn how to drive."

Chapter Eleven

66 This is why I don't want to do this!" I said slam my hands against the steering wheel scaring myself as I hit the horn. Finn laughs so hard it induces a hiccup fit. Apparently, my complete inability to drive pulls him out of his funk. I narrow my eyes at him. "I'm so glad you're finding this so amusing." It's been almost two hours of this and we've barely moved more than five feet. No exaggeration.

He has to catch his breath from all the laughter.

"I'm sorry, Pumpkin, but you're pretty bad."

"Then can we stop?" I plead with a hopeful smile. There's a reason I've never done this.

He shakes his head, "Nope, this is an important rite of passage and you're overdue."

"I hate you," I mutter as I put the car back into drive. We're driving around the empty parking lot at an abandoned supermarket in New Shiloh. The concept of such a big building being empty in Harpersgrove is unheard of, but it's the only way I won't kill someone or cause serious damage to anyone's property. He's brought me here to hide my shame.

"No you don't, you love me," he says with a smile. That makes me blush, but I do my best to hide my face in my shoulder. He doesn't seem to notice the pink in my cheeks, than God. I've really come to like Finn and it's cosmically unfair.

"Okay, so nice and slowly, move your foot from the brake to the gas." The car drifts a little when I move my foot and I get scared and slam back on the brake. Finn flies forward, nearly hitting his face against the dashboard.

"Woman, you're going to kill me."

"I'm sorry! I don't want to do this!" I shriek again. I throw my face into the steering wheel, once again forgetting about the damn horn. The squeak that erupts from my throat makes him giggle and my skin flush.

He loosens his seat belt and encourages, "Well, we're not going anywhere until you at least kind of get it. And you're going to get your license if it kills you."

"Well, I think it's going to kill you the rate we're going," I mumble, taking a deep breath. "Can we break for just a second?"

"You're foot's already on the brake," he teases sarcastically.

I stick my tongue out at him, "You know very well that that's not what I meant," I say as I put the car into park. I sigh and rest my head back against my seat.

"So," I begin, interested for a change of subject. Something that's not about driving, or his mystery girl, or my family. Something else. "What are your plans for next year?"

His head cocks to the side and eyebrows raise. "What do you mean?" He releases his seat belt and twists toward me.

I shrug, "Well, you're a senior. I'm a senior. We have important things to consider about our futures."

He ponders this a moment.

"Well," he begins, letting a deep breath out through his nose. A bird perches on the hood of the jeep, intent and ready to listen as I am to Finn's answer. "That depends on who you're talking to."

My eyebrows knit together. "I don't understand."

He smiles, pulling his foot up onto the seat and resting his arms on his knee.

"If you're talking to my father, I'm going Ithaca and studying pre-law and then going to Yale for law school. Join the family business. Get married. Have 2.5 children and a golden retriever and die from a heart attack before sixty."

"Oh, your dad has expectations, huh?" I ask, even though I knew the obvious answer. I wonder what's it's like to have parents that interested. Mine are only writing the check.

Finn sighs, running a hand over his face.

"They're all corporate lawyers, all of them. My grandfather, my great uncles, my aunts, my dad and my brother. My father's firm is Wise and Wise."

"Your brother works with him," I deduce, chewing on hangnail killing my thumb. Chewing the skin around my fingers is an awful nervous habit of mine. He nods.

"Yep, and once Kathy graduates from law school I'm sure that she'll be joining the firm too, making it Wise, Wise and Wise."

I laugh aloud. "And if you join, it'll be-"

"Wise, Wise, Wise and Wise," he finishes for me.

I put my hand over my mouth, trying to muffle my laugh.

"Oh, that's just awful." A laugh peeks out from behind his voice.

"I agree."

"Okay, so that's what you hear if you talk to your dad, what about if I ask you?"

He smiles that tragically beautiful, lopsided smile and says, "Well, as far as what I'd study I don't have that completely set, but I want to go to UCLA."

I choke on my own breath. "Me too!" I squeak.

"Small world." His eyes are so intently locked on me, like everything I have to say is important. Normally, it would embarrass me, but I love the way he looks at me.

"Why there?" I inquire, trying to steady myself.

"To be honest, because it's on the other side-"

"Of the country!" I finish for him.

He laughs and nods. "You've got it, exactly." He pulls down on the ends of his hoodie, dragging my eyes to his waist and my eyes kind of linger there. I remember back to that brief glimpse I'd received of his body when when I'd dropped the pie on him. Warmth rises up through my chest as my eyes stay settled on his waist.

"Okay," I continue, pulling my gaze away from his appealing waist-line. "If you could do anything, anything in the world and money was no object. Making an honest and reasonable living was no object, what would you do?"

He thinks for a moment, pursing his lips as he does. "That's an interesting question. I guess I'd kind of like to be a social worker."

"Really?" That's not what I was expecting at all, but as I let myself think about I know that Finn would great in that role. I doubt anyone would have trouble talking to him. I'm sure he could get anyone to open up.

"Yeah, I like helping people and I think that if there were more people who could, or wanted to do that job maybe we could help more kids. I like kids."

I smile. "Yeah, I guess I can see you doing that. You'd be good at it."

"But my father would quite literally flip his lid if I did. It's a bit of a step down in pay grade from a corporate attorney." My parents have never put any pressure on me to go one way or another in my field of study. Maybe every family has its own issues.

"Yeah, but it's your life." It seems like such and Eleanor thing to do. Yet my mother seems to have no opinion at all on the subject.

He groans. "Oh, God, I wish it were that simple. I really do."

"But who am I to talk, right? My mom wouldn't notice if I pulled a Richard Pryor and lit myself on fire." She'd only notice if my hair was out of place when I did it.

He stays away from that pleasantly dark thought and asks, "Well, what would you do? If money were no object?"

I smile, coyly turning my attention to my hands. What I want seems silly and has changed so drastically over the last few months. "I'd run a pie shop."

He laughs uncontrollably and my cheeks flush deep. I know it's stupid. "Oh come on, really?"

I sigh. "I know what you're thinking, but that place has completely changed my life and it's made me really like pie." I exclaim with a laugh.

"Well, it is good pie," he admits as he reaches out to tuck a loose piece of hair behind my ear and my breathing halts.

We're silent for a moment, and it isn't awkward at all. Finally he breaks the quiet. "Okay, enough stalling. Back to the driving."

My lips turn down in a frown. We were having such a lovely time. "Fine." I put the car back into drive, but keep my foot firmly on the brake.

He places his hand on mine and my breathing quickens. "Take it nice and slowly. You won't wreck the car, just don't push too hard on the gas."

I take another deep breath and slowly lift my foot. As the car begins to crawl, I see Finn brace himself from the corner of my eye, but I don't slam on the brake. I let my foot gently touch the gas, and it doesn't jerk forward! We begin to roll at a whole ten mph! I've never been more excited about anything in my life!

"You're doing it!" he exclaims joyfully, hopping up out of his seat.

"I am! I am!" I squeak. Holy crow, I'm driving! Maybe, I get why people like it so much. It's quite an accomplishment when you finally get it.

I slowly lift my foot and rest it gently back on the brake. When we're fully stopped I put the car into park and can't stop myself from grinning like an idiot. "I just drove a car! A real car! Thank you."

But Finn isn't smiling anymore. He looking at me like he never has before, like he's memorizing my face. "What is it?" I ask, turning in my seat to face him.

He doesn't speak. He reaches out with one hand and places it against my cheek.

"Elle," he whispers softly as he moves toward me. I can't breathe. I can't think. I can't stop what's about to happen. I'm not sure I really want to anyway. The next thing I know, Finn kisses me. Not 3788. He kisses *me*. His lips are soft, warm, and more than I remembered. I put my hand behind his head and pull him closer to me, hungry for him. But suddenly my eyes fill with hot tears. I've already ruined this, broken it before it could start. I'm lying to him. Every moment we're together, I'm lying. I know who the girl of his dreams is. I'm her, but I haven't told him. I let him go on and on, pouring his heart out to me and I don't stop breaking his. I've ruined this.

I push back from him and try to hide my face so he won't see me cry, but I know that it's useless. I bite down hard on my lip to keep the growing in my throat contained.

"Elle," he begins, but I won't let him. I don't deserve to feeling any better and I won't let him try.

"Please Finn, don't." I cry, sniffling. God, how can I have done this? I'm so stupid. "Please don't be nice to me."

"I'm sorry, I thought it was okay," he apologizes, making me feel so much worse.

I shake my head. "No, you don't have anything to be sorry for, please. It's my fault." I know he doesn't understand, just like he didn't understand why I'd run the night of the dance. I reach down and grab the door handle, nearly forgetting to unlock my seat belt. "I'm so sorry," I cry again before dashing from the car.

"Elle!" I hear him call after me, but he doesn't follow. He lets me run. I need to get away, far away. So I just keep running.

I sit on the curb outside a 7-11 counting the cigarette butts floating in the murky puddle beside me. With a slurpee in one hand and some big taco looking thing in the other. It's disgusting, but it numbs me. It had been rather stupid to run from Finn in the middle of New Shiloh. I have no idea where I am. I'm forced to call the one person who I know can help me.

Blanche pulls up to a screeching halt in front of the store. She hops out of the magic pumpkin, but doesn't approach me.

"You're the saddest sight I have ever seen. You know that, right?"

She pushes her plastic sunglasses atop her head and shifts her weight in her sneakers.

I answer by bursting into tears. They get in my slurpee.

She slams the car door and sits beside me on the curb, her bright sneakers falling directly into the puddle.

"Elle, what happened?"

I wipe my eyes with the heels of my hands and take another bite of my taco hybrid. Blanche snatches it from my hand and tosses it in the nearby garbage can.

"Hey! That was mine!" I cry. My lip start to quiver as my heart breaks all over again.

She rolls her eyes, "You'll thank me for it later when you don't have cancer."

I pout, yep like I'm five and confess, "Finn kissed me."

"He did what?" Blanche exclaims. "Elle, that's great!" My eyes widen, how could she say that?

"No, no it's not!" I shriek as a mother and her children scurry by us, trying not to make eye contact. I can't blame her. I always wonder about people who hang out in the parking lots of convenience stores.

"Why not?" she demands. "Isn't this what you wanted? For him to like you, not the alter ego?"

"Because I didn't listen to you in the beginning," I sob into her shoulder, ruining her New Shiloh track shirt with my mascara.

She seems confused. I would be too. "Okay, I'm sure you're right. I am a genius, but you're going to have to be a bit more specific."

"I should have told him from the beginning who I was, but I didn't. I messed this up. I can't fix it now," I cry into my slurpee, which she doesn't take away from me, and I'm grateful.

She absorbs my words for a moment before she speaks.

"Okay, now, remember that I love you and that you're my best friend." She waits for some sign of recognition from me. "Michelle Antoinette Conner, that is the stupidest thing I have ever heard in my entire life," she snaps with an actual smile on her face and a laugh in her voice.

I lunge away from her, my slurpee spilling over my legs. The overwhelming aroma of artificial banana makes my stomach turn and sends a shiver through my body.

"What?" I exclaim. "It's not stupid, it's true!"

She lets out a sharp breath through her nose and hops back to her feet.

"You know what, I've tried to break you of your ridiculous delusions about all this crap, but you won't listen to anyone. So, I'm done, I can't do it anymore." She stomps back to her car and throws me a towel from her backseat to clean off my legs.

"I'm sorry this is so hard on you," I snap coldly. "But this is my life."

"And you're the one messing it up."

When I walk in the front door, using my key for the first time in too long, the house is silent. More than it should be.

"Mom?" I call out into the dark living room, but hear nothing back. She must be out somewhere, not too strange as of late.

I need a nap, correction I need a mini coma. I trudge slowly up the stairs and down the end of the hall. I pull the string to bring down my staircase and feel like my feet are full of lead. I need not to see anyone for a while. But of course fate is never so kind.

Tyler and Megan sit on the edge my bed, looking nervous and uncomfortable.

"I thought I told you two never to come up here again?"

They exchange nervous looks, speaking telepathically with their shared twin brain. I'm sure they think I'm going to kill them, and to be honest I'm considering it. I hate them.

"Can we talk to you for a minute?" Tyler asks.

"Why? Gathering more info for Lucy?" I clip, collapsing into my desk chair. I'm so not in the mood for this.

Megan looks like she's about to cry. Good. "No," she says meekly. "We want to apologize."

I roll my eyes. "Well, isn't that nice of you." The base of my chair squeaks as I twist back and forth. I need to fix that.

"Come on Elle-" Tyler begins, but I'm not going to let her finish. They have no power here.

"No, no, no, there will be none of that. I know that the three of us have never exactly gotten along, but what the two of you did to me is completely unforgivable." I shout. Angry and exhausted tears blur my vision. I'm spent.

"Can you even begin to wrap your mind around how that felt? I've been having a really hard time," I admit to them, the first time I really have out loud and my voice betrays me by breaking on its ends. I'm so tired. "A really hard time and then you go and do this so you can be popular?"

Now Megan does cry. Again, good.

"We were really stupid, I'm so sorry. We just wanted Lucy to like us so badly that we didn't think of anything else," she sobs.

"And now that you realize that she doesn't want you and that she'll never want you. You want me to forgive you?" I exclaim, my head beginning to pound. I really need to lie down. "Get off my bed."

They exchange confused looks and hold each other's hands tightly.

"Did I stutter? Get off my bed." They oblige and I flop down on my back, covering my eyes with my forearm.

"What can we do, Elle?" Tyler begs. "We'll do anything."

I want to tell her they can go to hell, but my phone starts ringing before I get the chance. I reach down and grab it from my purse. It's my dad. "Hello?" I say into the receiving end of the phone.

"Hey honey, how you doing?" he screams. The man has never understood the concept of speakerphone.

Well that's a loaded question, but I decide now isn't the time to have a talk like this with my father. "Fine, how are you," I answer instead.

"Oh, I'm fantastic. Got some really good news today," he responds a smile in his voice, it almost makes me smile. It's been nice to see such a happy side of him.

"What kind of news?" I ask. The twins squirm uncomfortably on the floor as I ignore them.

"Well, it was the strangest thing. Your mom came to my office today."

"And this is a good story?" I ask I flip to my side and stare at the glow in the dark stars on my wall.

He laughs. "I know, I was thinking the same thing when I saw her, especially considering the fact that Becky works five feet from me." Yep, that could have been bad. "But she actually said hello to Becky, nicely."

"Are you sure it was Mom?" I honestly question, unable to believe that the woman who gave birth to me could be so kind to the woman she sees as the destroyer of her family.

"I agree, but your mom was different today," he continues, unable to believe it himself it seemed.

"What happened?" I ask, turning away from my sisters. They have the most antsy and anxious looks on their faces and I don't want to see them.

"She signed the divorce papers." he answers simply.

I sit up straight in my bed.

"She did what?!" The twins sit forward, hoping to be included.

He explains further, "She told me that she didn't want me to think that she was only trying to make me miserable. That she could never move on with her life if she didn't remove herself from mine. Then she hugged me, wished me the best, and left."

My mouth hangs open. I can't believe it. I don't believe it.

"Again, are you sure this was mom? There are a lot of tall women with dark hair in this world dad."

"Trust me, dear. If there's one woman I know, it's your mother," he begins before picking up his phone and taking it off speaker. At least there won't be anymore screaming.

"Honey do you think you could drop by the house tonight? Becky has something she wants to talk to you about." Oh joy, wedding planning.

I nod, even though I know he can't see me.

"Sure, can you come by and get me?" After my recent driving experience I'm in no hurry to get behind the wheel anytime soon.

"Absolutely. How's seven o'clock?" he asks.

"Great." I say as I end the call and return my phone to my purse.

My head falls back against my pillow as I try to absorb the craziness of all this. It's incredible, impossible, completely out of character for Eleanor Conner. Perhaps my mother isn't the villain after all.

For only a brief moment I've been able to forget that the carbon copies are in the room. They're still waiting patiently for me to level their sentence. I take a deep breath and sit up on the edge of my bed to face them. Their spines straighten instantly like their bracing against a coming storm. I cross my arms over my chest, appearing as official and vicious as I can.

"I have a way you can start making this up to me."

I know that my sisters can't possibly be pleased about going to Dad and Becky's. I mean, they have vowed to never see either of them again. However, as we drive toward their apartment, the three of us and my dad in the car, neither girl seems too upset, just stone quiet.

"It sure is nice to have all my girls in one place," Dad says cheerfully as he hums along with the top 40 hit buzzing through the radio.

Megan makes some sound of disgust from the backseat and I flip around to glare at her. She clams up immediately. I can get used to this newfound power.

Becky waits for us at the top of the stairs. "Oh, I didn't know everyone was coming!" she sings gleefully. I have to give her that much, she's a genuinely happy person. As much as I had tried to convince myself otherwise in the beginning, she's a pretty genuine person all the way around.

"I was surprised too, honey," my dad begins, for some reason taking the stairs first. Not only is his middle aged and out of shape, but he's short as hell. All three of us could have made it up and down the stairs twice before he got to the top. "I got there to pick up Elle and she said the others wanted to come as well."

"It's good to see you, girls." Becky gushes as she welcomes us inside. Her hand lingers a moment on my shoulder and she knows I'm responsible for getting the twins here. Woman's intuition, I guess.

The girls mumble a "hello," but I ignore them. "Becky," I start, patting her hand on my shoulder. "Dad said you wanted to talk to me about something?"

"Oh, yes," Becky says with a smile. "But first, can I get anyone something to drink? Soda, tea, water? Anything?"

The girls shake their heads and so do I, but dad requests more of that viciously sweet iced tea. I guess, it's growing on him. My dad motions to the living room area for us to take a seat, which of course we do. The twins on the love seat, holding each other, me in the armchair and Dad and Becky on the sofa.

"What did you want to tell me?" I ask Becky again as I fiddle with the fluffy corner of a pink, Hello Kitty pillow.

She exchanges a smile with my father, but there's a bit of a nervous edge to it. I suppose, that since she hadn't been expecting my sisters, whatever she has to say, they may not be ready to hear.

"Well, considering the fact that your mother has decided to move forward with the divorce-"

"She what!?" Tyler and Megan exclaim together, there messy top knots flopping in horror. I suppose whatever delusions the twin are holding to that the separation is temporary between our parents are officially crushed.

"Oh, yeah," I interject dryly, my eyes still on Becky. "Mom agreed to sign the divorce papers."

"What?" Megan says again, a squeaky edge to her voice. She seems devastated and I feel a little bad. She is my little sister, after all.

"We'll talk about it later." I answer, really just to shut her up. "Go on, Becky."

I can tell that she doesn't want to say any more, not if it's going to upset my sisters further, but I egg her on with my eyes. This is our reality now, time for the girls to grow up a little like I've had to do.

"Well, your dad and I have decided to move up our wedding."

"To when?" Tyler asks, gripping Megan's hand tightly for support.

Becky locks her big brown eyes on me as though my opinion is the only one that matters. "Two weeks from Saturday."

"When?" the three Conner children exclaim together. I don't want Becky to think I disapprove, but man that seems hasty. And honestly impossible.

"I know it's soon, girls," my dad takes over, putting his arm around a nervous Becky. Her shoulders instantly settle from their stiff position with her guy there to protect her. "But we don't want to wait anymore."

"Wait," I begin, waving my hands in front of me to temporarily stop the madness. "There's no way you can possibly get married that soon. I mean legally, just because mom agrees to the divorce doesn't mean that there are magic fairies that make it all happen in an instant."

"Divorce fairies would be a bummer," Megan adds absently, laying her head on Tyler's shoulder.

My dad chuckles and Becky smiles. I'm not totally sure if they're laughing at me or with me. Dad squeezes Becky's hand and responds, "Ever the brilliant one, my first born. You're right, we can't legally get married right now, so consider it more of a promise. Like a ceremony of our intentions."

"Like a really fancy and expensive promise ring?" I clarify, a chuckle of my own, but I'm most certainly laughing at them.

Becky giggles, visibly pleased that I get her idea. "Exactly," she exclaims as she leans forward a bit in her seat. "Besides, there's never a bad reason to have a party!" Ah, there's my valley girl. A few weeks before it would have bothered me and the urge to punch her in the face would have consumed me, but now I barely notice. In fact, I find her rather charming.

"You're not pregnant, are you?" I shriek, desperate for an immediate answer as the thought pops into my mind. "Because I'm just coming around to the thought of you two together at all. Please don't make me throw having a new sibling into the mix." My fragile mental state can't take any more punches.

Becky leans forward across the coffee table to take my hand and rub her thumb across my knuckles. It's funny how many women in my life project this maternal force in my direction. The only one who doesn't seem to is my actual mom.

"No, Michelle, I'm not pregnant. I just want to be with the man I love. I'm ready for the world to know, and for it to be official and real."

In the spirit of keeping the peace between us I decide not to mention that her restlessness is due to the fact that she and my father have been together for months, maybe longer behind my mother's back. That won't help this situation at all.

"Well, as long as you're sure," I say instead.

"Two weeks?" Tyler squeaks from beside me. Apparently the reality of all this hasn't yet set in for them. The bubble of their reunited family has been burst.

My dad turns to the twins. His glasses slip down his nose as he rubs palms against the legs of his dark washed jeans. "Yes, girls, and I'm sorry that this has been hard on you, but you have to face the fact that your mother and I are not getting back together."

Isn't this the way you worded the conversation when your kids are like five? Oh wait, I forgot who he's talking to, my mistake.

"I'll always love her. She's the mother of my children, but we're not right to be together anymore. And the fact that she and I broke apart does not mean I'll ever break apart from you. In fact, I hope we get closer."

He extends his arms out to them and they gawk at him like he's an alien. I decide to see if my new powers work in this instance too. I glare at them and as soon as they catch my expression, they practically jump into his arms. Oh yeah, I can get used to this!

I feel Becky's hand on my shoulder. "Why don't we give them a minute?" she whispers softly as it looks like my sisters are about to cry. They've missed their father too.

I follow Becky to the kitchen where she hands me a can of soda from the silver refrigerator. "So," she begins, opening a can for herself. "I was wondering if I could talk to you about something?"

"Okay," I say cautiously, waiting for her spill. I accepted the stupid post as maid of honor, so I've got to take what goes with it. I'm not jazzed about doing it at hyper speed, in two weeks and then having to do it again when they actually get married, but I've made my bed.

"Shoot."

She smiles brightly, hopping onto her kitchen counter and sits her soda can off to the side. "Well, what are you doing tomorrow after school?"

And so it begins.

Dad takes us home about an hour later. After listening to Becky plan out all of our "promise ceremony" preparations that need to be done so quickly and will probably take all of my time between now and then. I'm in desperate need of some sleep.

I kiss Dad goodbye and make my way into the house. The girls scurry upstairs, glad to be done with their penitence for the night, and I wander into the kitchen.

"Where were you?" I hear suddenly from behind. It scares me so much I grab the first thing off the counter (a sponge) to defend myself. My mother emerges from the darkness and cocks an eyebrow at me.

"What're you going to do? Clean me?" She flicks on the kitchen lights to reveal herself in a cut off sweatshirt and yoga pants. She looks about twenty-five years old. I hope I've inherited some of those genes, but I'll probably end up like my father's sister Claire who looked like an old woman at thirty.

I sigh and place my weapon down. "No, you just scared me."

"Where were you?" she asks again. I can see soft blue bags forming under her eyes and her hair hangs loose at her shoulders. I've never seen her so tired.

"We went to dad's for a little bit," I answer with a sigh, hoping it won't upset her too much. We have to start making it seem normal. This is reality now.

"You got the twins to go? Impressive," she says simply, fiddling with and rearranging the fruit in the basket on the breakfast bar.

I shrug. "Well, they kind of owe me." I decide to leave it at that. The rest of the story is too long and we're both too tired.

She nods slowly and sits down at the breakfast bar, her back to me.

"You know it was never necessarily that I wanted him to be miserable, not forever anyway."

She wants to talk to me. Normally I'd fight this like the plague, but after the big, grown-up steps she's taken for herself today, it's the least I could do.

"I know."

She laughs a bit, but there's no humor to her voice.

"No you don't, sweetie, and I don't blame you. You were right, that is how I made it seem."

Okay, so I know I'm right, but I'm trying to make her feel less crappy about it.

"Then, why did you do it?"

She doesn't look at me, but single tear escapes her eye and rolls down her cheek. My mother never cries.

"Because he embarrassed me. He humiliated me and I wasn't ready to just let that be okay."

"Mom-" I begin, but she cuts me off before I can try to comfort her.

"No, no, let me finish," she urges as I settle onto the stool next to her. "I love your father and I know that I haven't always made it easy for him. I don't make things easy for anyone, but I never thought he'd do what he did. And then he just dropped me, like I was nothing."

"Mom, that's not true. I mean, what he did was wrong and despicable and I don't want you to think that I condone that. But Daddy still loves you," I say and for the first time I really know it's true.

She scoffs at me and bites at the inside of her cheek, "Sure he does."

"He'll always love you, Mom. You're the mother of his children." It worked for dad with the twins. I hope the same line would work on mom. "But maybe, you're just not meant to be together like that." She sighs, sucking back more tears "And I know you don't want to hear this, but Becky makes him really happy." She rolls her eyes, a growl rumbling low in her chest. She doesn't want to hear this, but I need her to understand. "I know how that sounds and in the beginning I thought it was just because she was blonde, built, and twenty-two, but mom you should see him when he's with her. He's different, she really makes him happy."

"Why are you telling me this?" she asks, her voice soft and meek, quite un-Eleanor-Conner like. It's unfathomable that this woman who raised me, the epitome of strength and hard exterior, could be this quivering shell of a vulnerable woman sitting next me.

I take her hand, something I can't ever remember doing. "Because I want you to find it too. Dad's your past, let him be your past. I want you to go out and find your Becky, because you don't deserve to feel embarrassed and humiliated forever."

"You really believe that, Michelle?" she asks, her eyes focused on our intertwined fingers.

I nod. "Mom, I know we don't exactly get along, but that doesn't mean that I want you to be miserable. You're my mother."

Then she does something that she hasn't done since I was about six years old. She reaches out, pulls me in her arms and hugs me tight.

"Thank you, sweetie, I love you." She kisses my hair near my temple and I realize that this is what I've been missing. All the mothering gestures from other women were nice and much appreciated, but nothing comes close to my real mom. She's who I need.

I hug her back, my arms can almost wrap the full way around her thin frame. It's not going to fix everything or even anything, but it's a start.

"I love you too, Mom."

Chapter Twelve

I feel like an idiot. "Oh honey, you look beautiful!" Becky squeals as she swishes to me in her chic, form fitting pale pink dress. I stand on the platform in the bridal boutique, thirty- seven mirrors around me and a little Ukrainian woman poking me with pins as she makes her last minute adjustments to my dress. It's the brightest Pepto pink that I've ever seen. There are no straps, a huge detriment to my boobless figure and a huge pink bow on the back that should have settled above my butt, if I had one. The dressmaker added fabric to it because I'm so damn tall it only came to my shins originally. Becky's dress looks exactly like mine, only hers is a baby pink. I look like a freak. Becky looks like princess. Damn it. "You're going to look so beautiful tomorrow, Elle."

Two weeks have flown by faster than I thought possible. It's insane really, but I'm actually thankful to Becky and her insistent planning because it's kept my mind off other things that I'd rather not think about. Planning the event kept me from the pie shop. Normally it would have destroyed me to be away so long, but been it's necessary. I stole a copy of Blanche's track schedule and the only shifts I take as of late are ones when the New Shiloh track team are at an away meet or at practice.

I haven't heard from Finn at all since the afternoon in his car. Not that he would have been able to contact me considering he doesn't have my phone number. He does have an e-mail for me, only he thinks it's for

3788. But again, Becky's kept me so busy that I don't have time to think about him much. For that I'm grateful.

"Now, for tomorrow," Becky begins, pulling her massive binder from her duffle bag of a purse. "You need to be at my apartment at 7:30, or you're just welcome to spend the night, to get your hair and makeup done."

"Then I need to go to the florist and yell at Raul and make sure that all of the flowers get to the hall by ten," I repeat with a sigh. This is the third time we've been through the plan today, and that's just today.

She closes the binder and smiles at me proudly. "I really appreciate you doing this Elle. I know you're not super excited about having me in your family."

"I don't know, I'm kind of warming up to the idea." And it's surprisingly true. In fact, spending all this time with Becky has really made me come to like her. I'm trying my best to envision her in more of a big sister role rather than stepmother. Maybe we will be able to be friends after all. Whatever she ends up being when the dust settles, I'm glad she's there.

"I don't ever expect you to see me as any kind of mother figure-"

"And as I have stipulated before, you don't have to worry about that, because that would be creepy," I tell her again for the thousandth time.

She sighs and says, "But maybe more like a big sister? I mean, everything you're going through in your life, I've probably been through-" Oh, like having a boy in love with you, but him having no idea that it's actually you he made out with at a dance, but then he made out with you again in reality? Yeah, doubt it. "And for me, as you know, it wasn't that long ago, so I have advice. I'm a good listener. I just want to be here for you, as a friend, as anything."

"I know Beck, thank you." And again, I mean it.

Becky drops me off at the house after the final fitting, my dress drapes over my arm as I unlock the door. Becky doesn't dare come in and I don't blame her. My mom might be doing better, but there are boundaries to her tolerance.

My phone buzzes like crazy in my pocket. I pull it out and inspect the number. It's not one I recognize. "Hello?" I say into the receiving end.

"Hey," a deep male voice says back to me. It's pained and sad, but easily identifiable.

Oh good lord.

"Are you there?" Finn asks again.

"I'm here," I manage to squeak out. My throat is dry and my knees might give out on me. "How did you get my number?"

"Blanche didn't exactly want to give it to me, but I can be quite persuasive," he answers, a chuckle hidden in his voice.

"I have no doubt," I respond softly, leaning against my front door with my hip, not ready to go inside.

"Why are you avoiding me?" he snaps sharply. I know he's hurt by having to ask.

"What do you mean?" I lie. I'm a terrible person. Hell has a toasty, warm seat ready and waiting for me.

He lets out a long breath into the phone that rasps in my ear. "Come on Elle, you haven't been at the shop in forever, every time I come by they say you aren't there. Blanche won't tell me anything. So why are you avoiding me?" he demands. I'm sure he's frustrated. He has every right to be.

I take a deep breath and tell him as honestly as I'll allow myself, "Finn, I'm not good for you. Can't you just let it drop?"

"No, and that's stupid," he responds simply. "Come on, even if you don't like me that way-" Is he joking? "I'd like us to at least be friends."

Again, my every impulse is to just tell him. Tell him the truth about me, but I can't. My fight or flight index kicks in, and as is so typical of me, I pick flight. Damn chicken. "I'm sorry Finn, I've got to go. My dad and Becky are getting married tomorrow. Well, not getting married, dedicating themselves to each other or something, and I just have a lot to do. I'm sorry." And I click off the call. It's rude and cowardly, maybe even cruel, but I don't know what else to do.

He tries to call me back right after and again and again after that, but I don't answer. He can't see it yet, but pushing him away from me is the best thing that I can do for him. I'm a liar and fraud, and Finn deserves so much more than that. He deserves more than me. I pick up my keys and run my fingers along the new key chain I made from the three simple glass beads to remember the dance where everything had come together and subsequently fallen apart.

I force Megan and Tyler to pick dresses to wear to the wedding. They know they still owe me big time for the Lucy thing, but they're fighting going to this ceremony with every impulse in their bodies. I remind them that all they have to do is attend. I'm in the damn thing.

"But we don't want to," Megan whines with a stomp of her foot.

"And I forgot to care," I inform as I search through their closet. Good lord, you can clothe every child in Africa with all they have.

"Did you invite Finn to come with you?" Tyler asks as she holds a pretty white dress that contrasts perfectly with her dark hair, to her slender frame.

Megan grabs it from her and criticizes, "You cannot wear white to someone else's wedding you dumb-dumb."

"Um, it's not their wedding," Tyler fires back, taking the dress in her hands. "Besides, Becky isn't even wearing white."

"No, Finn is not coming," I say curtly, hoping it will end this line of conversation. As little as I want to discuss my love life, I want to discuss it with them even less.

They exchange confused glances and Tyler asks, "Why not? You obviously love him. We read your letters, remember?"

I roll my eyes, trying to force a mint green dress onto Megan. "I do not love him. He was someone of interest once, but he's not anymore. End of story."

"Far from it," Megan shoots with a laugh as she obliges me and slips the frilly green over her body. "You're enamored-" Whoa! Who gave my sister a dictionary? "And you can't hide it."

"I am not, and stop using big words, it's freaking me out," I hiss, collapsing on the mountain of clothes that used to be Megan's bed.

Tyler laughs as she debates between two navy blue dresses that are exactly the same. "Oh yeah, she's in love!"

I drop the pile of clothes in my arms next to me on the floor and mumble, "Well, on that note, I'm leaving. Please pick something nice and appropriate please."

And as I flee the inquisition, they sing to my back, "Elle and Finn sitting in a tree K-I-S-S-I-N-G!" I sprint away.

"No Raul, you know she's going to have an aneurism if you put the carnations before the roses." I hiss at the florist as he makes last minute touches to the church. Things are going quite swimmingly overall. My hair piles high in curls seven feet over my head. I'm six feet tall already and prancing around in four inch heels so I look a bit like a sideshow attraction. Come one and all and see the Galloping Giraffe. I'm acting as cruise director for the guests and I'm obsessing over flowers. This is a moment straight out of my childhood nightmares.

"I'm sorry, miss, but she's so picky." Raul, the sweet and patient florist, apologizes as he rearranges the flowers for the forty-ninth time in twenty minutes.

I sigh and pat his shoulder. "I know, and I'm sorry, but it is her day." Gag, who am I?

A hand taps my shoulder. It's my dad. "Honey, Becky's ready for you. She wants to start." The place is full to its limits. How on earth Becky got so many people to agree to come to this with only two weeks notice, I will never understand. She must be some weird breed of Jedi or something.

I nod and let Raul off the hook, telling him the flowers are fine. The little fella runs so fast from me to freedom that he kicks up dust behind him. I take my own bouquet, filled with roses and a bunch of other flowers I don't recognize and rush to the back of the church. My dad and my Uncle Billy, who flew all the way from Denver just to be here (as he's reminded us over and over all morning), stand together at the front.

Becky looks amazing, not that I'm surprised. She too has her hair piled up on top of her head in curls, but she doesn't look like a muppet. "You look great, Beck," I tell her with a smile.

She grins sheepishly, unsure of herself. "You think so?" she fishes for a compliment and for today I can oblige.

"I know so. It's going to be great. You've done a fantastic job." I squeeze her hand tight. "You ready?"

Her smile brightens as she straightens her shoulders. "As ready as I'll ever be."

Before I turn to the open doors I tell her, "Welcome to the beginning of the process of becoming a Conner." And then my intro starts and I make my way down the aisle.

With the exception of my sisters, who look elegant by the way, I don't recognize a single person. No one in my father's family, including my Nana and Pop-Pop, agreed to come to the ceremony. They don't approve. I think that's why Uncle Billy makes sure we're all very aware that he came and agreed to be dad's best man. But it isn't important, even dad doesn't seem to notice.

Becky takes my father's hand and she looks at him with more love than I can comprehend and it makes my heart swell. I'm nearly giddy, I'm so happy for them. Such a turnaround from only a month before when I hated that Becky even existed. But she's good for my dad and she loves him. My only stipulation is that they can't have a baby right away! Other than that, I'm sure we'll be okay.

The officiant, a friend of Becky's who was only there for show, smiles at the congregation and then turns his focus to my father and future stepmother. "We are gathered here today to hear the intentions of Rebecca and Anthony to pledge their lives to one another." It sounds nice. "Anthony," he says to my dad. "Repeat after me. I, Anthony,"

"I, Anthony," he repeats, love gleaming in his eyes. He never looked at my mom that way.

"Intend to take you, Rebecca," the officiant continues.

"Intend to take you, Rebecca."

"To be my wife."

My father brightens even more. "To be my wife."

"Now Rebecca, repeat after me," her friend says to my stepmother. "I, Rebecca,"

Becky fights to keep her composure, but she does it well. Her make-up is too perfect to ruin. "I, Rebecca,"

"Intend to take you, Anthony."

"Intend to take you, Anthony," Becky repeats, a huge smile in her voice.

"To be my husband."

Her voice breaks a little, but she keeps it together, "To be my husband."

The ceremony goes on, with pomp and circumstance that's just fluff to make it longer than two minutes and for the most part everyone stays engaged, everyone, but me, that is. All I can do is look at my dad, who beams at his future wife. And a thought occurs to me. Maybe society looks at them like they're inappropriate. Like a man my father's age should only be with someone like my mom, but you know what? Screw society. He's the happiest I've ever seen him and that's what really matters.

"Anthony and Rebecca have declared their eternal love for one another," the officiant announces, pulling me back into the service. "And it is my pleasure to declare that they are on their way to becoming husband and wife." Tears spring to my eyes, actual tears. He turns to my dad, "You may kiss your soon to be bride." The congregation erupts in applause as the happy couple kiss and I almost drop both my and Becky's flowers I'm clapping so hard. In the congregation the twins are on their feet; maybe they've started to get it like I have.

Becky and Dad make their way down the aisle, Uncle Billy and I close behind, and I absorb the happy faces as they gaze upon the happy couple. Nothing can break this happy feeling in me.

I'm incredibly wrong. For sitting at the back of the room in the very last row is a face I had not all been expecting to see today.

Finn Wise stares right at me.

We stand behind a set of closed doors at the reception hall, waiting for our grand entrance. Finn had made no attempt to approach me in the church and there's no way I can be certain that he'll crash the reception. I want to sneak in the back, but Becky insists on it being this way. Double damn it. If Finn is in fact crashing my father's pre-wedding, no doubt he'll decide to crash the part with the food. I mean, I would. Uncle Billy stands next to me mumbling to himself as he types feverishly on his phone. Probably in a bidding war for his precious Star Trek action figures that he covets more than his wife. A gentle roar on the other side of the door makes me swallow hard. I already made it down the aisle in one piece. It seems to be pressing my luck to try it again without falling on my face.

"Honey," my dad says to me, touching my arm. "Are you sure you're okay?" He and my uncle are almost identical in their small stature and round bellies. On the other hand, Uncle Billy has an unkempt beard and a permanent sourpuss and my dad's sporting a hipster haircut and sunshine in his eyes. Clearly, genetics only take your looks so far.

I nod, slower and more believable than I had to Becky and answer, "Peachy, Dad. Really, I'm good." I put my arm around his shoulder and squeeze him tightly. He only comes to my shoulder when I'm in heels like these. The hair oil Becky's buying for him smells like sandalwood and it comforts me. My daddy comforts me.

And then there's no more time to think, because they call my name and it's time to go. The double doors open and I enter the enormous room, my flowers death gripped into my fingers. I try to focus on the ground in front of me, knowing that if I look up at anyone who may or may not be around I'm sure to fall. Everyone applauds and I smile the best I can, intent on keeping my eyes locked to the floor. Raul has done a wonderful job on the flowers here too. It's a heck of a lot of pink, but it smells like a spring meadow in the middle of a crisp fall and it awakens my senses.

I reach my seat in one piece and sigh. I made it! Safely! And hadn't fallen on my face. I can chalk this one up to victory. I kick my shoes off under the table. No more need to look like a newborn baby giraffe in those heels.

I feel a hand grip my elbow and pull me back. I stumble and fall, but the other hand steadies me, pulling me into its owner. Finn doesn't appear necessarily happy to see me, even though I try to smile at him. He's hurt and confused and that breaks my heart.

He keeps both his hands on my arms and holds me to him. What is it with men and sandalwood? Finn smells like it too. I feel safe and warm in his arms. Oh why, oh why, did I have to screw up any chance we have together?

"What are you doing here?" I finally demand, waiting for the explanation of the century I'm sure.

"Becky invited me," he says simply, his face impassive and unchanging. Well that makes sense, she invited everyone else. My stepmother seems like the Cupid type. I'm sure she sensed the attraction between us. Maybe she sees it as doing me a favor. A poor, misguided favor.

"Of course, she did," I say, tucking a loose curl awkwardly behind my ear as Finn still holds my elbows. As I duck my head forward, my skin brushes his stubbly chin. Clearly he hasn't shaved in a few days. Is that because of me?

"I only took the invitation because I wanted to see you," he admits, his fingers flexing against my arms. I can tell it's taking everything in him not to squeeze me too hard. "I don't know what's going on Elle. Will you please explain it to me?"

His voice is calm and even and all I want to do is cry. I rest my forehead against his strong chest and realize how much I've missed him.

I nuzzle myself a little deeper into the comforting smell of his clothes and I'm so glad he doesn't push me away. If anything he grips me tighter and pulls me a little closer.

"I don't know what to say."

"Tell me what happened in the car. What did I do wrong?" he pleads as he squeezes my arms and shakes me gently. Maybe he can shake some sense into me. I breathe in more of his heavenly scent as he balances his chin onto the crown of curls atop my head. "I swear I thought it was okay to kiss you."

"Oh Finn, you didn't do anything wrong. It was me." I open my mouth to tell him. Why hide it anymore? But I don't get the chance.

My father's voice sounds through the nearby speaker.

"Before Becky and I share our first dance, I have a special request of someone here tonight." He sounds so musical, so blissfully happy. I'm incredibly jealous. "From the day my oldest daughter was born I promised her that she and I would dance to a very special song on her wedding day. I am aware that this is not actually a wedding and not hers, but I can't wait anymore. Ellie honey, where are you?" he asks, searching for me.

"Wait here, please," I say before breaking away from Finn's grasp and moving to where my father can see me. "I'm here, Dad."

"Would you share a dance with your old man, sweetie?" he asks, extending his chubby sausage fingers to me from the dance floor.

"I'd be delighted." And as my dad takes my hand the crooning styles of Mr. Stevie Wonder's hit "Isn't She Lovely" hum from the speakers overhead. Dad and I begin to dance and a sickening realization hits to me. A memory that propels me back a few weeks, to the night of the New Shiloh High masquerade dance. This exact song had been playing when I danced with Finn. I told him that it was my father daughter song for my wedding. Oh, my God. I try to keep my attention on my father, who beams at me proudly, but my focus drifts to the peripheral to see if Finn noticed. But I don't see him anywhere.

I can't breathe. I can't think. I can't stay in the moment. Luckily the song ends as quickly as it does. I kiss my father on the cheek and Becky takes my place as a much softer and sweeter song begins to play.

I flee to the crowd, looking for Finn. He must have remembered, he remembers everything. I need to explain. Where has he gone? My shoulders slump in defeat when I find him nowhere.

"You know, I had a girl once tell me that song was to be hers and her father's on her wedding day," a voice says from behind, with a cheerful nip to it.

I spin around to see him still here, he hadn't left. His hands are stuffed into the pockets of his khaki dress pants and his purple tie sits crooked against his pale blue dress shirt and navy sport coat. He's lovely, gorgeous and perfect.

"Finn, I can explain," I begin, taking a deep breath, no turning back now. "I'm the girl. I'm 3788." I feel the tension leave my body with the secret I've held too long.

He flashes me that lopsided grin he's so famous for and begins to laugh. Well, that catches me off guard to say the least. What can possibly be funny?

"Yeah, Pumpkin, I know." My knees buckle, ready to give out on me.

"What do you mean, you know?" I demand, anger, shock and embarrassment all flood my pale cheeks. "How long have you known?"

He keeps smiling, oh god what a perfect smile... FOCUS MICHELLE!

"Well," he starts again, running a hand through his coal colored hair. "I'm not going to lie, I didn't know for sure right away, but you made it kind of obvious."

I had not!

"I did not." I stomp my bare foot like a toddler.

"Oh, come on Elle, you obsessed over getting the keys back. You were way more invested in the situation than any other girl would be. And let's be honest, how many six foot tall girls are there that spend enough time at a pie shop to get key chains and have a best friend who just happens to go to New Shiloh." He makes a valid point. "But I didn't know completely until I saw you cry," he touches my face like the tears are still there, "when Lucy claimed to be you."

I knew that would give something away!

"And then when you started avoiding me, I had the Ghost," my mind flutters back to the pasty ginger who delivered my first letters, "see what locker number you had. I was too curious then. And of course he found that your locker was-"

"3788," I finish for him.

He nods slowly. "Yep that's the one." Hot tears sting the backs of my eyes, but I don't let them through, not yet.

"Why didn't you say anything?" he urges as he takes me by the arms again.

I press my lips hard together, have to keep the tears inside.

"Because you're you and I'm me," I yelp, letting my real fears be heard out loud. "I mean, I didn't want you to be disappointed that your mystery girl was just a plain old ordinary girl from Harpersgrove. Look at you!"

He cocks an eyebrow at me. "Elle, that's the stupidest thing you've ever said." He almost seems mad at me. He grips my arms a little harder and rests his forehead against mine.

My skin breaks into goose bumps under the heat of his hands.

"I don't know what to say. I had this image in my head of the kind of girl you should be with and-and look at me, Finn!" I shout, drawing a few looks from people at a nearby table. "I'm not her."

He drops his hands from my arms and I miss him instantly. He takes a step back and stares at me like I'm a stranger. It hurts so much I'm sure I'll implode.

"Did you even read my e-mails?" his voice disgusted.

I rack my brain trying to remembering anything I've gotten from him, but nothing comes to mind. "What e-mails?" I beg, lost for some kind of answer.

He swallows hard and fierce emotions flood his eyes. "If you didn't even take the time to read them then I don't know what I'm doing here," he hisses as he turns away, running a hand through his perfect hair.

I grab his arm and pull him back to me. I've spent all this time avoiding him and pushing him away and now I'm terrified that he'll actually go.

"Finn, just tell me what the e-mails said. I don't-I don't understand."

He pushes a rogue curl that's fallen loose behind my ear and his fingers linger a moment on my cheek before he pulls me into him. He kisses me deeply and fiercely with more intensity than he has before. One hand is in my hair, the other grips me around the waist as his tongue parts my lips. I've never been kissed like this. He's kissing me like it's the last time and I drag him closer to hold on as long as I can.

"Figure it out, Pumpkin," he whispers against my mouth before he slips from my grasp and leaves me standing alone and vulnerable.

My hand remains stretched out for a few moments too long as though I'm willing him to come back to me. I already knew that I messed up, but seeing him, feeling his rejection is more than I can fully swallow. I slump into the nearest chair and sad tears blur my vision. I set my sights on my hands that knit together in my lap when another hand covers them. I glance up just enough to see my father crouching down to my level. His soft gray eyes full of concern as he asks, "You need me to kick his ass?"

A sputter of laughter erupts from my lips as I wrap my arms around his broad shoulders and drop to my knees out of the chair. I push my face into the crook of his neck and breathe in the scent of salt and cologne. He's startled for a moment and his arms remain at his sides before he enfolds me in them and runs his hand up and down my back.

"Shh, shh, sweetheart," he murmurs into my ear, pressing a kiss above my ear. "It's okay, you're okay. I've got you."

"I messed up, Daddy," I cry into the collar of his shirt. I knew that people have to be staring, but for the first time in a long time I just want my dad. Let them stare. "I don't know how to fix it."

He smiles against my temple and it makes me squeeze him harder. I wish that I was still a child and small enough for him to scoop into his arms and hold me on his lap like he used to do. As it stands now, it would probably be easier for me to do it to him. "You'll figure it out, sweetheart. You're the smartest person I know. Is there anything I can do?"

I pull back and wipe underneath my eyes. "Would you be okay if I left? I'm just not really in a party mood."

He smiles and places his thick hands on my slim cheeks. "I wouldn't mind in the slightest, just give me a moment and I'll drive you home."

I shake my head sharply and say, "Absolutely not, this is your party, you can't leave it. I'll get an Uber."

He pats the top of my head like I'm still his little girl. "You are most certainly not getting an Uber. I'll come back to the party after I get you home safe. Just give me a second to tell Becky."

Twenty minutes later I explode through the front door of my house, tripping over my own feet in the four inch heels, in such a hurry to get up to my room and my computer. The puppy barks in protest when I don't scoop him up to go with me. There's no time!

I kick off my shoes in the upstairs hallway and rush forward to pull down the stairs to the attic. I crawl on my hands and knees to get up them faster.

I jump on my bed, hoping I don't pop it, as I pull my laptop across my satin covered legs. I tap my foot impatiently as the computer boots to life. After what seems like an eternity I load my e-mail and scan for anything from Finn. My heart catches in my throat when I don't find a single thing. I search my spam and junk folders and nothing. I run my hands through my crunchy hair sprayed curls and almost lose hope until I remember the e-mail I created for 3788. My fingers fly as I type in the address for the other e-mail. Tears spring to my eyes and my breath catches in my throat as e-mails flood my inbox. All of them from Finn.

I click on the first one. It arrived right after the last e-mail I'd sent. It's message is simple, "You're wrong, you know, you're more than good for me. You're perfect and I'm going to prove it to you."

Chapter Thirteen

I start reading. E-mail after e-mail of all the stupid things we've ever talked about in the shop and so much more. I find out his favorite movie is *Say Anything* and subsequently his favorite song, *In Your Eyes*, by Peter Gabriel. He's a sucker for chick flicks and loves the smell of PineSol and desperately misses his mom. He tells how he feels about me. How my rejection hurt him. And then I read where he figured out it was me all along and that's where everything stops. His last e-mail is simple and breaks my walls down in an instant.

3788 was a sweet and awesome girl and I liked her a lot, it begins as I force my eyes to not skip ahead. *But you're so much more, Elle. I like 3788, but I love you. Stop running from me, let me catch you.*

I close the lid on my rose gold laptop and settle back against my wall. Ignoring the tears that ruin my mascara, I focus instead on the pounding of my heart in my chest. Finn Wise loves me, not 3788, me. He knows who I am. He's connected the dots between mystery and reality. He's really and truly seen me, he can still say he loves me, and I feel I can finally let myself admit that I feel the same about him. I love him too. Suddenly, Miss Nancy and her last piece of advice jump to my mind from the day I'd gone back to the New Shiloh flea market. She told me that hiding from my problems didn't make them go away. Now I know she's right. Hiding myself from Finn hasn't kept me from loving him and apparently it didn't kept him from loving me. Finn asked me to stop running and let him catch me and that's exactly what I intend to do. I fish my phone out of my purse and press to call Blanche.

"Hey," I exhale when she answers. "Do you know where Finn lives? There's something I need to do."

"Um, well, of course I do," Blanche responds, her voice breathy and slightly wheezy. "But I don't think it would help you much."

"What? Why?" I demand as I search like crazy for my keys, and some pants!

"Because he's not at home. We're at track practice at school," she responds as the water in her bottle swishes in my ear.

"Okay, okay," I said zipping up the front of my dark gray hoodie and cringing at the crunchiness of my still mile high hair. I'm trying to justify the fact that I'm thinking about seriously going to New Shiloh High School looking like a reject from a cheap porno movie as I profess my love to Finn in front of his entire track team. "I'm on my way."

"Whoa, whoa, whoa," Blanche shouts into the receiver forcing me to bring it back to my ear and wait a moment for her to continue. I don't have a moment. "You don't want to come here right now. Wait and think about it before you come."

"What are you talking about?" I demand, waiting to confirm my Uber.

"Well it's not really an actual practice. Finn asked me to come run with him for a while, he's a little upset. I think it might just be best to give this some time. Maybe wait through the weekend before you say anything to him."

"I need to talk to him, Blanche," I murmur softly as I pull on my tennis shoes, even though it seems fruitless.

She sighs heavy on the other end. "I know you do sweetie, just give him a little time. When I'm done here I'll come over and we'll talk about it, okay?"

I fall back onto my squishy waterbed and pout in disappointment.

"Okay."

It's eleven o'clock before the pumpkin pulls up to my house. That's some run those too had. I'm trying like crazy not to be jealous. She hops out of the car in jeans and a sweater, clearly she's been home to shower and change, while I've been over here suffering.

"How you doing, sweetie?"

I'd taken the time to develop a plan in the hours since we'd spoken. It's corny and probably stupid, but to me it's perfect. I just need Blanche to drive.

"Get back in the car!" I exclaim as I hoist my backpack up my shoulder.

"Where do you think we're going?" she demands as she settles her hip against the door of her sad vehicle. "I thought we were going to talk about this."

"I've done enough talking, Blanche. For once, I need to act," I say as I crawl into the passenger seat. She peers at me uncertainly from the window. "I'm telling you that you've been right this whole time. I love him, Blanche." But a new reality had hit me while I'd waited for Blanche to arrive, something far more important than I realized. None of this, not a single thing that's happened over the last few weeks has anything to do with a boy. True, I want the boy, I really want the boy, but this isn't about him. Every moment of self-doubt I have endured hasn't been about Finn at all. I have spent my entire life living in a shadow cast by my mother and sisters and the confidence they exude. Maybe they haven't always been the most beautiful people inside, but they have never doubted their worth. This entire situation with my parents has thrown that on its ear. If they don't know who they are now, how could I figure it out for me? I've grown up feeling less than and no amount of praise from my friends could fix the doubt I felt in me. It's not about people telling you you're awesome or beautiful or special, it's about believing it yourself. I never realized they weren't the same thing. Of course I pushed away something I wanted, something that seemed too good to be true. I've always known that if things seem too good to be true, then they usually are. I have spent my life convincing myself that it's okay that I'm only normal, average, ordinary, that it's fine that I'm nothing special. What I realize now is that all of that, every thought like it is a load of shit. I am spectacular, amazing, beautiful and worthy. I have friends that I would literally die for and I know they'd do the same for me. I'm at the top of my high school class with my pick of colleges and a future so bright it's blinding. I have a quirky sense of humor, a winning personality, and a collection of salt and pepper shakers that show me I'm unique. I'm special because I'm me. Finn didn't fall in love with me because of a lie or a fantasy. He fell in love with me because I'm me and that's more than enough. So, none of this is because of the boy, but now I know it's okay to want him as much as I do, because if he's something I want then I know I deserve it. "I love him," I say again, more for my benefit than for Blanche's.

She smiles and hops in beside me. "I can't believe you finally said it!"

I roll my eyes at the pompous ass as I click my seat belt. "Yes, you're a genius. Now drive!"

Twenty minutes later we sit outside a McMansion in one of the numerous developments that have moved into New Shiloh in the last decade. This house sits with four others in a round cul-de-sac at the end of a long, windy street. Finn's jeep is parked in the driveway and the scene is quiet and serene. I'm about to change that.

My breathing quickens as I start assembling the pieces of my project and grand gesture. Blanche gnaws on her lower lip.

"Are you sure about this?" she asks. She has this little waving Chinese cat suction cupped onto her dashboard and I'm trying to convince myself that he's making me brave.

"You loved the idea two minutes ago!" I shriek as I drop everything back at my feet.

"No, no, it's a great idea," Blanche soothes. "You just seem really nervous."

"Of course I'm nervous, but I have to do it." My hair is still in ridiculous curls and my makeup is insane and I realize I more resemble 3788 right now than I do Elle. Maybe it's the combination of both of us that will make me strong enough to do this.

I gather my things and step out of the pumpkin onto the driveway. I hop up to stand on the hood and Blanche sticks her head out the window and barks, "This was not in my contract! Get off my car."

"Shut up! The pumpkin's fine!" I yell back as I connect my phone to the small bluetooth speaker in my hands. I lift the phone above my head and hit play for Peter Gabriel's "In Your Eyes." One by one, lights flicker on in nearby houses and blinds flutter as people stare out their windows at me. I keep myself focused on the darkness of the only home that matters. "Come on Finn," I mutter to myself. "I know you're in there."

Finally a light inside blinks to life and I swallow hard as the front door opens to my beautiful guy. He's shirtless, wearing only running shorts and it's hard for me not to fall over. He jogs out to me in the driveway. His face is to about my belly button as I stand on the hood of Blanche's car. He looks confused, but not unhappy to see me. Blanche has hidden herself under the steering wheel to give us some semblance of privacy. Sweat glistens his forehead and down his neck and I swallow a little harder. He's so incredibly beautiful I can barely breathe.

"I'm sorry," I shout over the music. "I didn't have a big boom box, this was the closest thing I could do." I know I look like a crazy a crazy person. From the speakers, to the hair to the smeared hot pink lipstick and mascara all the way to my sweats. I'm sure he thinks I'm off my rocker. I probably am.

He wraps his arm around my waist and lifts me off the car as I slide down his body. My heart has officially stopped. I'm pressed up against his bare skin. He reaches up with his free hand and pauses the music as I bring my arms down. "What are you doing?" he asks, confusion knots between his perfect eyes, a curious smile lingers on his lips. That gives me hope.

"*Say Anything*," I answer with a shrug. "You said it's your favorite movie and that's how it ends. John Cusak holds the boombox over his head playing *In Your Eyes* for the girl of his dreams."

The smile grows a little brighter as his fingers flex against my back. He still hasn't let go of me. "When did I say it was my favorite movie?"

I raise a shaky hand to move my ridiculous hair out of my face and continue, "In your e-mails. I read them all." He bites his lip, still waiting for me to say something. "I swear to you Finn, I stopped looking at that e-mail account right after the dance. It hurt too much. I had no idea that you had sent me those things."

He cocks his head to the side and asks, "Did you read the last one?" I can smell his sweaty, salty skin and desperately want to lose myself in him.

I'm unable to fight the happy smile that hints at my lips as I let my hands settle on his chest. His heart pounds under my fingers.

"Yeah, yeah, I did."

He places his palms on either side of my face, his thumbs grazing my cheek bones, "My crazy, crazy girl, what part of you could ever think that you weren't good enough for me? That's complete insanity."

I grab his wrists to keep his hands in place, trying not to giggle with glee at the fact that he's touching me.

"I don't know, years of self-loathing from constantly playing second fiddle to my sisters, but I'm just spitballing." I vow to be nothing but honest with him from this moment forward. There have been enough secrets between us to last a lifetime.

He pulls me closer to him, his face serious as places a gentle kiss against my forehead. "You, Miss Conner, will never play second fiddle for me. You're the leading lady, top of the pack."

A few of the tears escape past the gates. "So, you're not disappointed?" I squeak out, knowing the sobs are on their way.

"I mean, I know that you said all those wonderful things to me, but I just want you to be sure."

He digs his fingers into my over shellacked hair and rests his forehead against mine. "Listen to me," he whispers softly. "Like I told you in the email, I really liked 3788. She was cool, but Michelle Conner, you're beyond incredible. So far from anything I've ever dreamed. I'm in love with you."

And then he kisses me, hard and I welcome it. I put my hands on his cheeks, my arms around his neck, my fingers on his chest, touching him everywhere I can.

When he finally pulls away he pushes the tears away with his thumbs and smiles. I smile too. I push my lips together, it feels like a dream.

"I love you, too."

Off in the distance, nearby church bells chime to signify the dawning of a new day. As the clock strikes midnight, it's just us. No masks, no secrets, no facade. We see each other beyond our mystery. It's me and the boy I love, 3788 and the Mystery Man., Elle and Finn; all rolled into one.

I don't have to have to run anymore, I've finally let him catch me.

THE END

About the Author

At eight years old I sat down at my kitchen table with a box of Crayola 64 count crayons and off white construction paper to create a picture book full of colorful images for my mother. Sitting her down, I walked her step by step through an epic tale of a flower that gets blown away from a field to journey on the wind. That was the day my mother knew I was destined to be a story teller. She always said I was natural performer, never without a skip and a song. But on that day, she knew writing would be my destiny. Now, over two decades later, I'm so excited to finally share my stories with the world.

My name is Katelyn Marie Brawn, I'm a born and raised Baltimorean since the year 1988. I come from a loving family of two rock steady parents and a younger brother that is the coolest young man you'll ever meet. My favorite creature on the entire planet is my five year old mutt Rosie. I honestly think I like her more than most people (if you knew her you'd be forced to agree with me). Besides Rosie, there's nothing is this world I love more than a hot cup of tea, a blanket to crochet, and an old rerun of *Murder, She Wrote*. Yes, it's true, I was born a ninety year old woman.

Just to spice things up I sport a tattoo addiction to go along with my pleated skirts and double string of pearls. I'm involved in many things. I teach artistic roller skating, craft beaded jewelry, and can bake a mean cupcake. I love mentoring my group of skaters. It's the greatest gift I've ever given myself. These girls are the true inspiration behind the books that I intend to write. *Pumpkin Pie* is the first of these stories.

I love fairy tales! However, I'm certain there's more substance to the story beyond the traditional tale. Using a modern context and setting, I want to show girls that happily ever after isn't out of reach, even in the darkest of situations. I want them to see that they aren't alone in the issues they face every day, both big and small. My mama says I was destined to be a storyteller. I hope to do her proud.

CPSIA information can be obtained
at www.ICGtesting.com
Printed in the USA
BVHW071933300921
617863BV00011B/345

9 780998 681139